W9-BYA-640

THE LOSERS' CLUB

John Lekich

THE LOSERS' CLUB

By John Lekich

ANNICK PRESS

TORONTO + NEW YORK + VANCOUVER

Copyright © 2002 John Lekich

Annick Press Ltd.

All rights reserved. No part of this work covered by the copyrights hereon may be reproduced or used in any form or by any means – graphic, electronic, or mechanical – without the prior written permission of the publisher.

We acknowledge the support of the Canada Council for the Arts, the Ontario Arts Council, and the Government of Canada through the Book Publishing Industry Development Program (BPIDP) for our publishing activities.

Edited by Barbara Pulling
Copy edited by Jennifer Glossop
Proofread by Robin Van Heck
Cover and interior design by Irvin Cheung/iCheung Design
Cover photograph by Lorne Bridgman/Westside Studio
Cover models: Nicholas Constantine, Leroy Stanisclaus, Sun Quach, Eduardo Barbosa, Miro Wagner

Cataloguing in Publication Data

Lekich, John
        The Losers' Club

ISBN 1-55037-753-1 (bound)—ISBN 1-55037-752-3 (pbk.)

        I. Title.

PS8573.E498L68 2002   jC813'.6   C2002-901126-4
PZ7

The text was typeset in New Baskerville and Gills Sans

Distributed in Canada by	Published in the U.S.A. by	Distributed in the U.S.A. by
Firefly Books Ltd.	Annick Press (U.S.) Ltd.	Firefly Books (U.S.) Inc.
3680 Victoria Park Avenue		P.O. Box 1338
Willowdale, ON		Ellicott Station
M2H 3K1		Buffalo, NY 14205

Printed and bound in Canada

visit us at **www.annickpress.com**

For my parents

CHAPTER

ONE

They say misery loves company, which is why we decided to form the Losers' Club in grade nine last year. Sometimes we'd sit around at club meetings and wallow in things only losers can appreciate. For example, we could spend a good half-hour trying to pinpoint the sound that perfectly expressed loser abuse at Marshall McLuhan High. There are lots of showy sounds to choose from — begging, pleading, even the occasional shriek — but for me personally the definitive loser sound is hearing Winston Chang's voice coming from inside his own locked locker.

Now, it's not unusual for certain kids to get stuffed inside their lockers at our school. It happens all the time, especially to Winston, who's shorter than, say, a baritone sax. In fact, Winston must have held the grade-nine record for being stuffed into his locker. He's had the same locker for two years in a row now. He refers to it as his "tin can condo." He even has a pillow in there with a special loop so it can hang on a coat hook — just in case the janitor takes a little longer than usual with the hacksaw.

Our janitor's name is Mr. Winecki, but he's sawed off so many of Winston's locks that he lets Winston call him Walter. Winston often goes down to the janitor's room to help Mr. Winecki with his collection of foreign beer labels. "I scrape the labels off the bottles for him," says Winston. "Sometimes Walter's hands get a little shaky."

One afternoon last fall Winston was scraping off beer labels when Walter asked why Winston had a pillow in his locker.

Winston told him, "Just because someone goes out of their way to make you feel uncomfortable doesn't mean you have to *be* uncomfortable."

I guess this made an impression on Mr. Winecki because during the Christmas break last year, he took all the shelves out of Winston's locker. When Winston asked him why he went to the trouble, Mr. Winecki said, "A growing boy like you needs more headroom." This made Winston feel pretty good because he is always afraid he'll never grow another inch. Plus, since Winston made it a point to use as few books as possible, he really didn't need the shelf space.

Winston was so grateful for the janitor's kind gesture that he let Mr. Winecki use the hacksaw to cut off his locks — which is more than I would do. I mean it's no secret that Mr. Winecki drinks on the job. Don't get me wrong. I'd probably drink if I cleaned toilets for a living. I just didn't think it was a great idea to let Mr. Winecki play with sharp objects.

Once I suggested to Winston that he simply call out the numbers of his combination through the locker vent. That way, Mr. Winecki could open the locker the regular way.

Winston got all indignant on me. "I can't give my combination to just anybody. There's valuable stuff in that locker."

"Like what?" I asked.

"Like *me*."

After Winston calmed down a little, he explained his point of view. "You don't understand," he said. "Walter needs to use the hacksaw. It makes him feel important."

In case you're wondering, Winston is a lot smarter than he seems. On the surface, he doesn't appear to be the sharpest knife in the educational drawer. He never studies, his grades are pathetically low, and he has transformed daydreaming into an art. Winston says the only reason he carries a book bag is to "blend in with the other book bag drones."

Some of us other drones will check out a book from the school library occasionally, if only to get a smile from Ms. Maculwayne, our intensely gorgeous librarian. She is the pinnacle of grace and beauty at Marshall McLuhan High. I've seen guys struggle with piles of books they have no intention of reading for the sole purpose of impressing her. Winston is generally too lazy to be one of those guys. Like many of his fellow losers, he comes across as what you might call "emotionally underdeveloped."

But don't let Winston's frivolous side fool you. Just when you think he's got to be the most emotionally underdeveloped fifteen-year-old on the planet, he'll say something semi-profound like "Immaturity is the ultimate form of rebellion" or "If you can't be cool, then play the fool."

Sometimes Winston can be surprisingly observant. For example, it was Winston who first noticed that Julie Spenser was giving me extra-long looks in history class last spring. She is one of those aloof girls who are always wearing black — black jeans, black sweater, black mascara. It's too early in the year to tell what she'll be like in grade ten, but I think she's one of those people who tries to hide how smart she is by being emotionally frosty.

Mr. Yankovitch, our overly peppy English teacher, was kidding around this week in an effort to break the beginning-of-the-school-year ice. Mr. Yankovitch poses so many questions that some students like to call him "Mr. Why." He asked Julie to explain the reason she was so crazy about the color black. Julie looked him right in the eye and said, "Because I can't find anything darker." When Mr. Why asked us to fill out a data sheet on our personalities, she listed her major hobby as "brooding."

Personally I thought that was funny, but not everyone appreciates Julie Spenser's view of life. My friend Manny Crandall says she creeps him out, and Winston says that it's downright antisocial to wear that much black unless you're the lead in a Kung Fu movie or something. In fact, Winston thinks Julie Spenser is so different that she might even find me romantically interesting. Manny thinks this is a crazy theory, but, as Winston says, Manny is about as romantic as a pile of vomit.

To appreciate Winston, you have to understand that he's used to going his own way. He has his own personal code of behavior, which he sticks to no matter what. For instance, Winston never told on whoever was stuffing him inside his own locker. He always smiled and informed the principal that he was practicing to become an escape artist. He was very cool about it. He would only start yelling when his legs started cramping. He was always concerned that someone nearby might be taking a makeup exam or trying to enjoy a few moments of peace in the washroom.

Even before we became friends, I respected this attitude. So, whenever I was out on an early hall pass, I'd check the little vent in his locker to make sure he wasn't looking up at me from the other side. After a while, Winston trusted me enough to let me have his combination.

I should explain that I'm currently the only kid at Marshall McLuhan High with a hall pass that gets me out of class a full five minutes early. That's because the administration thinks I might get trampled by a stampede of "thoughtless individuals" if they let me out at the same time as everybody else. For years, I've been using metal crutches to get around. I'm what you'd call "permanently disabled," if you were being polite. People are not always polite.

I don't like being disabled, of course. The crutches make a creepy hollow sound when I'm moving down the empty halls, and certain thoughtless individuals are always offering to help me down the stairs so they can get out early and be first in line at the cafeteria. I never let anybody help me that way. It's one of my rules.

Besides the hall pass, the only good thing about walking on crutches is that nobody tries to stuff me in a locker. Even Jerry Whitman, who runs a very profitable extortion ring and intimidates a decent cross section of the losers in the student body, refuses to shake me down for my share of "loser bucks." While Jerry relishes loser bucks more than any other kind of money, he says it's bad public relations to injure a poster boy for the handicapped.

Maybe this is why the school administration is under the sad illusion that Jerry Whitman is filled with love for all humankind. "Jerry Whitman is golden," says Manny. "Jerry

Whitman is *so* golden that if they erected a statue of him on the school grounds, even the pigeons would go out of their way not to crap on it."

Manny may be exaggerating a little, but it is true that Jerry Whitman does not look like your average shakedown artist. When Whitman puts on his "teacher's face," he gives the impression he would happily adopt every starving orphan in the world, if only he had enough spare change in the pockets of his neatly pressed khakis. You would never guess that he hates losers of all varieties. Jerry is careful to protect his image among the non-loser populace.

Not that Whitman doesn't have his ways of getting to me. He once saw that old-time comedian Jerry Lewis hosting the Jerry Lewis Telethon for muscular dystrophy. This is where Jerry Lewis wheels out a bunch of little kids in wheelchairs and goes on and on about how we should give money to "Jerry's kids."

Whitman, who has a very warped sense of humor, began calling his extortion victims "Jerry's kids." I made the mistake of asking him to lay off a kid once. After that, it didn't matter that I don't even have muscular dystrophy. Whitman would see me in the hallway, pat me on the head and say stuff like "I ask you, Sherwood, what would we do without Jerry's kids? Don't you agree that it would be a much *poorer* world?"

See what I mean about Whitman getting to me? It's one thing for a misguided head-patter to believe that he is patting someone on the head for good reason. It is quite another when the head-patter is doing it as a crafty form of humiliation. This may sound crazy, but sometimes I think it would be easier to get degraded, shamed, and occasionally beaten up, like everybody else in my crowd. Maybe that way I would have some privacy.

Ever since Jerry and his goons began to leave me pretty much alone, I have formed a kind of public safety zone for all the other kids who were being bullied, robbed, and generally made miserable. You can always tell when one of Jerry's kids is about to crack under the strain. Their eyes glaze over, and they look like an alien from some science-fiction movie. Whenever I see that look on a person, I make sure to sit beside them in the cafeteria. It's not much, but it gives them a break

That's how I got the nickname Savior Sherwood. My real name is Alex Sherwood. But when word got around that I was willing to do the occasional good deed, every one of Jerry's kids started to use the stupid nickname. They would say things like "I got dibs on sitting beside the Savior at tomorrow's assembly." I mean, they would actually argue about it.

I blame Manny Crandall for this. Don't get me wrong. There are a lot of things I can appreciate about Manny. For instance, he's the best artist in the school. He's always drawing these really great cartoons that make me laugh. In addition, even though Manny is a very big guy, he tries not to let his above-average girth get to him.

Manny likes to call himself an activist for the horizontally challenged. His motto is "I'm wide and I'm here." Sometimes when he knows that Jerry and the boys aren't watching, he'll wave his fist in the air and shout, "Fat Power!"

So what's the problem? Manny's extra weight makes him one of Jerry's favorite targets. That's why Manny started to follow me around like some sort of horizontally challenged shadow. When I called him on it, he said, "Can I help it if you are an oasis from constant torment?"

Manny even offered to pay me to eat lunch with him. "I would rather give my loser bucks to you than to Jerry," he said. "It's way less humiliating."

When I refused Manny's money, my reputation as a do-good-er began to spread. That's when my life changed for the worse. I went from being a grade-eight loner to being very popular with the more pathetic element of Marshall McLuhan High. Everywhere I turned some zit-faced loser wanted me to be an oasis from constant torment. How could I refuse? After all, *I* was a zit-faced loser, a zit-faced loser that Jerry Whitman liked to pat on the head. Let's face it. Whether I wanted to admit it or not, guys like Manny and Winston were my kind of people.

But it is never easy being a do-gooder, especially when you are up against someone as wily as Jerry Whitman. If there's one thing Whitman knows, it's how far to push a loser. He usually leaves your borderline losers alone. Or cuts them precisely enough slack so that they won't go running to someone like Mr. Matchesko, Marshall McLuhan's wrestling coach.

Manny says that Jerry has a built-in psychic telepathy when it comes to zeroing in on those unfortunates who are only too glad to pay up in silence. Plus, Whitman is very big on loser research.

"Jerry Whitman knows your complete personal statistics," gushes Winston, who can never help being impressed by any sustained mental effort that isn't his own. "He knows every-thing from what scares you to what sets off your allergies."

Manny adds, "Most importantly, Jerry Whitman knows the places you like to hide on collection day."

But Jerry knows much more than that. He knows what makes your average loser want to blend into the background with the soft drink machines, the badminton nets, and the trashcans. I wouldn't be surprised if he also knows the exact reason that I don't turn him in to the school authorities. Even though I consider it one of life's more embarrassing personal mysteries.

Manny says that if you are a loser, the worst thing you can do is give in to the temptation of confrontation. Manny calls confrontation "the Big C." Most losers avoid the Big C at all costs. As Manny says, "The Big C never fails to spell disaster."

I understand. That's the reason I try to stay in the background and do as much good as I can. I quickly discovered one problem with doing good was that I couldn't do good in two places at the same time. No matter how hard I tried, I couldn't be around Winston every time one of Jerry's boys wanted to rip him off or stuff him in his locker. I suppose that if I had to rate who was the most popular target in the school, it would be Winston Churchill Chang.

Winston lives with his older brother, Neville. Their dad is a heavy-duty businessman who lives in Hong Kong. Winston's house has a big-screen TV, a games room, and a bunch of other perks. Winston claims there are so many guestrooms in the house he can go for days without sleeping in the same bed twice. Manny says the whole thing sounds like something out of an old Richie Rich comic book.

Although Mr. Chang is never around, he makes sure his youngest son has plenty of spending money. When Winston came to Canada in grade eight, his first mistake was trying to be popular at his new school. He flashed a big roll of loser bucks in a very uncool way. This naturally attracted the attention of Jerry Whitman, who made Winston's cash flow his top priority. That's been the case from September to June for two straight years.

The best thing about summer vacation is that Winston and the rest of us losers get a much-needed break from Jerry and the boys. Manny says Jerry is too busy hiking and water-skiing in July and August to bother with the administrative headaches of extortion. So the final official act of the Losers' Club last year was to adjourn for the summer.

There were even times over the summer when I managed to forget that Whitman would come back twice as strong in September. Rested, relaxed, and ready to squeeze the last dime out of the poor unfortunates I call friends.

Winston always hoped he might grow a couple of inches over the summer. For three straight years, his version of hello on the first day of school has been "Do I look taller?"

My answer is always the same: "Maybe a little bit." It isn't much of a lie, and it makes him feel better.

There was one noteworthy thing about Winston's first grade-ten locker-stuffing. I could hear him dialing his cell phone, but that wasn't really out of the ordinary. Sometimes, when things got to be too much, Winston would call Neville on the cell and his brother would pick him up and take him home. He'd spend the rest of the day going from guestroom to guestroom and messing up the beds. It was boring, but nobody tried to take his money.

No, the unusual thing was the sound I could hear between the beeps of the cell. Winston was crying. It wasn't the sort of crying you would normally do if you were in Winston's situation — you know, like from frustration. It was something else. Something I recognized.

Winston was pretty embarrassed when I opened his locker. So I pretended it was no big deal.

"Someone's frying onions in home ec," he said as he wiped his eye. "Those fumes can be very irritating in a confined space."

I wiped my eye as if I knew what he was talking about. "Is Neville coming to pick you up?"

"Neville's been in California since August. I was trying to get Walter on his beeper, but he must have shut it off." He looked at his cell phone in disgust. "What kind of person has only one number on his speed dial?"

"Back up," I said. "What's Neville doing in California?"

Winston smiled. "He's made it past the first round in that big karaoke contest."

Neville lived for karaoke, which was basically about a bunch of people singing stupid songs in a bar. Neville had a very good voice, even when he was singing ancient songs like "Raindrops Keep Falling on My Head," but the thought of him singing always made me laugh. He never failed to close his eyes when he sang, which made him look as if he was passing a kidney stone or something.

Winston could tell I was about to laugh. "What's so funny?" he asked. "This could be my brother's big break."

When you got right down to it, Winston was very proud of his brother. I changed the subject. "Does your dad know about this?"

"No," said Winston, whose father was very strict. "He'd kill us both."

"Who's staying with you?"

Winston shrugged. "I'm all alone, I guess — unless you

count Cola." Cola was Neville's pet Doberman. Cola, a one-man dog, never paid any attention to Winston unless Winston was waving around a steak or something.

There was something melancholy about Winston standing there outside his locker. I'd never seen anybody look so forlorn. Winston told me that the set-up for the international karaoke competition was very complicated. "I'm not sure how long Neville will be away," he said. "This could drag on longer than the hockey play-offs."

That's when I first got the idea to move in with Winston. You see, I had this secret that nobody else knew. I was all alone too.

CHAPTER

TWO

Y ou don't know me that well yet. So you might think my urge to move into Winston's empty mansion would be a passing phase — the way some girls at school change boyfriends about once a week. Nothing could be further from the truth, however. And it's not because Winston has a Jacuzzi or even because my apartment is the size of the average phone booth. It's because, in my own small way, I'm a secret rebel.

You know how some kids are addicted to stuff? Maybe it's cigarettes or alcohol or always having to get the top mark on a test. Well, I have an addiction, too. I'm addicted to freedom.

That's right. Freedom is my drug of choice. I'm hooked on the thrill of doing whatever I want whenever I want. Don't get me wrong. I don't lounge around in my underwear chugging beer or anything. Mostly it's little things like eating nothing but barbecue-flavored Doritos for dinner or staying up late to watch an old Marx Brothers movie on a school night.

You could say I'm different. For example, I'm crazy about

Groucho Marx, a movie comedian even older than Jerry Lewis. Groucho had a couple of brothers named Harpo and Chico who would do crazy slapstick things in black and white. But rolly-eyed Groucho, who wore a phony-looking moustache and carried a big cigar, was my absolute favorite. Whatever he said came out funny. He even walked around in the same hunched stoop I get when I'm really tired — except on Groucho it was kind of cool.

The thing I liked most about Groucho was that he pretended to do what everybody else asked and then went ahead and did whatever he wanted. I'm not as cool as Groucho. But you might say that I've sampled the sweet taste of independence on the smorgasbord of life. And once you've tasted freedom, there's no going back. You can't turn around and say, "From now on, I'm going to keep regular hours and eat liver every Wednesday." At least I can't.

I can hear you saying, "But where are your parents? Do they not object to your staying up until two in the morning with barbecue-flavored Doritos dust on your lips?" Good question. Part of the answer is that my mother is dead. I don't like to think about it. But it's been a few years now and — aside from the memories in my head — I've gotten used to the idea that she's gone for good.

This leaves my dad. My dad is not dead, although he's come close to blowing himself up a few times. One day he was conducting an experiment in the garage he rents for the purpose of refining his inventions. I can't remember what invention he was working on. It could have been Perma-Paint ("The car coating that doesn't scratch, crack or peel, even when you hit it with the biggest hammer in the toolbox!"). Or it could have been Insta-Dye ("The surprisingly easy way for the man of distinction to banish his gray hair!"). Whichever it was, he got too close to the Bunsen burner and deep-fried his eyebrows. Do you know how long it takes for a set of eyebrows to grow back? These are the kinds of things I am forced to consider as the one and only son of Sam "The Shovel" Sherwood.

Part of the reason they call my dad the Shovel is because he invented something called the Pocket Shoveler. It's a little shovel with a handle that folds up so you can carry it around in your pocket. That's the invention that got my dad into infomercials, those cheesy ads on late-night TV where they sell stuff that looks good but is actually crap. He would go on television and say things like "Friends, have you ever felt the sudden urge to dig a hole and found yourself with nothing but your bare hands to dig with?"

Then he would bring out some pathetic guy who worked in a pet cemetery to talk about how the Pocket Shoveler had changed his life. ("I've found that this handy tool is perfect for placing your smaller household pets at rest!") Talk about embarrassing. The entire thing gave me the sudden urge to dig a hole with my bare hands and crawl right in.

It didn't help that my dad had this assistant named Connie who did nothing on TV but smile and point. Dad refers to Connie as "my lovely associate." I suppose there must be more than a few sleep-deprived viewers who think Connie looks pretty hot. Personally I don't understand the attraction. For one thing, she should be in *The Guinness Book of World Records* for having the longest, reddest nails in the universe. My dad says that I don't understand the delicate balance between glamour and salesmanship.

In some ways, I have to admit that my dad is on the smart side. He says there're a whole bunch of anxious shoppers out there who prefer to purchase items while normal people are fast asleep. They like to buy things because it helps them forget about their problems, which is why they can't sleep in the first place. My dad calls them his "pajama army."

By now, you may have guessed the other reason for my father's nickname. He may not be Thomas Edison, but he can really shovel the BS. In fact, it's surprising how many members of the pajama army felt a sudden urge to purchase the Pocket Shoveler. They were so eager to forget their problems that they couldn't wait to get their hands on what is basically nothing more than a giant spoon. That's when I figured out that people will buy almost anything if they happen to be lonely and awake in the middle of the night.

My dad even made a second commercial. In it Connie would point and smile while he read testimonial letters from his many satisfied customers. He still carries one particular letter in his wallet. It reads,

Dear Mr. Sherwood,

I wanted to write and tell you that I think the Pocket Shoveler is the greatest invention known to man! I am a senior citizen and find conventional shovels to be both cumbersome and an unwelcome invitation to back strain. In my advanced years, I have discovered that there are many reasons not to put your trust in banks or other financial institutions. Consequently, I have buried many of my valuables at clandestine locations around the neighborhood.

Often, I will think of a new location before falling into my

nightly slumber. I am proud to say that I sleep with the Pocket Shoveler under my pillow for the sake of such occasions.

You have given an old man peace of mind. Who could ask for a better gift? If there's ever anything I can do for you, you have only to ask.

I remain your humble servant,
Sanford T. Barrington III

My father says he looks at that letter every time he feels he hasn't lived up to his potential as a man of ideas. He's read it to me so often that I have it memorized.

Even when he's not on TV, my dad likes to talk as if a camera were following him around. He will often hand me a line about how his next invention will put him firmly on "the road to greatness." Although I'm not proud of myself, I admit I get somewhat sarcastic about his aspirations. For example, around the time he had that little accident with the Bunsen burner in the garage, I said, "I don't think they allow you on the road to greatness without eyebrows."

Dad looked at me all hurt and said, "Sometimes I wish you could be more like Sanford T. Barrington III."

"You want me to start burying my valuables at clandestine locations?" I asked.

"I want you to be a little more appreciative of your old man," he said.

Believe me, I try to be appreciative of my dad, but he doesn't make it easy. He's always pestering me about my own goals and aspirations. His favorite question is "Why don't you have a *project*?" And then he'll start talking about how the road to greatness always starts with a project.

The hardest part of my dad talking about goals and aspirations is that he always has to give examples. The example he uses the most is how he tried out for the track team in high school and ended up winning a bunch of medals. "I wasn't the most natural runner," he says, "but I had a *goal.*"

When my dad starts talking about his youth, it makes me think we have absolutely nothing in common. For instance, he's always saying how the high school years were the most carefree years of his life. This thought really scares me. I start to think, "Maybe the high school years are the most carefree years of *my* life and I'm just not noticing."

Recently I made my views on the subject known. I probably should have asked my dad, "How can I be carefree when all you ever talk about is having goals and aspirations?" Instead, I looked at him and said, "You mean life gets *worse* after high school?"

That's when my dad took me to his old high school. In the main hall, there was a display case filled with his medals and ribbons. There was also a black-and-white picture of him as a teenager. He looked a lot like me, only in a track uniform and without the crutches.

My dad wore a proud expression. "It's too bad you don't go this school," he said. "You could walk past the display case every morning and be reminded of my glory days." And then his expression got prouder still and he added, "I could inspire you in absentia." "In absentia" is a fancy way of saying that you're someplace else when you're supposed to be at home. Dad is in absentia a lot.

I know I should have been happy that my dad had a big display case to himself. But the whole thing felt so weird. It was as if somebody had trapped the best part of him behind glass and there was nothing I could do to let it out. The more I looked, the sadder I got. I kept looking until it became pretty much the second-saddest day of my entire life.

Now is as good a time as any to tell you that I was born with cerebral palsy. You know how your brain tells your body to do things like walk and you get up and do it? Well, in my case, the signals that my brain sends get a little scrambled. It's as if I've got a short circuit somewhere in the walking department. I can take steps but my foot doesn't always land in the place I want it to. Mine is a fairly mild case of CP. I mean, everything else works normally, but I sure won't be running any races.

Mom used to say that my crutches were my two best friends, because they helped me get around. That was my mom, always looking on the bright side. Actually, unless you count the supreme aggravation of Jerry Whitman, crutches are the ultimate pain in the butt. End of story. On the other hand, as inventions go, they're way more useful than a shovel for burying your smaller household pets.

I've come to terms with my disability. I guess it's because I was born this way. I don't know any other way to be, and that helps a lot. In fact, sometimes I think the way I walk is more of a problem for everybody else.

My dad never says anything about my disability. But it's not hard to get the idea that I let him down just by being born. He always says that his success at track came through hard work and determination. But his own dad was also a fast runner. So I think my dad thought speed was in the family DNA or something. At least until I came along and screwed up his theory.

Often my dad is so busy talking *at* me he doesn't notice we actually do have a few things in common. I'm interested in building things, which is sort of like inventing. I like to read books on architecture, construction, and building design. I've even sketched out plans of a few imaginary buildings when nobody's looking. The thing is, my dad definitely lacks focus when it comes to my interests. He says I daydream too much, and they don't give out medals for daydreaming.

I don't think my dad noticed how sad I was the day he showed me all his running medals, either. He had prepared an inspirational speech about how he went to university on a track scholarship and ended up falling in love with science. "All those years," he waxed, "I thought I was running toward the finish line, but I was really running toward a new beginning."

The trouble was, though my father loved science, science didn't always love him back. He'd managed to earn a fair amount of money on the Pocket Shoveler, but this only made him more ambitious. He took his profits and put them into developing Perma-Paint.

For a while, Perma-Paint sold very well. My dad was so pleased he said we might be able to buy a condo. I was starting to think that maybe being the son of an inventor wasn't so bad after all.

But then Dad took the profits from Perma-Paint and put them into Insta-Dye, this stuff in a spray can that was supposed to "*safely* banish the gray in a gentleman's hair." I emphasize the word "safely" because that's what it said in the directions. Also my dad would go on TV and say, "Insta-Dye is scientifically tested to be 110 percent safe. I am so sold on this product that I can hardly wait for my hair to turn gray so I can use it."

At first, it looked as if my dad was a genuine genius. Insta-

Dye sold way better than his first two inventions. Dad was ecstatic about this stroke of good fortune, because he had taken development money from an outside investor named Big Garry.

Big Garry was a used-car salesman who made commercials in the same studio as my dad. It was hard to miss Big Garry on TV. He would lean against the hood of an old pink Cadillac while dressed in a giant pig costume and shout things like "Help me bring home the bacon!" and "I'll squeal for a deal!"

Big Garry was the only guy I could think of who was more embarrassing on television than my dad. Dad didn't talk about him much, but when I mentioned I had no respect for a grown man who would stoop so low, he said, "Don't let the pig outfit fool you. You don't want to mess with Big Garry."

Apparently Big Garry had a fiery temper. Once he took a sledgehammer and smashed the windshields on half a dozen of his used cars. "Somebody remarked that he'd gained a lot of weight," Dad told me. "When he is not wearing the pig costume, Big Garry is very sensitive about his appearance."

At this point, I should also explain that Big Garry had a lot of gray hair underneath the cowl of his pig suit.

Anyway, it seemed for a while that Insta-Dye was going to make us all rich. But then everybody's hair started to fall out. Well, not everybody's, exactly. It happened only to Big Garry and the other gentlemen who used Insta-Dye to banish the unsightly gray. There was even an article in one of the local papers with a headline that read "Hair Today, Gone Tomorrow." The article was accompanied by a picture of a totally bald Big Garry. He was quoted as saying, "When I catch up with Sam Sherwood, I'll personally pluck each and every hair from his head."

Suddenly all my dreams of condo ownership went up in smoke. It turned out that there were very few actual *gentlemen* among the users of Insta-Dye. My dad, who was hiding out in a series of local motels, was threatened with a pack of lawsuits from the pajama army — not to mention Big Garry's vow to give him a very painful makeover.

I can't say for sure, but I think the hair dye was the same scientifically tested formula as the car paint. That being the case, my dad could have used a smart lawyer. Unfortunately he had spent the money he had saved to test-market a female version of Insta-Dye called Color Me Gorgeous. Translation? The Sherwood boys were practically broke.

My dad knew he couldn't avoid Big Garry for long if he stayed in town. So he decided to go underground with Connie — just for a few months, until things cooled off. He figured that if they kept moving, no lawsuit or government official or angry investor could give them trouble. So he took off early in July. It wasn't the best solution, but I think Dad was scared of going to jail. Or maybe he was scared of Big Garry finding him *before* he could make it to jail. Anyway, I was told never to ask where he was calling from.

I admit that I miss my dad sometimes. He calls me from a phone booth every couple of weeks or so. ("Remember, son, my code name is Uncle Vito.") "Uncle Vito" sends cash whenever he can. But when I ask him where he gets the money, he tells me not to worry. "My needs are simple," he says. "And Connie is happy as long as I buy her a new nail file once in a while."

Luckily we had credit at the neighborhood grocery store. I'd also saved some money from a few odd jobs. This gave me a bit of a financial cushion. You might say I found life quite manageable, unless you counted my babysitter, Francine Flermer. Francine was the housekeeper my dad hired last year to look after me. She'd stay over sometimes while he was busy inventing things well into the night. Then while Dad experienced what he liked to call his "vacation from incarceration," he asked Francine to move in and take up the slack.

Francine was one of those babysitters who didn't like to be called a babysitter. She felt that the term would stunt my emotional growth. "Don't think of me as a babysitter," she once said. "Think of me as a roommate who holds the balance of power."

Francine was a free spirit who held up her jeans with a piece of rope. According to her many tales of romance, she had fallen in love more times than I have broken out in acne. Everyone in the building had an opinion on Francine. Mr. Sankey, who managed our apartment, called her flakier than a piecrust. The last time I was down in the laundry room, he said, "That Francine, she really colors outside the lines." Mr. Sankey is the kind of guy who can belch his way through the entire alphabet. But he had a serious point.

Francine was a dedicated zit-gazer who helpfully pointed out the arrival of each new pimple on my face. She was also keeping a journal on everything I did so that she could "truly understand the mind of a male adolescent." She followed me around the apartment in "observation mode." She stared at me, then wrote things down while I ate my breakfast cereal.

When I asked why she was staring, Francine said, "I would like to encourage you to share your inner feelings." When I told her that I *had* no inner feelings, she simply smiled and said, "Maybe not yet. But you wait. Soon those inner feelings will come pouring out of you like tea from a little teapot."

Even though my dad always paid her a few months in advance, Francine claimed she had no need for money or the creature comforts of life. She said she only accepted the use of my dad's former bedroom because her back had to be in good shape for her weekly tango lesson at the Nice and Easy Academy of Dance. Francine was very serious about the tango. She plastered the floor of Dad's bedroom with rubber footprints that had little numbers on them so she could practice between lessons. In addition to driving me crazy, my babysitter had a real talent for dancing with imaginary men.

In the middle of August, Francine ran off to Argentina with her tango instructor, Ramone. I was thrilled at first. She left some of the advance money my dad had paid her in an envelope. So I was happy about that, too. I don't want you to think badly of Francine for taking off on me. After all, she was in love with Ramone and — from everything I've heard — love is one of those emotions that can really screw up your sense of obligation.

I made up some story about my dad phoning to say he'd be home in a couple of days. In the meantime, I told her I could stay with friends. Francine was so hot to catch the next plane to South America that she believed me straight off. I didn't have a stopwatch or anything, but she was probably out the door faster than my old man could push off the starting block back in high school.

I could have stayed in the apartment by myself. But I was beginning to suspect that a strange man in a hat was following me around. I would look across the street and he would be standing under a lamppost, pretending to be doing nothing. The next moment, I would look again and he'd be gone. The whole thing creeped me out.

One afternoon, when I was trying to convince myself that the man in the hat was a hallucination, "Uncle Vito" called.

"Alex?" said my dad. "I want you to go over to the window and look outside." Since the phone was cordless, this was not hard to do. I stuck the portable part in the pocket of my jeans.

"Are you at the window?"

"Yes, Uncle Vito."

"Do you notice anything suspicious?"

Across the street the man with the hat was standing under a lamppost. "I think someone's been following me around," I said.

My dad coughed. "It could be a private investigator certain parties have hired to find a very close friend of your uncle Vito's."

"What sort of parties?"

"Could be lawyers for a lawsuit." I could hear Dad sigh before he added, "Or it could be a silent partner who has decided to stop being silent." I knew that my dad meant Big Garry.

"Uncle Vito?" I asked. "Are you okay?"

"Oh, sure," he said, brightening up in a fake way. "You want to say hello to your Aunt Bernice?"

"Aunt Bernice" was the code name for Connie. The last thing I wanted to do was talk to Connie, but I could tell my dad was stressed out. It put him in a good mood whenever Connie and I were polite to each other.

"Put her on," I said.

Soon I could hear her over the phone. "Hi, Al," she said.

"Hello, Aunt Bernice," I answered. "How are your fingernails?"

"They're hot pink at the moment," she said. "Thank you for asking."

For a few seconds, I couldn't think of anything to add. Finally, I said, "Well, don't break any."

"I hope you mean that, sweetie," Aunt Bernice said.

She put my dad back on the line. "Things are getting more complicated than I expected," he said. "I'm going to have to make myself scarce. It may be a while before I can talk to you again."

"I understand," I said.

"No, you don't," he whispered. "I think your phone may be bugged."

I didn't say anything, so my dad broke the silence with, "Are you listening?"

"Yes."

"Good," said Dad. "Did you know the handles of your crutches are hollow?"

"No."

"Well, they are. When you have a minute, I want you to unscrew them. *Both* of them. I left a little surprise in there for you."

"Uncle Vito? Maybe I could meet you somewhere."

"Bad idea, Alex. Don't worry about the guy following you around. He wants me. How's Francine?"

"She's out buying some special soap for my skin," I said. "I might stay with a friend for a few days. Francine says it's okay."

"That short kid?"

"His name is Winston."

"Right," said Dad. "Listen to Francine, okay?"

"Will you write?"

"I'll be back as soon as I can," he answered. Then his voice got louder. "Oh, hell," he said. "I love you, son. Can you hear me?"

"I can hear you, Dad," I said. But by then all I could hear was a dial tone.

I went into the bedroom and got my Swiss Army knife out of the desk drawer. I thought I'd better unscrew the handles of my crutches and discover the surprise that my dad had left inside.

The screws were very small, but I was patient. I got the first fat handle off, and as my dad had said, the inside was hollow. I didn't have a clue what was in there. But then my finger came across two chubby bundles of paper. I used the tweezers in my knife to pull out the surprise.

There were two rolls of tightly wrapped hundred-dollar bills. I counted them, and they came to a total of $2000. I stuck them in my shirt pocket and unscrewed the handle from my other crutch. There were two more bunches of bills, totaling another $2000. This time, there was also a note:

Remember how your mother used to say that your crutches were your best friends? Well, now they really are! But seriously, son, this is your nest egg. Be responsible!

Dad.

It's not often that I have $4000 in the pocket of my shirt. To be honest, I've *never* had $4000 in the pocket of my shirt. I couldn't stop looking at all the hundred-dollar bills, even while I put the handles back on my crutches. But mostly I was wondering why my dad would leave me with all that money if he planned to be back anytime soon.

CHAPTER

THREE

Sometimes, when I need to get away from the pressures of being Savior Sherwood, I hang out at Barney's Bagel Land after school. The restaurant features a big mural of cartoon people doing things with bagels: fairy princesses wearing bagel crowns, a circus strongman lifting a giant bagel over his head, even a baby carriage with little bagel wheels. The people in the mural are doing everything with bagels but eating them — which, considering how lukewarm I feel about bagels in general, makes perfect sense to me.

So, you're probably thinking, if you don't like bagels, why would you go to Barney's Bagel Land? Well, mostly because Jerry and the boys never set foot in the place. Since there's a senior's center and a medical clinic down the block, the only people who go to Barney's Bagel Land have blue hair and like their cream cheese extra soft. Don't get me wrong. I am not putting down the elderly. On the contrary, since many of them have canes and walkers, I feel quite comfortable in their company. They don't go strange when they see my crutches. They just nod and smile, as if we're all part of the same club or something.

I even talk to the occasional old person. There's this one lady who wears the exact same flowered dress every day. We don't know each other's names or anything. All we talk about is the weather or how certain kinds of bagels are easier on her dentures than others. But she is always smiling and saying stuff about how she is a "full-fledged eccentric who particularly enjoys exchanging pleasantries with young people." Once she mentioned that she used to have a son my age. I don't know whether her son is still around or not. But since she only has one dress, I try to cut her a little slack. I mean, it doesn't cost anything, right?

Alvin, the guy who owns Barney's, is an okay guy. Every so often he gives me a free bagel, because, he says, I'm one of the few young guys around who doesn't treat his customers like they're terminal droolers.

I feel so at home there that I've often considered taking Manny and Winston along. But I can get pretty selfish sometimes. I suppose I've kept the place a secret from them because they would try to turn it into a hidden lunch spot. Then all the losers would discover it and my private sanctuary would be ruined.

I should explain about hidden lunch spots. These are places around the school where it is too inconvenient for Jerry and the boys to track the rest of us down. A good example of a hidden lunch spot is underneath the auditorium stage. It's a very popular area for losers who want to eat their sandwiches in peace. Although it is dark, dusty, and crowded, there is a plus side: Jerry and the boys do not like crawling around in there because it gets their neatly pressed pants all dirty. Unless, of course, it is a collection day. On collection day, all bets are off.

As you can imagine, the best hidden lunch spots have a way of filling up fast. Manny is always trying to think of a hidden lunch spot that is still more or less virgin territory. Last year he went so far as to attend a few noon-hour meetings of the Future Teachers Club. Mr. Matchesko, the club's sponsor, is probably the only person who intimidates Jerry Whitman. Unfortunately Manny shot off his mouth about how he had discovered this excellent oasis from torment. After that, every loser in the school developed a sudden interest in the teaching profession.

Things have gotten so bad that even a five-minute head start doesn't help much. Sometimes Manny claims that I forget to stake out a hidden lunch spot because I feel sorry for all the losers who don't have a hall pass. Then he ends up apologizing for this theory. "I am a desperate man," he says. "The action in the cafeteria upsets my digestion."

Anyway, the other day we ended up in the cafeteria at high noon. Winston, Manny, and I were sitting in what Manny likes to call "the safety cluster." This means Manny never strays more than a few inches away from me at a time. He also makes sure I sit directly between him and Jerry's boys, in case Jerry tries the flying doughnut trick.

The flying doughnut trick sounds more complicated than it is. Simply put, it is Jerry throwing a stale cafeteria doughnut at the loser of the day. Often the loser of the day turns out to be Manny, who provides a broader target than the rest of us. You can't say many good things about Jerry Whitman, but his throwing skills are practically major-league quality. He can throw nearly anything and make it hurt. Manny says that sooner or later he is going to suffer the ultimate degradation of "death by cupcake."

Whitman's projectile of choice is a cafeteria jelly doughnut, which has a certain amount of heft to it because it is *always* stale. I have never taken one in the side of the face, but Manny tells me it is surprisingly painful. "It's not so much the filling as the sugar glaze," he says. "After a few days of sitting around waiting to be purchased, it hardens like concrete."

This is not your typical case of cafeteria exaggeration. I once made the unfortunate mistake of biting into a school doughnut. The action convinced me that I'd have a more rewarding culinary experience with a jelly-filled chunk of cement. That's why I felt so guilty about going to the washroom during lunch and leaving Manny practically naked. I mean, Manny was so anxious that he wanted to go *with* me to the washroom.

"I feel the sudden urge to comb my hair," he said.

Naturally I did not allow Manny to follow me into the washroom. After all, the human male has to have some privacy. I should have known better. While I was being extra sanitary and washing my hands, Jerry was getting a clear shot at Manny with a cinnamon roll the size of a Frisbee.

Later Winston told me that the perfectly round pastry went sailing across the room like a flying saucer aimed at Manny's head. "He never saw it coming," said Winston. "It caught him right above the ear as he was finishing off a slice of pickle."

The next thing that happened will clue you in on why I put up with so many of Manny's complaints. Manny can be gross. But every once in a while he'll do something that's both totally disgusting *and* totally inspiring to the loser contingent at Marshall McLuhan High. Such was the case after he got hit with Jerry Whitman's cinnamon roll.

Winston said it took Manny a few seconds to recover from the unexpected assault. But Manny is not what you'd call a slow thinker. He didn't want to give Jerry the satisfaction of a wimpy reaction. So he took the cinnamon roll and shoved the entire thing into his mouth.

Winston said you could hear everybody in the cafeteria gasp. There were even a few girls who seemed more than a little upset. But Manny kept right on chewing. He made it look as if he was really enjoying himself, even though the roll probably tasted like something left behind at a construction site.

Anyway, here comes the best part. Manny turned in the direction of Jerry — his mouth still half full of chewed up-pastry — and made a very courageous remark.

"Hey, Whitman!" he shouted. "Thanks for the complimentary dessert."

Back at our lockers, I asked Manny how he had managed to eat the whole pastry in one go. He told me that he imagined he was a monster from his favorite Japanese horror movie who was biting the head off Jerry Whitman. And then, after making sure none of Jerry's boys were around, he shook his fist in the air and shouted, "Fat Power!"

Everybody knew Jerry would jack up Manny's weekly "protection fee" for that little stunt, but some stunts are worth it. Winston said it was one of the coolest things he's ever seen a loser do. It was almost enough to convince Manny's fellow losers that Manny wasn't a loser at all. Of course, losers are generally more understanding than the rest of the school population.

Manny says if it weren't for me, he'd be nothing but a walking bull's-eye. In fact, he can get surprisingly sentimental when the mood strikes him. Just before school let out last year, he looked at me and said, "I want you to know that I think of you as more than a human shield." For Manny, that was a very emotional statement.

One thing I have always appreciated about Manny is his sense of humor. "I hate the cafeteria to the depths of my soul," he says. "It is like hell — only with colder pizza."

Some people don't like Manny because he's overweight and from New York. Manny's real first name is Rupert. But he likes Manhattan so much I gave him the nickname of Manny. After a while it stuck. Not even Jerry and the boys call Manny by his real name any more. Manny prefers to refer to Rupert as "the R-word." "Is Jerry Whitman capable of mercy?" Manny will often ask. "No! But at least he does not use the R-word."

Manny says New Yorkers are more tolerant of people who stretch the law of physical averages. In fact, he gets so homesick for Manhattan that he sometimes brags about how great it is. This sort of talk really irritates Winston, who likes it right where he is. "I know the Fat One is miserable," says Winston, "but that's no reason to keep talking about someplace we've never been."

You may have sensed a certain tension between Manny and Winston. I know things are getting especially tense when the two of them start using pet names in a bad way. Winston will call Manny "the Fat One" and Manny will call Winston "the Short One."

Every so often, Manny accuses Winston of being prejudiced

against people who carry a few bonus pounds. "You, Short One, are a fat bigot," he will say. And then he will go on and on about how he, Manny Crandall, is a fat activist who will someday make a great artistic statement that will amaze one and all.

There are times when Winston does pester Manny about stuff like exercise and self-control. For instance, he will say, "Manny, why don't you jog, jump up and down, or eat more lettuce?"

Then Manny will glare at Winston and retort, "It's possible that one day I'll lose weight. But no matter how hard you exercise, you'll never be taller."

Lunch can get nerve-wracking even when the subjects of weight and height are not on the table. To illustrate, here is a sample conversation between Winston and Manny, with me in the middle.

Manny: "I would kill for some real New York pastrami from Nate's Deli."

Me: "Is New York pastrami from Nate's Deli really good?"

Manny: "New York pastrami is the *only* pastrami."

Winston: "The *only* pastrami?"

Manny: "Especially from Nate's Deli of Manhattan."

Winston: "What's the difference? Pastrami is pastrami."

Manny: "Alex, please tell the Short One that he knows as much about pastrami as he does about being tall."

Winston: "Alex, please tell the Fat One to go jump in the lake."

See what I mean? I try to keep the peace. I try to point out that, if we can't rely on each other, what chance do we have against the forces of Jerry Whitman? But this doesn't stop

Manny and Winston from bickering like a couple of old guys on a park bench.

Privately I urge Winston to cut Manny some slack. In addition to being horizontally challenged, Manny has other problems. His dad has remarried and still lives in New York. "He has a skinny new wife and a fat new baby," says Manny. "If you are a baby, it's A-okay to be as fat as you want."

Manny and his mom moved here to live with Manny's grandmother. Unfortunately Manny's grandmother died soon afterwards. Manny says, "After that, I knew it would be a lot harder for my mom to put on her lipstick."

I should mention that Manny's mom is a heavy drinker, much worse than Mr. Winecki. I got this directly from Manny, who notes that his mother's current occupation is "getting up and falling down." Manny says that his mother likes to call herself a "stay-at-home mom." He also says that she can be more accurately described as a "stay-in-bed mom." Things are so bad that the two of them pretty much live on his dad's support payments.

"My mom says she feels like a broken-down old truck that's been traded in for a new sports car," explains Manny. "She says I should take her to the used wives' lot and leave her there to rust."

This is why I don't want Winston to pick on Manny. But sometimes it's no use trying to convince him. One day they even argued about who had more of a right to get drunk — Mr. Winecki or Manny's mom.

Winston naturally took the side of Mr. Winecki. "Walter has way more stress," he said. "He has to maintain the physical integrity of the school."

"Yeah, well, my mom has *me*," retorted Manny. "And I don't

have physical integrity." The way he said it made Winston shut up for the rest of the afternoon.

The strange thing is that, deep down, Manny and Winston sort of like each other. Case in point: after getting hit with the cinnamon roll, Manny was really down in the dumps. "It's only the first *week* of grade ten," he said. "I have about a hundred more flying doughnut tricks to look forward to and I've already used up my best comeback."

This touched Winston, who decided he would try to cheer Manny up. While the rest of us were coloring maps in geography class, Winston worked on an anonymous note for the school suggestion box. Marshall McLuhan High has a no-weapons policy, which is something you have to understand before getting Winston's joke. Anyway, Winston wrote this note that proposed all cafeteria baked goods be banned from the school since they were hard enough to qualify as lethal weapons.

The last part of the note was so good I remember it by heart. It read: "Do we have to wait for someone to lose an eye from one of the cream puffs before this administration takes action? How much longer must the more vulnerable segments of the student body be pounded with the pound cake?"

Even Manny thought it was a reasonably hilarious way to end a weekday afternoon. "I hate to admit it," he said. "But the Short One makes me laugh like nobody else."

While Winston and Manny can be a pain in the butt, they are also very trustworthy. That's why I decided to tell them about Francine departing for Argentina and the situation with the man in the hat. Winston was extremely sympathetic to the fact that I was left alone in my tiny, Jacuzzi-less apartment while some strange guy was shadowing me. Before I could suggest that I move in with him, he came up with the same idea.

Manny did not agree with this plan, which he made plain to me. Personally I think he was jealous that I was the one moving into Winston's palatial abode.

"Are you sure some strange guy is following you around?" asked Manny. "Perhaps you are hallucinating because you are so deliriously happy over your babysitter's abandoning you."

"The Fat One is just jealous because we are going to be leading mature, independent lives in one of the city's better neighborhoods," said Winston, who could be surprisingly snobby at times.

"I'll be old enough to drive next year," proclaimed Manny, in defense of his maturity. "I am already saving for a big American car. It will not only gain me respect but also suit my generous proportions."

"Big deal," said Winston. "Some kids who live on farms learn to drive tractors when they're, like, *eight.*" He began to tell us about a story he had read in some magazine. "There was this one kid whose dad's barn was burning while the dad was doing something in town. The kid hopped on his tractor and got the fire department."

"Didn't the farm have a phone?" asked Manny.

"I don't know," snapped Winston, who hated to be interrupted. "The point of the story was that the kid was only half our age and he was already good enough to drive in one of those monster tractor rallies."

"Everybody gets to have fun but us," said Manny.

Manny and Winston went on like this for a while, but this time I was grateful for the distraction. The stranger following me around was making me nervous. My normally sunny disposition was getting rained on, and it showed. Winston, finished on the subject of tractors, turned his attention to me.

"Your skin is *so* bad," he said.

Manny inspected my forehead. "All that time with the babysitter has retarded your manhood."

"I think I *should* bunk in with you for a while," I said to Winston. "At least until my skin clears up."

"Excellent!" said Winston.

Manny looked glum, as if I had betrayed him or something. "I'll have to start calling you Mansion Boy," he said.

"Come on, Manny," I replied.

"So long, Mansion Boy," said Manny. He was trying to be sarcastic. The thing was, you could tell he was nothing but lonely.

CHAPTER

FOUR

Two days later, on a Sunday afternoon, I took a cab to Winston's C. Chang's house. Winston was so excited at my impending arrival that he was waiting for me out front. He took my bag, then unlocked the big front door and started to punch in the code for the security system. Neville had thoughtfully ordered the new security system before taking off to seek his karaoke fortune.

"You can relax, my friend," Winston said. "Now that the new system's in, chez Chang is completely Whitman-proof." He punched in the final number and continued, "Not to mention protected from the Beast."

"The Beast?" I asked.

"I'll explain once we are safely inside," said Winston.

I had been to Winston's house before. But without Neville practicing his karaoke, the place felt huge and empty. I glanced around the hallway. The only place I'd seen with a bigger entrance was the airport.

Winston put my bag down in the foyer. There was a giant

chandelier hanging directly over us. The tinny tapping of my crutches on the marble floor sounded spookier than it did at school.

Winston bowed and said, "Welcome to my humble home."

Cola, the Doberman, came bounding toward us. For a couple of seconds, I thought he was going to knock me over. Then he saw who we were and turned around, disappointed. He slunk away like the saddest dog on earth.

"He keeps thinking Neville's going to walk through the door," explained Winston. "Cola misses him so much he sleeps beside one of Neville's slippers."

Winston explained that, when Neville was there, Cola was a very mild-mannered Doberman. "Jerry Whitman came to the house once to collect his weekly extortion fee and all Cola did was wag his tail," he said. "Jerry even patted him on the head." But since Neville's departure, Cola had slipped into a deep canine depression.

I sat down on the hallway bench to take off my shoes. Winston kept talking, pleased to have company. "There are only two rules here, which are actually more like safety regulations. First, do *not* try to take Neville's slipper away from Cola. He gets very angry and upset."

"What's the second rule?" I asked.

I thought maybe Winston was going to say something about not tripping over Cola's water bowl. But he got all ominous on me and said, "Stay clear of the next-door neighbor."

"What's so special about your next-door neighbor?"

"Nothing," said Winston. "He is just your everyday, garden-variety psycho, that's all."

"You've been watching too much cable TV, Winston."

Winston ignored my comment. "I don't know his real name," he said. "But the little kids around here call him the Beast."

"Has he got one eye in the middle of his forehead or something?"

"He looks more or less like a normal guy," said Winston, "but he prowls around his house like it's a cave." And then, as if the next part was a very big deal, he added, "The Beast hates noise."

"So?"

"So the man killed a perfectly good lawnmower."

"How do you kill a lawnmower?"

"Well, if you're the Beast, you pound the hell out of it with a hammer while it is still trying to cut grass," explained Winston. "Some poor gardener from a couple of houses down nearly had a stroke."

"That's bad," I admitted.

"It's not just lawnmowers," said Winston, warming to his subject. "The Beast hates other things too."

"Like what?"

"Like dog crap."

"*Everybody* hates dog crap," I pointed out.

"Not like the Beast," said Winston. "The Beast hates dog crap as if getting rid of it is his mission in life."

Winston explained that Cola had a habit of crapping only on the Beast's lawn — as if the Beast's property was the Doberman's private commode or something. "Cola is kind of exclusive in his toilet habits," said Winston. "I've tried to modify his behavior, but he is very stubborn."

In retaliation, the Beast had gone so far as to walk into Winston's unlocked storage shed and steal a piece of Chang family property, one of those little cannons that spat back tennis balls so that you could practice your swing if you were alone on the court.

"I wouldn't mind so much if he used the thing to fire tennis balls," said Winston. "But he doesn't."

Instead, Winston's next-door neighbor had modified the tennis cannon to fire back the waste Cola kept leaving on his lawn. "The Beast calls it his crap cannon," said Winston, rolling his eyes. "I'm telling you, it's *gross*. You never know when the stuff is going to come flying over the fence. Plus, he keeps switching positions and angles. So you never know *where*, either. It's like being under constant crap attack."

"Have you tried talking to him?" I asked.

"Talk to the Beast?" exclaimed Winston. "I'd rather poke a rabid grizzly with a sharp stick."

"He does sound unusual," I admitted.

"Yeah, if 'unusual' means crazy," said Winston. "He has this wild look in his eyes, and he only comes out of his house to scream at little kids to be quiet. He put an evil Tahitian curse on the paperboy."

"Come on, Winston," I said. "Why would anybody do that?"

"Because he's *mental*," Winston urged. "The paperboy says he has a gun."

Winston said the Beast was so infamous that the little girls who skipped rope in the neighborhood had made up a rhyme about him. Winston was only too glad to recite it while pretending to skip an imaginary rope.

"He walks like a bear
And he talks to himself.

He never cuts his hair.
There's a gun on his shelf."

Winston recited the next part in a sing-song-y voice that reminded me of Neville doing karaoke.

"How ma-ny bod-ies in the base-ment?
One, two, three, four…"

I started to laugh, which Winston thought was uncalled for. "I am trying to warn you about this psycho," he said hotly. "Neville says the Beast is seriously bringing down property values."

"So all he does the whole day long is sit around serving back dog crap, putting curses on the paperboy, and bashing in lawn mowers?" I asked.

"He's a *writer*," said Winston, making it sound like another reason to view the Beast with suspicion.

"He must be a pretty good writer to afford this neighborhood."

Winston was not amused. "He's babysitting the house," he said in an exasperated tone. "My real neighbor — the normal one — has gone to Europe for a year or so. I'm telling you, the Beast is seriously deranged. I wouldn't be surprised if there *was* a body in the basement."

I said nothing, which made Winston shrug. "What am I talking to *you* about weird for?" he asked. "Not only do you think Julie Spenser is close to normal, you also find her humorous."

"She's okay."

"You *like* her?" asked Winston, amazed.

"At least she treats Jerry Whitman with appropriate disdain."

"She treats everybody with disdain, " said Winston. "That doesn't mean Jerry Whitman wouldn't like to change Julie's attitude and add her to his vast harem of girlfriends. You should be very careful about her."

"What do you mean?" I asked, trying not to sound too interested.

"Have you seen the way she studies you in Mr. Why's class?" he said. "This is the second year in a row she has confused your face with map."

"Maybe Julie Spenser is a zit-gazer," I said. "Like my former babysitter, good old Francine."

"There are plenty of other zits to gaze at in English," said Winston. "Anyway, why are we talking about this? Is there a bigger waste of time than trying to figure out Julie Spenser?"

Winston decided to give me a refresher tour of the main parts of the house so that I wouldn't get lost. It seemed like ages before we hit what he called "the formal living area." The formal living area was about three times as big as my apartment. You could toss a football around and not hit anything.

Winston showed me the space with a grand sweep of his arm. "This is my parents' favorite room when they're in residence. They can put on a show of being together but they don't have to make contact."

Next we saw the games room, which contained a pool table, a shuffleboard court, and a miniature bowling alley. From there we went to a room with the big-screen TV and the exercise room. Winston pointed out that the exercise room featured "his" and "hers" treadmills, which his parents never used at the same time. Finally, we ended up in the kitchen. It was almost as big as the living room, but the first thing you noticed was the mess. There were dishes and glasses everywhere. The odor of leftover food hung heavily in the air. Winston was kind enough to guide me to the source of the smell.

"There's nothing like a slice of cold pizza before bed-time," he said.

Judging from what was in front of us, this was an obvious statement. On the giant kitchen table, pizza cartons were arranged like greasy cardboard building blocks. They stretched toward the ceiling to form a pizza-carton skyscraper. An impressive number of more or less empty cartons from Chinese food and KFC and McDonald's hamburgers were stacked up alongside to form buildings of various sizes. Everything had been placed with great care. For all its grossness, you had to admire the structural integrity.

"How long did this take you?" I asked.

"Neville and I started it together," said Winston nostalgi-cally. "Before he left. What do you think? It's a little thing we like to call Take-Out City."

"Very impressive," I nodded, noticing a carton that seemed to be the home of a very dark bug. "You know who would get a big kick out of this? Manny." I moved closer to look at the bug, which turned out to be a slice of black olive.

"You think the Fat One would appreciate my sense of scale?" asked Winston.

"Absolutely," I said, as the ghostly odor of long-gone pep-peroni assaulted my nostrils. "Do you think we could move to another room for a while?"

"Where are my manners?" said Winston. "Let me show you where you'll be staying."

Winston took my bag and began to climb a huge staircase

with a polished banister. He was so short that he had a little trouble carrying my bag up the stairs. There were a couple of times when I pulled ahead of him. I was taking some pride in that when we arrived at my room. That's when my jaw dropped open.

I've seen some impressive bedrooms while reading magazines in the dentist's office. But standing in one is a different thing altogether. The carpet was so thick you could hardly see the tips of my crutches. In addition, there was a desk that looked wide enough to sleep on. There was also a TV, a huge closet, and a deep leather armchair. On one wall was a wood-burning fireplace, and by a huge bay window was a big brass telescope for gazing at the stars.

"Keep your curtains closed," Winston advised. "That window looks directly over the Beast's place, and he likes to work at night when there are no lawnmowers about."

I looked out the window. There was a hedge between the houses, but I could see right over it into a room of the house next door. In the room, I could see lots of books and a big oak desk. There was an old-fashioned typewriter on the desk, like the kind you see in black-and-white movies, and a huge ashtray filled with cigarette butts, but the Beast was nowhere in sight.

Anyway, I wasn't worried about the neighbor spotting me. My room was so large that all you had to do to disappear was step back a bit.

In the middle of the sea of carpet sat the biggest bed I'd ever seen. Winston pushed a button on a control panel sitting on the side table, and the top half of the bed rose up. He insisted I try all the different settings so I could find the best position from which to watch TV.

"This is one of the smaller guest rooms," Winston apologized.

"But I gave you this one because I haven't had a chance to mess it up yet."

He opened the door to my very own bathroom. "This is the bathroom with the bidet," he warned. "It's what the French use instead of toilet paper." He showed me how the bidet worked, pressing a plunger to release a stream of water that shot up from the toilet bowl like a fountain in the middle of a shopping plaza.

"Too bad the school washrooms don't come with bidets," he said. "We wouldn't have to bend down so far when one of Jerry's boys decides to give us a dunking." He laughed and then looked at me funny. "Is anything wrong, Alex?" he asked. "You don't have to *use* the bidet. We have plenty of bathroom tissue."

"It's not that," I said, noticing that Winston had lined up three different kinds of toothpaste on the counter. "I just wasn't expecting all this."

"All what?" asked Winston. "This is nothing. My old man has a custom-designed shower head that could take the paint off the walls."

Winston was so used to the luxurious nature of his surroundings that he didn't get what I meant. So I switched the subject. "Are you hungry?"

"Getting there," said Winston. "What do you feel like? You want to add a twelfth floor to the pizza tower?"

"What's in your fridge?" I asked.

"I never look in there," he replied. "Neville cooks a couple of times a week."

"Let me check it out." I said. "Maybe I could whip up a little dinner."

Winston looked shocked, as if I had said I might grow a third hand.

"Do you have any dishwashing liquid?" I asked.

"I don't know. Neville washes the dishes."

"What about the laundry?"

"Neville doesn't trust me with the laundry," he said. "He says I turn his underwear purple."

"What do you do for clean clothes, Winston?"

"When something gets dirty, I buy another one."

"Wouldn't it be easier to do the wash?"

Winston shrugged. "Neville will do it after the contest."

I was beginning to understand why Neville was taking so long in California.

I told Winston to leave it to me. He went to his room to get some rest after a hard day of trying his best to fall asleep at school. "Now and then, I come close to dozing off in class," he said. "But there's generally too much commotion to get a good nap going."

Downstairs in the kitchen, I located a box of dishwasher detergent behind a dozen or so bottles of pop. I loaded the machine with dirty dishes and turned it on. I checked the fridge, throwing away the brown stuff that had turned green and the green stuff that had turned brown. I had better luck when I opened the freezer. It was filled with frozen steaks, chicken, and chops.

Now, to be honest, I am not the greatest cook in the world. Nobody is going to give me a medal for anything that comes off the stove under my supervision. On the other hand, if you don't mind simple dishes, I won't poison you either. So I was fairly confident when I took out a couple of frozen steaks and thawed them in the microwave. I managed to find a few potatoes that were still good, plus a half-decent selection of vegetables. It was really no big deal.

Still, it was fun moving around in the spacious kitchen and pretending to be a major cook. I even discovered a roomy apron that said "World's Greatest Chef." Indoors, I can generally get around on one crutch. It leaves one hand free to do kitchen-type things. If I lose my balance, I can always grab a piece of furniture.

In no time, I was frying the steaks on the stove's fancy grill while everything else bubbled away in expensive-looking pots.

It must have smelled good to Winston. He came downstairs, looked at my apron, and said, "Honey, I'm home!"

We decided to eat in the dining room. Winston's Take-Out City took up too much room on the kitchen table to dine comfortably. Once we were settled, Winston noticed that I'd forgotten to take off my apron.

"You're not going to go all housewife-y on me, are you?" he asked.

"Certainly not," I said. I slipped off the apron and hung it on the chair beside me.

Winston ate a forkful of mashed potatoes and nodded his approval. "Well, maybe a *little* housewife-y is okay."

"Tomorrow I'll make chicken," I said.

We finished the meal and started on the ice-cream cake I had thawed out for dessert. Winston was blissed out. He said he felt that I had ushered in a whole new set of culinary standards.

"I think it's time to get out the wrecking ball," he mused.

The wrecking ball was really a tennis ball that Cola liked to chew on. Winston positioned himself in front of Take-Out

City, tennis ball in hand. Then he passed the ball to me.

"You know what? I think you should do the honors."

I wound up and threw the ball at the tower of pizza cartons. It teetered for a second and then came down with a very cool crash, wiping out a number of surrounding chow mein buildings and hamburger huts. In the aftermath of Take-Out City's demolition, a small cloud of take-out dust rose up from the ruins.

"Nice shot," said Winston.

"I got lucky," I said.

Winston moved closer to survey the wreckage. He was wearing slippers that made a sticky sound as he walked.

"Have you noticed that the floor's getting dirty?" he asked.

"Maybe you should get someone in here to clean."

"We have an account with Merry Maids." Winston showed me a brochure with a picture of two smiling cleaning ladies in uniform. "But I told them to stop coming."

"Why would you do that?"

"They always sent out a couple of Merry Maids who are not very merry," Winston said. "I don't like being outnumbered by grumpy women."

I finally got Winston to agree to call them and get them to clean while we were in school. After that, we went down to the washer/dryer and I gave him his first lesson in the laundry arts.

Later we folded laundry in front of the giant TV, then I decided to do some homework.

"I'd join you in your pursuit of academic excellence," said Winston, "but it wouldn't be true to my code."

Instead, Winston decided to take Cola for a short walk. I thought this was highly energetic of him, but he explained he was basically motivated by fear.

"If Neville comes back and finds Cola fat and slow, I'll totally lose the respect of my older brother," said Winston. "He made me swear that I'd walk Cola every day. Don't be concerned if we're gone a long time," he added. "Cola is a slow walker. He keeps looking for Neville in the bushes."

"That's what I call a faithful dog," I said.

"It's weird," said Winston. "Whenever the phone rings and it's Neville, Cola *knows*. It's like he can tell from the ring or something."

While Winston was walking the dog, I went up to my room. I lit a fire in the guestroom fireplace using a handy Presto-Log and spread my books out on the desk. When I'd finished my homework, I ran a bath and enjoyed the silence. I soaked for a while, feeling goofy with freedom.

By the time I got to bed, the fire was dying out. I set my alarm for 7:00 a.m., because Winston had confided that he had to be at school every weekday morning by 8:00 to have bacon and eggs with Mr. Winecki in the janitor's room. When I asked him how he managed to get out of bed so early, he said, "Walter counts on me to start his day with a few laughs."

Maybe it was the unfamiliar surroundings, but I woke up in the middle of night and saw that I had forgotten to shut the curtains. It was a clear night with a generous sprinkling of stars, and I found myself pushing open the big window.

You could still feel the warmth of early September. Everything was so still that I could hear faint music in the distance. Somebody was playing the saxophone in front of a full orchestra. I'd never heard music like that before. It was sweet and beautiful and sad at the same time. The kind of sound that seemed made especially for a sky full of stars.

It didn't take long for me to realize that the music was coming from the Beast's place. His blinds were up, and he had the lights on. The window featured a good view of his back, which looked 100 percent normal unless you considered that it was covered by a Hawaiian shirt with an ugly pattern of tropical fruit on it. Occasionally his shaggy head moved from side to side as he tapped away on the old typewriter. Cigarette smoke rose gently to form a kind of halo around him.

I don't know why I used the brass telescope to get a closer look. Maybe it was because the Beast seemed to be in his own private world, and that world looked intriguing. Anyway, I aimed the telescope at his window. By the time I had second thoughts about doing it, it was too late.

Since Winston's telescope was powerful, I could see a lot of detail. About a dozen Oh Henry! candy bar wrappers made a scattered patch of bright yellow on the floor. To my surprise, there was a big poster of Groucho Marx, which didn't seem to fit in with the décor in the rest of the room. There was also a scale model of the Chrysler Building, which I recognized from some of the books I'd seen on architecture. It sat off to the side and looked about three-quarters done.

Normally I would have spent time looking at the scale model or the poster of Groucho, but once I spotted the gun on the desk, I couldn't take my eyes off it. It was the sort of pistol you see in old army movies — big and black and sitting there like it was part of the furniture or something.

The curious side of me wanted to keep watching, but I finally made myself go back to bed. I tried to go back to sleep, but I couldn't stop thinking about the Beast.

CHAPTER

FIVE

For the next couple of nights, once I'd finished my homework, I watched the Beast through the telescope. The first night he kept busy writing, but the second night he mainly stared at his typewriter. After a while he switched off his desk lamp and buried his face in his hands. Following that there was no smoke and no music — just a guy sitting in the dark, waiting for nothing to happen.

I didn't mention my surveillance of the Beast to Winston. I told myself that I should keep an eye on the guy because maybe he was going to blow his brains out with the army gun that was always on his desk. But that was only an excuse to keep watching.

I wish I could tell you that I took a break from spying because I'm an ethical guy, but the truth is, Winston and I threw ourselves into the independent bachelor life with such enthusiasm that it started to use up extra energy. We played table tennis, pool, and shuffleboard. We spent time miniature bowling. We stayed up late to watch videos and play the latest computer games. As I said to Manny, "Life at the mansion is exhausting, but somebody has to do it."

Manny was clearly unhappy that Winston and I were having so much fun while he was stuck looking after his mom. His jealousy was especially bad the first Friday after I'd moved in. Friday was collection day, and Manny made a special point of calling me Mansion Boy all afternoon.

Jerry Whitman and the boys had established a routine over the years. But every so often — just to teach all of Jerry's kids "to expect the unexpected" — they would change collection day to a Tuesday or a Thursday. But mostly Jerry enjoyed collecting his extortion fees on Friday because it gave him extra cash for the weekend.

Jerry considered himself something of a ladies' man. He always maintained a showcase girlfriend for display purposes. There were also a few spares on the side, waiting to move up when he got bored with the main attraction. This meant he spent his money on a whole bunch of girls, which I'm told can be very financially demanding.

In addition, Whitman's status as a ladies' man required that no female loser should ever pay protection money. Some thought this was one of the few rules of goodness that Jerry Whitman lived by, but Manny said it was simply another way to humiliate guy losers by making them wish they were the opposite sex.

Either way, Jerry had no problem with depriving male victims of their weekend spending money. The result was a vicious circle of loserdom. Manny expressed the dilemma perfectly. "With no money for movies or video games or assorted reading material, there is nothing to do," he said. "Nothing to do but sit around and remind yourself that you are a bona fide loser."

Winston also resented the Friday collection day. "Why does it have to be on *Friday*?" he would ask. "Friday should be the best day of the school week by far." He felt so strongly about this that he used to pay Jerry on Thursdays. That way Friday could have "the right tone of impending relaxation."

Mind you — the Jerry Whitman situation aside — Winston is pretty relaxed on any day of the week. In fact, he is the most academically relaxed person I know. But just because a person is easygoing doesn't mean they can't have principles.

Anyway, Winston soon discovered that his early payments had a negative effect on his fellow losers, many of whom had enough trouble making the Friday deadline. So — not wanting to make anyone of the loser persuasion worse off than they already were — he'd reluctantly switched back to the regular day.

"I am lucky," says Winston. "Unlike the Fat One, I do not have a cash flow problem."

Friday collection is especially hard on Manny because he has the entire week to blow his loser bucks on junk food. "I always start off with good intentions," he points out. "But the Twinkie machine gets me every time." Manny explains that the Twinkies in the Twinkie machine are "sealed for extra freshness." He says that, compared to cafeteria doughnuts, the Twinkies taste as if they were baked inside the machine by kindly little Twinkie makers who live for no other reason than to answer the Twinkie call of Manny Crandall. "I try to think of what Jerry is going to be like on Friday if I don't have his money," he says. "But on a Monday, Jerry is no match for golden sponge cake with gooey cream filling."

Whenever Manny gets short of cash, I help him out with a

loan. I can do this because, for some reason, Jerry and the boys never hit me up for money. As a matter of fact, I'm the only non-girl loser that Whitman excludes from payment.

This used to puzzle Manny greatly. "You are an official loser in every way but shelling out to the Jerry Whitman fund," he would say. "To me, this is a bigger mystery than the Egyptian pyramids."

At first, Winston thought Jerry was being soft-hearted by letting me off the hook. "You are neutral," he would speculate. "You are the Switzerland of losers." Then he remembered that Whitman has no heart. Finally, we figured out why I didn't have to pay protection money. Stay with me on this point, and you'll begin to appreciate the cunning of Jerry Whitman.

"Jerry is not soft-hearted, but *you* are," said Winston. "That's why it bothers you so much to see one of Jerry's kids running the gantlet."

"Running the gantlet" is what happens when a loser falls behind on his payments. Miss a single payment, and Jerry will usually let you off with a stern warning, plus a wallet-draining boost in additional interest. Miss any more than that, and the boys make sure you run the gantlet from Monday to Friday. Your life will be total misery for five straight days.

A good percentage of losers who are set to run the gantlet will suddenly develop what Jerry and the boys call "the gantlet flu." But staying away from school only makes the inevitable agony worse. There is nowhere to hide once you've recovered from the gantlet flu. The boys will shove you in the hallway and splatter your books. They will trap you in a quiet corner of the library stacks and destroy your homework. They will snap towels at your vulnerable butt while you are getting ready for gym class.

If you get caught in the washroom alone, they will hold your head in the toilet and treat you like a human cigarette butt.

After a week of this, most losers are more than happy to pay up. Occasionally someone is stubborn or just plain broke. Under these circumstances, Jerry normally uses the Watertank to collect his fee. The Watertank's real name is Duane Waterton, but Duane is so massive that everyone calls him by his nickname. The Watertank is Jerry's faithful enforcer. He is so good at enforcing that he has never failed to bring back a fee with exactly the right amount of interest. Of course, there are times when he has to give the loser in question a black eye or some other lingering injury so that the person will remember to have money the following Friday.

I am ashamed to say that I was a close friend of Duane Waterton's back in the golden days of elementary school. One day in grade six, I even saved the Watertank's life. Manny often says that if it weren't for me, Duane would never have gotten big enough to be compared to a major appliance.

Here's what happened. Duane was sitting in the school lunchroom wolfing down a hot dog. I was sitting beside him, joking about the gross stuff that was supposed to be in the average wiener. All of a sudden, Duane started to choke. He stood up, but he was really having trouble breathing. That's when I remembered this thing I had seen on TV, where you stand behind a choking victim, put your arms around them, and make a fist underneath their rib cage. After that, you push up a couple of times.

So that's what I did. It must have looked ridiculous, because I forgot all about my crutches and was leaning against Duane pretty hard. The thing is, my TV maneuver worked. A sizeable chunk of hot dog flew out of Duane's throat and landed beside the soup thermos of some little kid who started screaming for his mother. After the kid stopped screaming, everybody started saying what a hero I was. There was actually an assembly where the principal thanked me for my alertness.

But the best part was Duane's reaction. After the assembly, he took me aside and got all serious. "We're gonna be friends for life, man," he said. And then, for emphasis, he added, "For *life.*"

Of course, back then I had no idea that Duane was going to become Jerry Whitman's major goon. In his darkest hours, Manny will speculate on how much easier our lives would be if Duane's chunk of hot dog had stayed where it was. "I wouldn't have wanted him to *die*," Manny says, "but maybe it could have stunted his growth or something."

It wasn't hard to see Manny's point. The Watertank is easily the biggest guy in grade ten. In a way, Duane's extreme size keeps things peaceful. Most of the time, he can be a very effective goon through the simple art of intimidation. In fact, when comparing levels of torment, there are more than a few losers who prefer a private session with the Watertank to the more lengthy degradation of running the gantlet.

Even when he's forced to get physical, Duane can still cut a guy some slack. There was the time a hard-core loser named Davey Swanigan was so far behind on his payments that he was supposed to get punched in the face. As it turned out, Davey had a very important part coming up in an English class production of *Julius Caesar.* He kept saying, "Please, Tank, not in the face. The Romans are vastly superior warriors and they are not supposed to look beat up. Everyone in my group will get a lower grade because of my inappropriate physical appearance."

Moved by this artistic reasoning, the Watertank decided to punch Davey Swanigan hard in the shoulder. It left an ugly bruise, but Davey managed to hide it by wearing a T-shirt under his Roman toga. Manny pointed out that Duane's gesture bordered on classy. "Plus, the Watertank's punishment is *quick*," he added. "Which is more than you can say for running the gantlet."

It is a terrible thing to observe Jerry and the boys doling out such treatment. And Winston says Jerry knows I would much rather run the gantlet than not have to pay protection and watch. "He realizes that you feel deep sympathy for your fellow losers," explains Winston. "So he has devised the ultimate psychological torment for a sensitive person such as yourself."

I must admit that the guilt of not having to pay protection eats at my gut. It eats at my gut so much that I offer regular loans not only to Manny but to other needy losers as well. I charge a modest rate of interest, which I put directly into floating other loans. Occasionally I have loans out to three or four losers at a time. What is the first thing seasoned losers tell a new member of Jerry's kids? "Go see the Savior," they say. "The Savior is always good for a loan."

Winston calls this the ultimate irony. "What a sweet deal for Whitman," he says. "On top of the general aggravation, he is squeezing way more money out of you than if you had to pay him directly."

How can I afford to keep giving out loans? Well, there is more honor among losers than you might think. Even though the guys I help are always short of cash, they somehow manage to pay me back on time. Winston says it's because they know the money is going to help their own kind.

Now and then one of Jerry's kids thinks he can let one of my loans slide. When this happens, his fellow losers give him the silent treatment. I don't encourage such treatment, because I feel it's merely an indirect way for Whitman to spread around his special brand of misery. But as Manny says, "The only thing that makes contributing to the Jerry Whitman Fund bearable is knowing that we have the Bank of Sherwood as a safety net."

Still, it's no picnic being one of Jerry's kids. On Fridays, the air of doom is thick enough to cut with one of Mr. Winecki's hacksaws. Everywhere you look, Jerry Whitman is getting secretly paid off. A loser will pass Jerry a copy of *To Kill a Mockingbird* with cash as a bookmark. Another loser will lend him a pen with a tightly rolled up bill inside it. Whitman has more pens — and does less writing — than anybody I know.

Manny says he often racks his brain to figure out why Jerry Whitman is so evil. He finds it especially perplexing since Jerry's family is the type you see pictured on boxes of granola. The Whitmans are what you might call terminally wholesome. Apparently Jerry's grandmother was once Miss Pacific National Exhibition. And Jerry's dad — Jerry Whitman, Sr. — has been the top-selling real estate agent in town for eight years running. How do I know this? Because Jerry Senior's face is plastered on practically every bus-stop bench in the city. Underneath a picture that shows all his gleaming Whitman teeth is a caption that reads: "Number one for eight years running!"

Jerry Whitman, Jr., is so admiring of his dad that he will regularly quote Jerry Senior's favorite sayings. For example, in the halls he will tell someone, "My old man says that the two dirtiest words in the English language are 'second place.'" Or in the cafeteria he will be heard remarking, "My old man says there are two kinds of people in life: the ones who kick ass and the ones who get their asses kicked." Whenever Whitman makes this last comment, Winston always whispers to Manny and me, "Gee, I wonder which category *we're* in."

Jerry is oblivious to everything else when he is mouthing off on the topic of his dad. Manny calls it "being in the Jerry Whitman, Sr., zone." In class, Whitman is always going on about how he and his dad do things together — like fishing, fixing up old cars, and other assorted guy stuff. Winston said that he once saw Jerry's mother buying gourmet cheese in the gourmet cheese store. "Not only does she have superior taste in dairy products," he reported, "she also looks like a high-fashion model."

"I don't get it," said Manny. "Whitman is tall, good-looking and completely zit-free. His parents are as perfect as he is. Why doesn't he leave us alone and go about his business of being ideal?"

"Because being ideal is not enough for Jerry Whitman, Jr.," said Winston. "Being perfect is so perfect that it's boring."

"But why does he have to take his boredom out on us?" asked Manny.

It was a similar exasperated question that had led us to develop the concept of the Losers' Club in the first place. In the early days of grade nine, Manny and Winston and I would hang around Winston's house and complain about how Jerry and the boys were making our lives a living hell. One afternoon Manny said something especially interesting. "I wish there was some way to get back at Whitman without him knowing," he griped. "There should be a Jerry Whitman dartboard where you can jab him right between his perfect eyes."

You never know when one little thing will to spark a chain reaction. That's what happened when Winston ran with Manny's idea. He had a full-length picture of Jerry Whitman from the school annual blown up, and he glued some corkboard behind it. What did he get? An official Jerry Whitman dartboard. I don't consider myself an overly malicious person. However, I experienced joys previously unknown while throwing darts at various portions of Jerry Whitman's anatomy.

One afternoon when we were over at Winston's place, Manny hit dartboard Jerry in a very private place. Since it was a Saturday, the day after collection day, the action gave him a bonus amount of satisfaction. "It would be selfish to keep this idea to ourselves," he declared expansively. "This would be great stress relief for countless other losers in the school. You know, like Jerry Whitman Anonymous."

That's pretty much how the Losers' Club got started. At first, it was just a bunch of Jerry's kids secretively gathering at Winston's house on Thursday afternoons to gleefully throw darts at the picture of Jerry Whitman. Then Manny came up with the Jerry Whitman voodoo doll.

The Jerry Whitman voodoo doll was really an old Ken doll that Manny had bought at a secondhand store. But Manny had made a few alterations, including a Jerry Whitman wig and Jerry Whitman loafers. Once you turned up the collar of the little Jerry Whitman jacket, it looked surprisingly realistic.

Manny developed a complete act around the doll. He would put on an old hat of his mom's that looked like a turban and pretend to be one of those ancient fortune-tellers on TV. Then he would stick a pin in a sensitive physical region of the doll. After a second or two, he would get a mystical expression on his face. "Where are you, Jerry Whitman?" he would moan. "Are you feeling an intense, mysterious pain in a precious bodily area?" The routine never failed to get plenty of laughs.

To anyone who wasn't one of Jerry's kids, the above might have sounded amazingly immature. But to veteran losers who had been abused, tormented, and financially drained since the beginning of high school, it was intensely liberating. After having to be so careful at school, we finally had a release for our Jerry Whitman frustrations. In private, it didn't matter whether it was stupid or babyish. After all, we were already losers. So what did we have to lose?

The dartboard and the voodoo doll also helped to create a bond among Jerry's kids that hadn't existed before. It wasn't long before we started to relax and compare notes. Finally, Tin Face Facelli, who has been wearing braces for half of his natural life, said something inspired.

"I wish I had been able to learn more about Jerry and the boys when I first came to Marshall McLuhan," he remarked. "It would have saved me a great deal of general turmoil and aggravation."

Tin Face was referring to the many things a loser can learn only from experience. For instance, if you know you are about to get beaten up by Jerry or the Watertank, it is very handy to wedge a large paperback textbook into your belt so that your gut area is protected. Once this is done, you cover up the textbook with a bulky sweater and hope for the best.

Not all paperback textbooks work effectively in this regard. Some are too thick and thus detectable when the Watertank's fist meets a particular loser's stomach. Others are thin and flexible but don't provide adequate shielding of the stomach area. It was Tin Face who found the perfect book for the job in the school library: *A Short History of Interior Design*. It proved both thick enough and wide enough to provide maximum coverage.

As soon as one loser returned *A Short History of Interior Design*, another loser would check it out. Ms. Maculwayne said it was the most requested volume in the history of Marshall McLuhan High. Due to its apparent popularity, she ordered several other copies of the book, but for some reason — known only to those pathetic enough to be behind on their collection payments — the books kept coming back lumpy.

Of course, sometimes it didn't matter what kind of reading material you used. Tin Face shook his head sadly. "A lot of inexperienced guys try the textbook trick under their shirts," he said. "But unless you have the bulky sweater, you might as well forget the whole thing."

This led to an earnest discussion of other mistakes that new inductees into the complex world of Jerry's kids could make. Rookies often bumped into Jerry and the boys several times a day, despite the fact that they did their best to avoid the experience. Senior losers, on the other hand, had learned to stay clear of Whitman's favorite hangouts around the school.

Howard Beal, who was going into his third year as one of Jerry's kids, had a color-coded chart that broke down Jerry Whitman's whereabouts on an hour-by-hour basis for the entire school week. Being a generous guy, Howard made an extra copy of the chart and used a special machine at his dad's print shop to laminate it. Manny said it looked so good we should frame it. But we settled for tacking it up beside the dartboard and the voodoo doll display.

Tin Face's comment got me considering how much intelligence, experience, and general brain power the senior Jerry's kids had. Why not pool our information for the good of all? That way, junior losers could benefit from the seniors' hard-won knowledge. I mentioned it to the others, and pretty soon the games room at Winston's house was a Thursday afternoon sanctuary for every loser in the school.

This development made a lot of sense. At regular Thursday meetings, I could arrange short-term loans for Jerry's kids away from the prying eyes of Jerry and his goons. In addition, losers who were about to crack from the strain of too much Jerry had a place where they could share their burdens with other like-minded individuals.

As the membership got bigger, we had to take certain precautions. People's exits from school were staggered, so that it wouldn't appear as if we were all heading for the same place on Thursdays. We were careful to make sure none of Jerry's boys followed us to Winston's, too. The number-one rule was, if anything looked suspicious, you headed straight for home. Manny said he was surprised no club member had broken down and confessed our secret in order to appease Jerry. But it didn't surprise me one bit. We might be losers, but all we had was each other.

Basil Whiting was so grateful for a safe haven from Jerry and the boys that he made a sign for us in grade-nine woodworking class. Basil has had a wood-burning set since he was five years old, and he's an expert at design. Even so, none of us were prepared for the elaborate way he spelled out "The Losers' Club" in Old English lettering. We agreed that it was a thing of rare beauty. Winston liked it so much he immediately hung it next to Howard's chart.

Inspired by this, Manny selected a special font on Winston's computer and typed out what he called "The Losers' Declaration of Independence." It began: "Give us your nerds, your geeks, your hard-core losers yearning to break free from the tyranny of Jerry Whitman Jr.!" We mounted this stirring document on the wall under the Losers' Club sign.

Next, Manny drew a series of hilarious cartoons that featured Jerry and the boys looking hopelessly stupid. My contribution was a saying from the great Groucho Marx, "I would never belong to a club that would have me as a member." Before long, we had a wall full of loser-oriented stuff.

Thursdays at Winston's was crowded with guys breaking out in nervous rashes or coming down with the first signs of the gantlet flu. It finally got so packed that Manny had to do interviews to determine if new applicants were pathetic enough to join.

This year, interviews for new inductees to the club took place on the first two Thursdays of the school term. By now, Manny has gained a lot of experience when it comes to sizing up the truly pathetic, and his interviews were very brief. They could be as short as one question. "What is the most satisfying thing you have ever collected?" Manny would ask. And if the applicant mentioned something along the lines of, say, "used bird nests" or "the postage stamps of Bulgaria," he was automatically a Thursday-meeting kind of guy.

Occasionally Manny didn't even have to ask a question. The applicant would start talking about how he was getting his sinuses drained the next afternoon, or how he had to walk his little sister home from embroidery class. Then Manny would simply say, "See you next Thursday."

Our school has lots of losers, all right — which makes it difficult to know why Julie Spenser singled me out from the crowd. Here is the most recent illustration of what I mean. The other morning I was standing around in the hallway minding my own business before classes started. I wasn't doing anything special, just reading a poster that was tacked up on the bulletin board outside the electronics shop. The poster was about this competition known as the Festival of Lights, which was sponsored by something called the Elvira Mumford Foundation. It read as follows:

Attention all high schoolers! Learn teamwork and initiative! Get into the Christmas spirit and foster family togetherness! Decorate your house with an exterior display of Christmas lights and delight children of all ages! Prizes! Cash! Scholarships! Your participation ensures a donation to the food bank.

At the bottom of the poster, someone had scrawled, "Attention, all losers!" in black felt pen. Somebody else had added, "Nerd alert!" in red ink. Below that, someone had underlined the part about the first-prize cash award of $1000 and printed "There's prize money, you morons!" Below that, someone else had underlined the part about the donation to the food bank and — in small, neat letters — had written, "You guys are so shallow!"

It was all very ordinary until Julie Spenser came up beside me. She stood there for a few seconds, making me uncomfortable.

Then, out of the blue, she asked, "Do you like Christmas lights?"

"I used to," I managed to mumble. "Back when I was a kid."

"Me too," said Julie, as if confessing some deliciously secret shame. "I used to like them a lot."

"Most little kids like Christmas lights," I said, hoping to take the edge off Julie Spenser's confession.

"Yeah," said Julie. "The rules were so simple back then. You wore your mittens pinned to the sleeves of your jacket. Cocoa was your beverage of choice, and Christmas lights were the absolute best. Remember?"

"Sure I remember." Suddenly I realized we were having a conversation. I turned to face her. Close up, the black mascara around her eyes made her look like a sad raccoon. "You ever miss being a kid?" I asked.

"Not exactly," she said. "I think the experience is overrated. In fact, it can be very boring."

"What do you mean?"

"I mean I miss the *buzz* of being a kid," she explained. She paused for a second, her eyes lighting up, and added, "The way the excitement was so *pure*. Getting worked up about something like Christmas lights. You can never get that back."

"Who says?"

"What?" blinked Julie Spenser.

"Who says you can't get it back?"

Julie gave me a funny little smile, as if *I* was the strange one. On the other hand, it *was* a smile. At that moment, it was easy to imagine little Julie Spenser with her little black mittens pinned to her little black coat getting all excited over outdoor lights. That's about as far as things would have gone if the Watertank had not happened by for his electronics class.

Suddenly Julie did something completely unexpected. First, she said, "I'll see you later, okay?" — as if she was really looking forward to later. Second, she leaned over and kissed me on the cheek, as if this was the most natural thing in the world. And then Julie Spenser walked off.

I stood there frozen. Even the Watertank was in shock. I saw Winston and Manny approaching out of the corner of my eye.

"Man," said Winston. "What was that?"

"That was more trouble than a fully loaded Twinkie machine on collection day," observed Manny.

"Way more," said Winston.

CHAPTER

SIX

Whenever I get worried about what's going to happen to my dad, I concentrate on reviewing the important events of the day. It takes my mind off the idea of Dad going to jail for fraud. Often I do my review late at night while soaking in Winston's king-sized Jacuzzi. But sometimes not even the soothing waters can melt my troubles away. At those moments, I realize how genuinely weird my new life at Winston's is.

Then I get to thinking about what it would be like to have the kind of family you see on those really old TV shows — you know, with some dad who works in an office but can hardly wait to come home and put on his slippers. Plus, a mom who vacuums all the time and bakes cakes for no particular reason. Manny says I should be grateful that I don't have a mom who hides bottles of vodka under her mattress. "There is no up side to your mom being a drunk," he points out. "Even the money I get from cashing in the empties goes straight to the Jerry Whitman Fund."

Manny can be pretty harsh about his mom's situation. He says he would move to Manhattan and live with his dad "in a New York minute" except for the fact that Babette, his dad's new wife, doesn't want him around. His last visit to his dad's place didn't go well. "Babette has invested in some very delicate modern furniture," he explained. "Unfortunately an individual in my particular weight class sort of clashes with the subtlety of the décor."

Winston is not keen on the subject of parents either. When his dad got hold of Winston's final grade-nine report card, he mailed him a report of his own. It was a ten-page financial summary of everything the Changs had paid to raise Winston since the day he was born. Fifteen years' worth of food, clothing, and shelter — not to mention a special category labeled "Amusements." All on official Chang Inc. stationery. Even Winston was surprised at how much he had cost.

At the end of the report, there was something called a "cost analysis statement." Mr. Chang had written: "We regret to conclude that, at this juncture, our son Winston C. Chang has shown a poor return on our investment! Solution? Better grades!" Below that, his mother had scribbled: "W.C.C. must live up to parental expectations!" Winston informed us that his parents like to use exclamation marks for everything, even their Hong Kong grocery list. "Get eggs!" he mimics. "Get butter! Fix W.C.C.!"

Still, both Winston and Manny have a definite soft spot for their parents. Manny says his worst nightmare is finding his mother permanently conked out on the floor of their condo. He makes jokes about his situation, calling the act of dragging his mom to the couch "the drunk parent workout." But Manny doesn't fool anybody. You can tell he is very concerned about his mother.

Manny says it's even possible to feel close to his mother in spite of her difficult behavior. One time she told him he was the only rose in an endless garden of bullshit. "My mother used to write poetry," he says. "Now she just sort of blurts it out."

Winston tries to hide the fact that he misses his dad by using humor. "The only time my father ever hugged me was when I got an A-plus on an arithmetic test," he says. Winston does an especially hilarious imitation of his dad. He hops around and shouts, "A-plus, Winston! A-plus!" Then he puts a serious expression on his face and goes, "It wasn't so much the A that got him excited. It was the plus."

Although Winston makes jokes about his parents, you can tell he feels bad at being practically deserted by them. I have seen him be very touchy about it on occasion. He will go out of his way to explain what he calls "the culturally unique per-spective of Asian big business." Winston says that in Asian culture it's not such a big deal to leave your kids alone in a huge house — even if it happens to be situated in a whole other country. That's when Manny starts feeling that maybe his own circumstances aren't so bad after all. "My mom's a drunk," he observes, "but at least she gets drunk under the same roof as me."

After a comment like that, Winston goes quiet. I think he has a lot of hidden anger about his parents. He told us once that in Asian culture one of the worst shames is not to do well in academics. "It's not your regular shame," he said. "It's like turbo-boosted shame." It doesn't take a rocket scientist to fig-ure out that Winston slacks off to get psychological revenge on his mom and dad. He feels guilty, but he says he's used to that particular emotion by now. "My parents serve up guilt like it's an ancient family recipe," he says. "Believe me, Winston C. Chang has eaten plenty of Guilt Foo Yung."

Nobody's parents are perfect, although my mom came awfully close. She took care of pretty much everything. "Your father is a dreamer," she used to say. "This is both his best quality and his worst one." After she got sick, she said, "You're going to have to be the practical one in the family. Can you handle that?"

I like to believe that I'm handling things well. Although I can't walk and push the shopping cart around at the same time, I've become quite good at organizing the household accounts. The first thing I learned about financial management on the home front was the following: when Sam "The Shovel" Sherwood gives you money, you use it to pay the rent in advance. Our building manager Mr. Sankey says that if all his tenants were as reliable as me, his ulcer would be under control.

Even though I've been staying at Winston's these past two weeks, I try to stick reasonably close to my regular apartment routine so as not to arouse suspicion. After school, I often go back to the apartment to check for messages. I've done laundry there a couple of times, so that I can touch base with Mr. Sankey.

At the best of times, Mr. Sankey likes to think of himself as a "live-and-let-live kind of guy." But recently he has been even less clued in on the comings and goings of tenants because he had begun doing extensive renovations for the building's new owner, a man Mr. Sankey refers to as "the Slave Driver." The Slave Driver is making Mr. Sankey do repair work inside and out. Several of the vacant apartments are being completely remodeled, and the outside of the building is being spruced up. As Mr. Sankey puts it, "The Slave Driver considers me a one-man work crew."

Mr. Sankey is so distracted that he has very little time to notice my absence from the premises — not to mention the disappearance of both Dad and Francine. This is pretty convenient, given my current domestic situation. Mr. Sankey is pretty cool, but you can never tell when an adult is going to have a severe attack of responsibility.

I like Mr. Sankey. He keeps his tools in the laundry room, and sometimes I'll go down there even when I don't have any laundry to do. Mr. Sankey has all sorts of old stuff stored in the basement from when his wife was still alive and they lived in a regular house. His collection of "invaluable antiques and assorted junk" includes an interesting array of outdoor Christmas decorations. There are cherry-nosed plastic reindeers and merry elves and many more unusual items.

My personal favorite is this gigantic sign from Fat 'n' Happy Turkeys, where Mr. Sankey used to work. The sign features one of those old-fashioned, hug-crazed families standing around a cramped kitchen table. On the table sit the picked-over remains of a Fat 'n' Happy turkey. The family members are happily watching the chubby, open-mouthed dad, who is about to chow down on a huge turkey sandwich. Underneath the picture — in two separate lines of plug-in neon lettering — it says:

From All the Boys at Fat 'n' Happy…
Wishing You a Happy, Closer Holiday!

Mr. Sankey's collection also includes a giant hula girl mannequin doing a holiday hula dance on top of a sandy patch of beach with writing on it ("Merry Christmas from the Island of Hawaii!"). Mr. Sankey says that his giant hula girl was originally part of a Christmas display for the Hawaiian Pineapple Company.

Mr. Sankey loves his outdoor holiday decorations, but I think he likes his giant hula girl the best. He told me that in his day no self-respecting automobile was complete without a pair of big fuzzy dice hanging from the rear view mirror and a little grass-skirted dancing girl swaying back and forth on the dashboard. That's why I enjoy hanging out with Mr. Sankey. You always learn something new about before you were born.

The last time I was down in the laundry room, Mr. Sankey was repairing one of the ancient dryers. There were dryer parts all over the floor and his butt was sticking out of the open door of the machine, right under the sign that says: "All monies found in the machines will be contributed to the detergent fund."

Mr. Sankey backed out of the dryer and turned around. When he saw me, he looked relieved. "I thought you were the Slave Driver," he said. "This is getting to be the only place I can find any peace."

Mr. Sankey looked tired. When I asked him what was wrong with the dryer, and he launched into his tirade. "In my day, they had clotheslines. Now nobody wants to hang out their unmentionables for public viewing." He snorted in disgust. "The world has gotten far too delicate for my taste." Mr. Sankey belched to emphasize the point, which he did often due to what he liked to call his "sensitive intestinal nature."

"Excuse my French," he added.

I gazed at the dryer parts scattered around Mr. Sankey's feet. "That looks complicated," I remarked.

"Not really," said Mr. Sankey. "You know what the most complicated mechanism is?"

I shook my head.

Mr. Sankey raised a finger in the air and made sure he had my full attention. "The human heart!" he proclaimed. "When that gets broken, you don't have the luxury of spreading the parts out on the floor." Mr. Sankey belched again before explaining, "I'm speaking metaphorically, of course."

I nodded and said nothing, which is often the best thing to do when it comes to Mr. Sankey. He took this as a sign to keep talking. "Not that I'm discouraging your interest in appliances," he said. "I figure that you know more about laundry than any kid I ever met. I mean that as a compliment."

"Thank you."

"Say, where's your old man? I haven't seen him in dog's years."

"He's on the road trying to drum up investors," I lied.

"Now that I think about it, I haven't seen Francine around either."

"She has a new boyfriend," I said. "They like to go dancing."

Mr. Sankey nodded. For a minute I thought he could tell I was hiding something. Then, as I placed my dirty clothes into one of the washers, he began fishing around in the top pocket of his overalls.

"Lifesaver?" he asked.

I looked at the roll of candy in Mr. Sankey's hand. There

was only one Lifesaver left. It was bright green and covered in pocket lint. I shook my head.

"Suit yourself," he said, putting the candy back in his pocket. "If you don't mind my saying so, you appear somewhat tense. Is Francine being her customary pain in the hind quarters?"

I shook my head. "I probably need more exercise," I said. "But this time of year there are a lot of leaves on the ground. I have to watch where I step."

Mr. Sankey nodded. "You know, there's more to life than getting your whites whiter," he offered. "Somebody your age should be having a few laughs now and then."

I put the soap in the washer and turned it on. It began to fill with water, making a hollow noise. This did not stop Mr. Sankey's inquisition. He simply got louder.

"You have a girlfriend yet?" he shouted.

I shook my head. I did not want to tell him that the mysterious Julie Spenser had kissed me. At the same time I thought that if I confessed an embarrassing fact, he might leave me alone. Something made me say, "Not good-looking enough, I guess."

"That's a load of horse shit," he yelled. I must have looked at him funny because he added, "I'm old. That means I can say anything I want. Let me ask you a question, son. Do you think I'm a good-looking man?"

Now, there is no way Mr. Sankey is even *close* to handsome. An unkind person might go so far as to say he's past the borderline on unappealing. He has plenty of wrinkles and a little strip of hair that waves around like a flag whenever there's a breeze. On the other hand, why would I want to hurt the feelings of someone who recently offered me his last Lifesaver? So I looked him in the eye and said, "Not in the obvious sense."

Mr. Sankey started to laugh like this was the best joke he'd heard in ages. "Well, I'll say this for you," he offered. "Your mother raised you right, God rest her."

Mr. Sankey pulled out his wallet. For a second, I thought he was going to give me a reward for being tactful. Instead, he pulled out a small photograph very carefully and said, "Let me show you something."

I looked at the picture. It was showed Mr. Sankey looking the same, only younger. He had his arm around a woman who was so beautiful she could have given Ms. Maculwayne a run for her money.

"That's me with my late wife, Eleanor," he said.

I could tell Mr. Sankey was waiting for a reaction. But I wasn't too sure about what to say. Mr. Sankey decided to help me out. "You're *shocked*, right?" he said. "Like, what is a guy who looks like me doing with a woman who looks like that?"

It was the kind of question that supplied its own handy answer. So I said, "Mr. Sankey, I have never been so shocked in my entire life." As answers go, it was not all that far from the truth.

You should have seen how happy my reply made old Mr. Sankey. "No less shocked than me, kid," he grinned. "No less shocked than Mr. Leonard T. Sankey."

"It's a puzzle, all right," I agreed, to be polite.

Then Mr. Sankey's voice went soft. "My wife got sick with the cancer. So I figured, why not ask her the big question. I said to her, 'Eleanor, you must admit that I am not beautiful in any cosmetic way you could happen to mention.'"

"What did she say?"

"She said, 'Leonard, I'll admit to that if you insist, because now is not the time for secrets between us.'" Mr. Sankey looked at the picture of his wife for a second and then kept on talking. "So I came right out and asked her, 'Eleanor, why did you marry me? In my estimation, we have always made a very odd-looking pair.'" Mr. Sankey blinked a couple of times without looking at me. "'Leonard,' she replied, 'would you say that I was a beautiful woman in the cosmetic sense?'"

Mr. Sankey seemed to have trouble continuing after that. So I helped him along with: "What did you say?"

"I said yes," answered Mr. Sankey. "Then she asked, 'Would you say that I've *always* been a beautiful woman?'"

There was a long pause. "You said yes?" I offered.

Mr. Sankey nodded. He was practically whispering now. "'Leonard,' she told me, 'I would have to agree. In fact, unlike you, I am a lifelong expert at being beautiful.'" Mr. Sankey looked me in the eye. "That's when she took my hand and said, 'You have no idea how little it means.'"

I watched as Mr. Sankey put the picture back in his wallet. "Women are the biggest mystery on earth," he said. "Especially *beautiful* women. In my experience, you never know what a beautiful woman is going to do next. Remember that the next time you encounter a beautiful person of the female persuasion."

"Mr. Sankey?" I asked. "Why are you telling me this?"

He smiled. "I guess I like your style."

"I have a style?"

"Absolutely," said Mr. Sankey. "For one thing, you score very high on laundry-room ethics."

"I didn't know there was such a thing."

"Oh, you can tell a lot about a person by the way they act in the laundry room," he said. "Remember that time you found five dollars in the dryer? What did you do?"

I glanced at the sign above the machines. "I put it in the dish for the detergent fund."

Mr. Sankey nodded. "Exactly. You automatically thought of the common good on behalf of your fellow laundry goers," he said. "There're more than a few people around who'd scoop up loose change from the dryer and take it for themselves." Leonard T. Sankey gave me a sly wink. "Some of them are even good-looking."

I checked my clothes in the wash.

"You go on upstairs," said Mr. Sankey. "I'll chuck that stuff in the dryer for you."

"Thanks, Mr. Sankey."

"You're welcome," he said. "And try to relax, okay? Have some fun! Otherwise you're going to end up in a room all by yourself thinking about the kinds of things you think about in a room all by yourself. You understand?"

"I think so, Mr. Sankey."

"Of course you do," he said. "You are not a stupid individual."

I suppose my conversation with Mr. Sankey stirred things up in me. I had my usual soak in the Jacuzzi that night, but I still couldn't sleep. So, for the first time in a while, I watched the Beast through Winston's telescope. Except for his desk lamp, all the lights were off. He had his chair turned to the side so that I could watch him staring into space. An unlit cigarette was dangling from his lips.

All of a sudden, he grabbed the gun off the desk and placed the barrel close to his face. You could safely say that was the scariest moment of my life. The strange thing was, I couldn't look away. I couldn't do anything. I couldn't speak. I couldn't breathe. I just watched.

The Beast pulled the trigger and a little flame popped out of the middle of the barrel. His cigarette caught fire as he puffed. For a second, a huge wave of relief washed over me. Then I noticed the Beast's expression. Even against the bright burst of flame, he wore a look of deep sadness.

At that moment, I realized that the Beast was a loser. He was harder to spot than some of us. He wasn't too fat or too short or walking on crutches. It was more like his loser status came from somewhere inside him. I don't know what he was thinking about, but I was pretty sure it was something a pile of candy bars couldn't solve.

CHAPTER

SEVEN

O f all the problems I had, one kept preying on my mind. I couldn't help wondering why my dad had left me with a nest egg big enough for a dinosaur to sit on. Neither of us had a bank account any more. When all the trouble started with Insta-Dye, Dad cleaned out our accounts and told me, "It's best that our remaining assets stay as liquid as possible."

I had thought about opening a new bank account for the money, but I'd decided to keep my $4000 inside my crutches. After all, they were seldom out of my sight, and a person would have to be lower than Jerry Whitman to steal them. What worried me more was that leaving me with this much liquid must be Dad's way of saying he wouldn't be home for months. So, although it was only the end of September, I began to wonder if I'd see him for Christmas.

When my mom was alive, Christmas was a major production in our family. We sang carols and drank eggnog and bought fresh tinsel every year. My mother decorated the apartment so that everywhere you looked there was something to remind you of the holiday season. She was the most festive person I have ever met.

Her favorite Christmas decoration sat on top of our Christmas tree every year. It was this elaborate angel that was missing a wing on one side. She actually *bought* it that way at some sale. When I asked my mom why she spent good money on an angel that was missing one of its wings, she said, "Just because something isn't perfect in one way doesn't mean it's not perfect in another."

But the thing my mom liked best of all was outdoor Christmas lights. When she was alive, we used to pile in the car and drive all over town to see the different houses lit up. Our last Christmas together, she was working three part-time jobs, even though the doctor told her to slow down. When I asked her why she worked so hard, she said, "Someday we're going to have a nice house with a big outdoor Christmas display."

It got to be a game we played that year. You know, fooling around because it made her happy. I'd ask her how big our Christmas display was going to be and she would say, "The biggest! People are going to drive from everywhere to see it. Our street will be jammed with traffic! But it will be so wonderful that even the neighbors won't complain."

My mom could get a little carried away when it came to the Christmas lights idea. Sometimes I would tease her about it, but she always stood her ground. "Everyone has a dream," she would say, "and this one is mine."

You might think it's a little odd for me to be thinking about Christmas in September. But to tell you the truth, I can make myself think about Christmas any time. It's my favorite way to remember my mother. So I probably consider the holidays more often than your average semi-mature individual.

This is the exact opposite of my dad. Ever since my mom died, he thinks Christmas is something you do your best to tough out — like a cold or something. Last year, he at least tried to get into the spirit of the season. I guess Connie had something to do with it.

Connie is the sort of person who does all her holiday shopping at Wal-Mart. She enjoys wearing red sweaters decorated with spangly-eyed snowmen. But she also has a practical streak. Last Christmas she gave me a Dustbuster and a pair of socks with Santa's reindeer on them. I didn't mind it so much, mostly because my dad was doing a half-decent imitation of being happy.

Anybody would have thought that Dad was having his best Christmas ever — except for one thing. Connie kept asking why we would put an angel missing a wing on top of the tree. You could tell it bugged her, especially since the angel sat crookedly off to one side. Finally, she went to straighten it out and my dad lost it.

"Don't touch that," he snapped. "It's *supposed* to be that way."

After that, Dad said he had to go to the washroom. He didn't come out for the longest time. But once he did, he was back to being cheery again. You would have had to watch him very closely to realize how down he was. I knew because I was feeling the same way.

I think having me around at Christmas reminds my dad of the way things used to be when my mom was alive. That's why I wondered if he was going to skip the whole thing this year and hide out with Connie. I didn't like the idea. But, as my mom would have said, I had to be sensible. Well, maybe not *too* sensible. I made up my mind I would get a tree and put the wingless angel on top, no matter what. It was a family tradition, even though I was running out of family.

Although it's nice to get that Christmas feeling back, I didn't mention my nostalgia to Manny or Winston. That's because for your average loser with a dysfunctional family, the Yuletide season is a major sore point.

Christmas is supposed to be like some snowy movie you see on TV, right? Where everyone is happy drinking spicy eggnog with the people they care about. Maybe it's the time of year you go skiing. Or maybe you get a kick out of buying a special present for your girlfriend or something. Your non-loser types may like to complain about the holidays, but deep down they're having a great time acting like kids again.

For a lot of losers, it's not like that at all. Some of my loser friends and their families don't celebrate Christmas, of course. Maybe they're the lucky ones. For losers, Christmas is a big shiny symbol for the things that have gone wrong in their miserable, loser lives all year long. They don't have girlfriends. They are too uncoordinated to ski. Or eggnog makes them break out in hives. See what I mean?

Winston says Christmas is an excuse for his parents to give him presents so they can feel less guilty about being workaholics who live in another country. But Manny is the one who really gets going about what a rip-off the holidays are. "My mother stays sober only long enough to make her special Christmas punch," he says. Then he gets highly sarcastic. "I believe in Santa Claus and the tooth fairy and that one day I will wake up skinny and be chased down the street by gorgeous super-models."

See why I avoid the subject of Christmas? Manny was in a bad enough mood already because Winston kept bragging about how great it was rooming together at the mansion "twenty-four-seven." Because of his various chores and responsibilities, Manny's visits to Winston's house were mostly restricted to the Thursday afternoon meetings of the Losers' Club. Still, those were enough to give him what he called "a taste for space."

Winston was so grateful for my company that he kept asking me what he could do to make my stay more comfortable. Throughout the school day, he provided Manny with a running commentary on how much fun the independent bachelor life was. How nobody told us what to do or what to eat. And how, the night before, I had done my homework in the Jacuzzi without getting my notes wet.

One morning in geometry class, Winston informed Manny that he was thinking of ordering more cable channels for the big-screen TV. He turned to me and asked, "Do you like stock car racing? Because they have an entire station with nothing but stock car races twenty-four hours a day."

Finally, Manny, who was trying his best to concentrate on obtuse angles, couldn't stand it any more. He rolled his eyes at Winston and proclaimed, "Why don't you just burp the guy and get it over with?"

Manny said this so loud that it was a little on the disruptive side. It forced Mrs. Loomis, our geometry teacher, to make a comment for the sake of classroom tranquility. Nobody likes it when Mrs. Loomis is forced to make a comment. You know it's coming because she looks at you over the top of her glasses after they've slid down her nose.

This time around, Mrs. Loomis looked over the top of her glasses and said, "Rupert?"

Now, it had been a while since anybody had called Manny the R-word at school. So he meant no disrespect when he didn't look up. Mrs. Loomis had to look directly at Manny and say, "Rupert, perhaps you can tell the rest of the class what you are discussing that's so much more stimulating than geometry?"

Manny always thought the best policy with Mrs. Loomis was total honesty. So he put on a sincere look and said, "Cable TV." And then he panicked and added, "But nothing with a restricted rating or anything."

Mrs. Loomis's glasses slid further down her nose. She looked at Manny sympathetically and said, "More concentration, less imagination."

Mrs. Loomis has what you might describe as an elementary-school twang. Unless she is talking about math — which she describes as "my absolute passion in life" — everything she says makes you feel like you're back in grade three. I don't mean that she's sarcastic or anything. It's more like she thinks we're still *cute*, even though that's the last thing any of us wants to be. Sometimes she will go so far as to talk about the importance of dressing warmly or eating a balanced breakfast.

Mrs. Loomis's gestures are from the third grade as well. If she is trying to explain a geometry problem that none of the class understands, she will often turn the invisible handle of an invisible water tap on the side of her head. "Turn on your brains!" she will urge, as if this was all we had to do to get the answer flowing smoothly through the pipes in our head. Mrs.

Loomis's class is early in the morning, a time when Manny says the pipes in his brain are still sluggish. The last time Mrs. Loomis told Manny to turn on his brain, he groaned, "My tap isn't working. I think I need some Drano for my brain-o."

Considering it was such a pathetic joke, this got a big laugh. Mostly because Mrs. Loomis makes us feel as if we should still be carrying around lunch boxes with cartoon characters on the front. But the laugh did not distract Mrs. Loomis from her great love for geometry. She bore down on Manny.

"Come on," she said. "You can do it! Go!" as if he were some kind of mathematical racehorse or something. Winston says that during Mrs. Loomis's class he has to continually fight the urge to break for recess. Manny says Mrs. Loomis makes him want to break for lunch.

Mrs. Loomis calls Manny, Winston, and me the Three Musketeers because we're always together. Manny is unhinged by this reference. Although Mrs. Loomis has pointed out that we are named after three great fictional heroes, this is not how Manny's mind works. "Say Three Musketeers to me and all I can think of is the candy bar," he explains. "Sometimes my textbook gets so wet from drool that I can barely see the equations."

Winston does an impressive imitation of Mrs. Loomis when the mood strikes him. He'll borrow his brother Neville's hundred-dollar sunglasses and perch them on the end of his nose. "We want *focus*," he'll say. "Not hocus-pocus." But surprisingly few people give Mrs. Loomis a hard time in class. That's because even though she chooses to ignore that some of us are old enough to grow beards, she's a very good teacher. She'll stay after school and work with any student who asks, no matter how long it takes to make them understand. She has also been known to drop by a sick student's house to see how they're doing and talk a little light geometry. The trick is to avoid asking her for inspirational advice.

Even Winston admits that Mrs. Loomis is a superior educator, which is a lot coming from him. Mrs. Loomis had Winston in algebra last year, and she is always giving him a hard time because she feels he's much better at math than his test scores indicate. Once she brought him in for a special math talk after school. Winston says Mrs. Loomis has been rhyming for so long that that she will often rhyme something completely by accident. Apparently, she got so frustrated during their meeting that she told him, "If you say you're trying, you're doing nothing but lying!"

Manny once suggested that Winston play dumb and tell Mrs. Loomis the finer points of mathematics were too much for his short little brain. "You don't want to be full of untapped potential and become Mrs. Loomis's pet project," he cautioned. "She'll never let you off the hook until she turns on your tap."

But the idea that he should act unintelligent greatly offended Winston's sensibilities. "I'm lazy," he said, "not stupid."

"What's the difference?" I asked.

Winston informed us that his approach to scholastic slacking was similar to marathon running. "I'm in it for the long haul," he explained. "Serious coasting takes more brain power than most people realize."

Manny understood the concept. "When it comes to avoiding serious effort, the Savior and I are mere sprinters in comparison," he said.

Winston C. Chang acknowledged the tribute with a slight

nod. "Unlike raw stupidity, long-term scholastic slacking takes genuine dedication. The key is to push the envelope while not arousing undue attention from parents, teachers, or similar authority figures."

"Maybe you should improve in geometry for a while," I suggested. "You know, throw Mrs. Loomis off the scent so that she moves on to someone else."

Winston rolled his eyes. "Mrs. Loomis is not your regular teacher," he said, as if he were talking about some highly worthy adversary in mathematical trench warfare. "If you improve, all she does is bear down harder."

Manny said this was absolutely true. He had heard a rumor that Mrs. Loomis's husband was also a math teacher at another local high school. "They sit around the dinner table discussing complex mathematical theorems," he said. "It's well known that they're fanatics for all manner of arithmetic."

Mrs. Loomis's mania for the teaching profession was no secret either. Manny had overheard a parent ask Mrs. Loomis if she had any children. Mrs. Loomis waved her chalk hand around the classroom and said, "I have thirty children per hour." Manny laughed. "It was as if she was calculating how far she could go on a tank of gas," he said. "Very serious but also very proud."

And yet, even though we could see the humor in it, the subject of Mrs. Loomis made us nervous. We could feel her keeping a special eye on Winston from behind her horn-rimmed glasses. And if she had an eye on Winston, it meant she had an eye on Manny and me as well. The two of us were nowhere near as unmotivated as Winston. On the contrary, my marks in math are quite respectable. But Mrs. Loomis had started to look at Manny and me oddly — as if we might have greater mental resources than she'd originally thought simply because we hung around Winston. Manny calls it "untapped potential by association."

"You watch," said Manny. "She's going to concentrate on our taps as soon as she's finished turning Winston's up to full blast."

That thought was enough to make us quiet down and at least pretend to concentrate on geometry for the next few classes. But at lunchtime Winston kept right on talking about how exciting the bachelor life was. And Manny kept getting more and more envious.

I had suggested to Winston that we invite Manny over more often. But Winston was less sure about having the former Rupert Crandall as a frequent houseguest. "We don't need Mr. Manhattan going on and on about his glorious former life," he remarked, one night at dinner. "Frankly, I am getting sick and tired of hearing how much he misses New York corned beef."

"It's New York *pastrami* he misses," I corrected. "Not corned beef."

"So what?" said Winston. "I happen to be very fond of Canadian bacon but you don't hear me mentioning it every five minutes."

"It's not the same, Winston."

"Whatever," said Winston. "We do not need Mr. Manhattan one going on and on while I am trying to unwind from a hard day of psychological warfare with Mrs. Loomis."

"Mr. Manhattan" was Winston's second favorite sarcastic nickname for Manny, after "the Fat One." Winston confided that Manny's extended presence might lead to genuine violence if Manny became too self-absorbed. "'Me' is the Fat

One's signature word," said Winston. "He has an ego bigger than his all-time favorite department store, which — as he tells us time and time again — is Bergdorf Goodman."

I didn't try to change Winston's mind or anything, but even he had to admit that the concept of Two Musketeers didn't feel right. It was what you might call a dilemma. Then, over lunch one day, Manny said, "My mother is the world champion of daytime napping. Maybe I could make some extended visits between feedings." So Winston and I agreed that Manny could visit after school whenever he was able to get away.

Once we had dealt with the issue of Manny's visits, I began to really settle in at Winston's. It got so that I slept as well there as I had in my apartment. In fact, I had the identical dream for three nights in a row. It was weird but also comforting in a funny way. It was one of those dreams that are so real you can practically touch them. One of those dreams that want to tell you something important, only you're never exactly sure what that something important is.

In the dream it was Christmas, and a whole bunch of cars and people were stopping by to get a look at this house that had a lot of unusual decorations. My mom was in the dream. From a distance, I could hear her say, "This is what Christmas is all about." She was excited and beckoned me over to get a better look. But every time I got closer, she would disappear — kind of blending in with the lights. But that's not all. Once my mom disappeared, the house came into sharper focus. It turned out to be Winston's mansion. I could even see the window of my room — all lit up against the dark.

CHAPTER

EIGHT

I've learned to appreciate the five extra minutes I get between periods when nobody else is in the hallway. As long as Winston isn't stuffed into his locker or some stray loser doesn't hit me up for a quick loan, it can be a very peaceful time to organize my thoughts.

It was shortly before lunch hour, and I was getting out of English class early. I decided to split the five minutes between trying to figure out my Christmas dream and trying to figure out if Julie Spenser was mentally unstable.

I had caught Julie looking at me a couple of times during novel study. Of course, it could have been my imagination. I planned to consider the idea on the way to my locker, but something happened to disturb my concentration.

The only thing wrong with having an early hall pass is that occasionally I'll bump into somebody who is skipping class. Usually it's someone I'd rather not see. And then, as Francine used to say, my whole aura of tranquillity is toast. Such was the case when I encountered the Watertank staring at Winston's locker with a look of genuine puzzlement.

As I said, the Watertank and I used to associate with each other back in elementary school. In those days, his name was simply Duane, and he was more or less a regular size. Now and then, the tank-sized Duane will get nostalgic for the simpler days of grade six and try to make out like we're long-lost friends or something. I'm proud of the fact that I cut him little slack in this regard — for he is one of Jerry's boys, plain and simple.

Whenever I get a warm feeling about the days when I used to go over to Duane's house and play Stratego or video games, I try to hold a certain picture in my mind. It is a picture of the Watertank with a bottle of extra-strength spray cleaner and a damp cloth. I should explain that Jerry makes Duane inspect the bus benches near the school, in case some mysterious loser has defaced the real-estate smile of Jerry Whitman, Sr., by blacking out his teeth with felt pen or drawing on devil horns and a moustache. It's Duane's job to clean off the black marks so that Jerry Senior looks wholesome again.

Not surprisingly, defacing the image of Jerry Whitman, Sr., is a popular team activity among the losers at Marshall McLuhan High. Manny approaches the task with such gusto that he holds the school record for the greatest amount of defacement in the shortest period of time. Here's how it works. A crowd of Jerry's kids will shield the guy with the industrial-sized felt pen while he draws very quickly. Most guys can't do much more than draw a few blackheads before one of Jerry's boys comes into sight. But even a few blackheads are enough to get Duane out with his spray bottle.

The Watertank gets very upset if he thinks you're staring at him while he is in the midst of his cleaning duties. Losers will hide behind issues of *Popular Mechanics* or *Scientific American*, pretending not to look while he is scrubbing away like some king-sized maid. But secretly they will be thrilled by the Watertank's public humiliation.

I can't help wondering why Duane would lower himself like that just to be one of Jerry's boys. Manny says that since we have never been even remotely cool, we have no understanding of how important it is to hang on to your cool status. I asked Manny what good it does to be cool if you have to be Jerry Whitman's slave at the same time — which — let's face it — is *not* cool.

Manny says I am being too philosophical. He says the important thing for a guy like the Watertank is to stay on Jerry's good side, because Whitman is both popular and all-powerful. "Besides," continues Manny, "it's not as though the Tank is your friend or anything. So why not enjoy his rare moments of personal degradation?"

Manny is right, I suppose. But much as I hate to admit it, there's still a small part of me that hates seeing my former friend acting so pathetic. Maybe that's why I try to avoid Duane whenever possible.

Unfortunately I can't manage to avoid the Watertank entirely, especially since my locker is next to Winston's.

So when Duane said, "Hey, Sherwood," I had to respond with something.

"Hello, Duane," I said. "Wiped out any good blackheads lately?"

Duane kept staring at Winston's locker. He stared for so long that I asked, "Winston isn't *in* there, is he?"

The Watertank shook his big head. "He is keeping up with

his payments very nicely," said Duane, almost as if he was reciting from a report card. "He has blossomed into one of our most co-operative clients." He looked at me directly and added, "Besides, I think he kind of *likes* it inside there."

I thought about all the extra space Winston had at home. "Maybe it's a refreshing change of pace," I said.

Duane looked confused but didn't move to go away. As I opened my locker, he said, "Jerry's in a real bad mood these days."

"Hey," I said, "there's a big surprise."

"He's in a real bad mood about *you*," said Duane. "Because you have a girlfriend."

"I don't have a girlfriend," I said.

"Are you *sure*?"

"Of course I'm sure. Don't you think I would know if I had a girlfriend?" And then, for good measure, I threw in, "Besides, what business is it of Jerry Whitman's if I *did* have a girlfriend?"

"Well," said Duane, "the girlfriend you say you don't have? Jerry has his eye on her."

"How can he have his eye on a girlfriend who doesn't exist?" I asked.

"That's just it," said Duane. "*She* says she does."

"Who?"

"Julie Spenser!" declared Duane, who was getting visibly frustrated. "She says you two are a definite couple. You go to movies together and the art gallery. "

"The art gallery?"

"That's what she says. The *art* gallery." And then he added, "Plus, I myself have seen her kiss you — which you must admit is solid girlfriend evidence."

"I don't even know Julie Spenser," I said, unable to keep the amazement out of my voice. "She's in my English class. That's all."

Duane scratched the back of his head to show how puzzling this was. "Jerry said it must be a joke. He said a girl with that much potential would never go for you."

"I hope you both had a good laugh," I said.

"Not really. Julie Spenser is a very convincing storyteller." He coughed. "I just wanted to let you know. Jerry would never admit it but the whole thing has him greatly perplexed."

"What's he so interested in Julie Spenser for anyway?"

"Jerry likes a challenge. He says underneath all that mascara and funeral wear and bad attitude, there's a babe worthy of Jerry Whitman waiting to be developed." He paused. "You think Jerry's right?"

"How should I know?" I said. It came out kind of cranky.

"Well, I wanted to clue you in," said Duane. "It would probably be better if you stayed away from Julie."

"I *always* stay away from Julie. I never go near her."

"That's good. Keep it that way."

"Okay," I said, still cranky.

"Don't mention this, okay?" asked Duane. "I'm not supposed to be talking to any losers unless it's collection-related."

"Your secret's safe with me," I said.

I thought Duane was going to leave, but he merely looked around to make sure the hallway was still empty. "What was the name of that kid who used to turn his eyelids inside out?" he asked. "The one who used to run around the playground scaring the girls?"

"Durwood," I said. "Durwood Mulvaney."

"That's right!" exclaimed Duane. "How could I forget a name like that? I wonder whatever happened to that crazy Durwood?"

"He's probably in a school where extortion doesn't run rampant," I said. "He's probably doing crazy things like spending his lunch money on *lunch*."

"What's with you?" asked the Watertank. "I'm only trying to tip you off about Jerry."

"Here's what's *with* me, Duane. I wish I could turn *my* eyelids inside out so that I didn't have to see all the crap that goes on around here."

The Watertank said nothing. Maybe it was that I didn't like Duane interfering with my quiet time. Or maybe I was upset by the actions of the mysterious Julie Spenser. But I kept right on going and managed to lose my cool.

"Who's running the gantlet today?" I asked. "Who are you going to dunk in the toilet until they cry like they're back in grade three?"

"Kid stuff," said the Watertank. "You know I never get heavy unless I have to."

"I've seen what you can do — enough to make our lives miserable but not enough to bring on any real heat from the school. Never a broken arm, right, Duane? Unless you count the 'accident' that Gordie Heffernan had in gym."

"That wasn't me."

"It was one of Jerry's boys," I said. "Or was it Jerry?"

Duane stayed low-key "It's business, Sherwood," he said. "Don't take it so personal."

By now I was more under control. So I said, "This is too much like a conversation for my taste."

"Excuse me for trying to do you a favor," said Duane.

"A favor?"

The Watertank blushed. "Yeah, you know," he said. "I wanted to pay you back for that hot dog thing."

"You think this is going to pay me back?"

"I don't know. It's a start, I guess."

"Do me a favor, Duane," I said. "*Don't* do me any favors."

I had put the lock back on my locker and was about to head for the cafeteria when Jerry Whitman himself approached. As always, Whitman was decked out in the latest fashions — suede baseball jacket, expensive loafers, designer jeans. With his good looks and his superior grooming skills, he looked like one of those carefree models in a commercial for the Gap.

Duane was obviously agitated because he and I had been caught talking.

"The Watertank's just looking for Winston," I said.

"Is he behind in his payments?" Jerry asked Duane.

"No," said Duane. "I just wanted to have a little fun."

"You should be concentrating on the clients who are behind," said Jerry. "Have fun with them first."

Most of the time Jerry Whitman seemed like a regular good-looking guy. The thing that gave him away was his butt-ugly smile. Whenever Jerry Whitman tried to smile, he looked like a nervous ferret. And Jerry Whitman was smiling now.

"You know what's funny?" Jerry said. "It's funny seeing the two of you together. How many legs do you count, Tank? Excluding me, I calculate no less than six."

"Nothing I like better than crutch humor, Jerry," I said. "It makes my day."

"Lighten up, Poster Boy," said Jerry. "You know how much I admire your pluck and determination."

The Watertank glanced at Jerry and asked, "How come you're out early?"

"Sometimes I like to survey my domain while the serfs have their heads down," said Jerry.

"That's pretty good," I said. "I'm surprised your marks in social studies aren't higher."

"I'm more of an entrepreneurial type," said Jerry. "Right, Tank?"

"Right," said Duane.

"Do you even know what that means?" said Jerry, looking right at Duane with his ferret-y smile.

"He knows what it means," I said. "He's big, not stupid."

Jerry turned to me. "You don't understand the kind of relationship the Tank and I have, Sherwood. We kid around, we play football—" Whitman put his hand over his mouth, as if he was on stage or something. "Oh, jeez," he said. "Here I am talking about sports-like stuff while you are permanently crippled. How thoughtless of me. That is, unless you've played football. Have you ever played football, Sherwood?"

"No."

"How about hockey or basketball?" he asked. "Those are fun too."

"No," I said. "I can't say that I have."

"I guess you're more the accountant type," said Jerry. "Or maybe a banker. Am I right, Sherwood?"

Duane said, "Can we go now, Jerry?"

Whitman didn't pay any attention to Duane. He was staring at me and saying, "You think I don't know about how you bankroll the losers?"

"What difference does it make?" I said. "It spends the same."

"You know something, Sherwood?" said Jerry, who was really playing with me now. "You've got *spirit*. The trouble is, your kind of spirit is bad for business. It's got a way of making losers think they aren't losers at all."

"So?"

"So the minute losers start thinking they *aren't* losers, I have to apply more pressure to get what I want. More pressure means more work and more hassle for my boys. Who knows? Within the next two years, we could have a full-scale loser rebellion on our hands."

"You're giving us more credit than we deserve, Jerry."

"Let's go, okay, Jerry?" said Duane.

"In a second," said Whitman. His eyes had gone cold. "First, I have to apologize to my disabled banker friend here for hurting his feelings with that sports talk. Do you accept my apology, Sherwood?" Jerry wasn't smiling any more, but he looked as ugly as if he was.

"Sure," I said. "No problem."

"That's great," said Whitman, smiling again. "I'd ask you to shake on it, but it looks like both your hands are busy."

"Come on, Jerry," said Duane. The bell had rung, and people were spilling out into the hallways, but Whitman didn't seem to want to move. Before long, there was a small crowd around us, waiting to see if anything would happen.

"You know, Sherwood," said Jerry, "there's something I've always meant to ask you. Say you wanted to put your arms around a girl while you were both standing up. How would you do it without falling over?"

I knew I was getting red in the face, but I just said, "I guess some things are worth sitting down for."

This made Jerry Whitman laugh. "I don't know why I find you so amusing, Sherwood," he said. "But I do." And then he patted me on the head.

Now, Jerry Whitman must have patted me on the head about a hundred times. But for some reason I couldn't take it on this particular day. I could feel myself gearing up for the Big C. As I have mentioned, confrontation is generally something that losers try to avoid. But this time around, I couldn't help myself.

"Don't do that, Whitman," I said — not really loud, but loud enough for everybody to hear it.

There was a decent crowd at this point, including an assortment of losers like Manny and Winston. Julie Spenser was standing at the back of the group like a curious piece of black licorice.

Jerry put up his hands, making a big production number of backing off. "Don't be so touchy, Sherwood," he said. "I was only trying to be friendly because you can't run or do sports or anything competitive."

"I could beat you at something," I said.

"*Something*," said Jerry, who was really enjoying my humiliation. "That's kind of a broad category, isn't it, Sherwood? Why don't you narrow it down?"

"What if I did narrow it down?" I asked, sounding more defiant than was probably good for me.

"All you have to do is name it, Sherwood," said Jerry.

"It can be anything?"

"I don't see why not. I can beat you at anything."

I'm sure if I had backed down at that point, nothing much would have happened. Except that I didn't feel like backing down. I saw the poster about the Festival of Lights out of the corner of my eye, so I pointed toward it and said, "That. I could beat you at that."

One of Jerry's boys went over and read the information on the poster out loud. It took a few seconds for the idea to sink in. Then the Watertank said, "A Christmas lights competition! Jeez, you might as well knit a baby sweater or something."

"What's the matter with you, Sherwood?" asked Jerry. "Has your brain been affected by too much milk and cookies?"

That got a big laugh until I answered, "You said you could beat me at anything. Are you backing down?"

Amazingly, Julie Spenser piped up. "You're not scared you might *lose*, are you, Jerry?"

Jerry gazed at Julie, who was giving him an awfully sweet smile for someone of her generally gloomy disposition. Jerry got an expression on his face that told me things were going to get serious fast. "I get to use my crew, right? Plus anybody else I want to bring in?"

"Sure," I said. "That sounds fair."

"Who do you get?" asked the Watertank.

"I'll take anybody you don't want," I said.

"That means you get the losers, right?" said Duane. The Watertank was looking me right in the eye, silently trying to convince me that I was making a dumb move.

"Shut up, Tank," said Jerry. "This is interesting." Whitman pasted a creepy little smile on his face. "It might not be bad winning some extra cash and appearing on TV. I accept your challenge."

There was a buzz through the crowd until Jerry added, "On one condition."

"What sort of condition?" I asked.

"I don't know yet," said Jerry. "But I'm not playing Santa Claus unless we raise the stakes and make it worth my while."

The whole thing must have been going to my head because the only thing I could think of to say was "Fine. You name the stakes and I'll accept."

After that, the crowd broke up. Manny and Winston stuck around. Manny was beside himself. "You know how I feel about Christmas," he moaned. "It sucks worse than cafeteria food, my birthday, and studying for a final exam *combined*."

He was so agitated I gave him money for the Twinkie machine. But that didn't stop him from worrying.

"Now we are losers and *elves*," he blurted. "How could things get more bleak and depressing?"

Winston, who had stayed quiet up till now, flashed me a dirty look. "Jerry Whitman will think of something," he said glumly. "You can bet your jingle bells on that."

CHAPTER

NINE

Jerry Whitman did manage to think of something, that very afternoon, something diabolical, even for Jerry. One of his boys passed me a note in English class that laid out the bet. If neither of our teams won the competition, things would remain the same. But if Jerry's team won, I would have to close down the Bank of Sherwood. As part of the deal, I would have to swear not to help my friends in any way — financially or otherwise. I would also have to swear never to hang out with them again. It would mean the end of the Losers' Club. The end of everything.

I knew Whitman would pull out all the stops in his determination to be the winner. So why would I be insane enough to accept such terms? Because, much to my shock, Jerry accepted the additional terms I scrawled on the note before sending it back. He agreed that if *my* team won, he would end his entire extortion ring. I mean, fold up the whole thing and leave every single loser in the school completely alone until graduation day.

I wrote, "I accept this challenge on behalf of my fellow losers" on the amended version of Whitman's note and signed my name at the bottom before adding, "Keep this confidential or the deal is off." I passed the note to Jerry's boy and tried not to think the worst.

That night over dinner I told Winston about the stakes that Jerry Whitman had set for the competition. It took him a minute to get his mind off the roast chicken I had made. But eventually he chewed, swallowed, and pronounced, "As the Fat One says, Jerry Whitman is lower than the lowest snake in a very low ditch. The guy gets more pleasure out of seeing us suffer than he gets out of the money." He shook his head in wonderment before musing, "How do you get these little potatoes so golden brown?"

I summarized my roasting method for him. And then I asked, "What do you think about the bet?"

"I think you would have to be crazier than the Beast to accept such terms," said Winston, his mouth full of chicken. "Without you to back us up, torment would run rampant in the halls. Plus, suppose that by some Christmas miracle we defeated Jerry's team in the contest? How do you know Jerry would live up to his part of the bargain?"

"I don't."

"Precisely!" said Winston. He rewarded himself by spearing another potato.

"But I think it's worth the risk," I said. "Besides, I don't want to back down."

"Why not? We're losers. Backing down is what we *do*."

"You think I'm going to forget about this, don't you?" I asked, not wanting to tell him that it was already a done deal.

"You are a rationalist," observed Winston, who liked to throw in the occasional big word to prove that he was a slacker by choice. "You will inevitably do the thing that makes the most sense for the good of all losers."

"I don't know," I said. "This feels important. It could be a turning point or something."

"Some turning point," said Winston. "You have turned us from dorks who only want to be left alone into dorks who publicly moonlight as Santa's helpers. This is a definite step up on the dork scale."

"Jerry and the boys will also be Santa's helpers," I pointed out.

"First, Jerry and the boys are not losers," said Winston. "They can do the occasional dorky thing and not have to worry about subjecting themselves to endless scorn. Second, Whitman is smart enough to realize that this Christmas contest is a public relations bonanza."

"What do you mean?" I asked.

"It's simple," explained Winston. "The administration already thinks that Jerry Whitman is golden. Once he gets through milking this Christmas lights thing, they will be ready to nominate him for sainthood." Winston was so absorbed in his reasoning that he was completely ignoring the potatoes now. "Inevitably he will be in an even *better* position to torment us."

"I never thought of it that way," I said.

"Of course you didn't," said Winston. He paused for a second. "Personally I believe thoughts of Julie Spenser are draining your brain."

"Maybe she is clouding my thinking a little," I confessed. "Why is Julie Spenser spreading rumors that aren't true?"

"Remind me to show you the escape room downstairs," said Winston.

"Why do you call it the escape room?" I asked, playing along. I knew that Winston would get back to Julie Spenser sooner or later.

"It's where my mother goes to escape my father when they have their arguments," he said. "There is also an escape room in Hong Kong. But the escape room here has a bigger table."

Winston stopped talking to eat some more. Finally, I got curious and asked, "What's the big table for?"

"The big table is for my mother's five-thousand-piece jigsaw puzzle of the Taj Mahal," said Winston. "It is the largest and most complex puzzle I have ever seen."

Winston spoke very slowly during the next part so that I would get the moral of the story. "And yet," he went on, "the Taj Mahal puzzle is like a six-piece picture of a baby calf when compared to the puzzle of Julie Spenser."

"Why do girls have to be so complicated?" I asked.

"It's not only girls," said Winston. "It's people in general." He looked at me nervously and said, "Can you keep a secret?"

"I guess."

"It's about Walter," said Winston. "He has this little fridge in the janitor's room."

"So?" I asked.

"So the fridge is full of root beer that isn't really root beer."

"What is it?"

"*Beer* beer."

"Which kind?" I asked.

"I don't know," said Winston, all urgent. "I didn't drink it. I *smelled* it."

"Maybe you shouldn't have gone into his private fridge."

"It looked exactly like root beer," explained Winston. "I was thirsty." He leaned in closer and added, "Walter makes and bottles his own beer. The caps are tight. The labels are those yellow ones that say 'Root Beer.' You can't see through the brown glass."

"How many did you open?" I asked.

"A few," he said. "I screwed the caps back on. There were a couple at the front that were actually root beer."

"Hey," I said. "Everybody knows Mr. Winecki drinks, right?"

"Sure," agreed Winston. "But he's been getting more shaky lately. Yesterday he burned himself frying our bacon."

"Maybe we should tell somebody," I suggested.

"They'd fire him," replied Winston. "Walter complains about work, but he loves being a janitor. He says the only reason he gets up in the morning is that he delights in making the school a cleaner place to be."

"Maybe they'd get him some help," I said. "He could take a leave of absence."

"Then they'd transfer him to another school," said Winston, shaking his head. "I don't want to tell anybody."

"But he's your friend."

"That means I get to decide," said Winston.

We stayed quiet until I said, "He doesn't sound as bad as Manny's mom."

Winston agreed. "Walter can still stand up," he said. "But he's been leaning on his mop lately."

"Do you ever worry about Manny?" I asked. "Because I do."

"I've got Walter to worry about," said Winston. "And now I've got Cola to worry about. Cola misses Neville so much that he's starting to turn down regular dog food."

Right then, the phone rang. Winston answered it, and his face lit up. He listened for a while, then said, "Third place. You were robbed, bro." As he was talking, Cola skidded into the room and started eyeing the phone receiver as if it were a big fat steak.

"When are you coming home?" Winston said into the receiver. He listened for a long time. Finally, he said, "Why can't you bring her over here?" It seemed like an innocent enough question, but Winston C. Chang looked distraught. "No problem," said Winston, trying to sound cheery into the phone. "Alex is staying with me. He cooks and everything."

Winston listened again and then said, "I'm okay. *Really*." There was a pause. "How can Dad find out? He's not coming here until Christmas."

Cola barked. Winston continued, "Yes, I'm being careful. Yes, *extra* careful.…Okay, give me a second." Winston held the phone to Cola's ear, and I could hear Neville's voice making baby noises. Cola's tail started beating on the kitchen floor. Eventually the noises stopped. Winston put the phone to his own ear, but Neville had already hung up. He set the phone back in the cradle and watched as Cola moved in the direction of Neville's bedroom.

"He's in love," said Winston.

"I'll say," I agreed. "I've never seen a dog so happy to hear his master's voice."

"Not Cola," said Winston. "*Neville*. He's in love with some girl from California."

"When's he coming home?"

"He's not sure." Winston seemed to be in shock. "He says

they're at a very delicate stage in their romance."

"So what?" I said. "Make him come back. He's your brother. He *has* to."

"But he sounded so *happy*," said Winston. "I haven't heard him this happy since Coca was alive."

"Coca?" I asked. "Who's Coca?"

"Coca was Cola's brother," said Winston.

"Neville had two dogs?"

Winston nodded. "I was walking Coca one day," said Winston. "Neville was paying me to walk him because he had to take Cola to the vet." He looked down at the floor. "I wasn't watching where I was going. Coca got away from me and was killed by a car."

"Neville must have been shook up."

"He was pretty cool about it, considering," said Winston. "But I always felt I owed him one. Maybe this will make us even."

"So he didn't say when he said he'd be back?"

Winston shrugged, but he was still looking down at the floor. "Who cares?"

"Winston," I said. "Your parents aren't coming back till Christmas. That's three months away."

"Maybe we should throw a party," said Winston, changing the subject abruptly. "You know, be spontaneous."

I went with the flow. "Who would we invite? Manny?"

"That's the best we can do?" scoffed Winston. "The Fat One!"

I thought of some other guests, but Winston seemed discouraged. "All losers," he said. "I'll bet we can't name one person who would come to our party who doesn't have some geeky thing wrong with them."

"Stanley Horton?"

"Asthma," said Winston.

"How about Rudy Zennetti?"

"Eczema," said Winston.

"Maurice Lieberman?"

"Stutters," said Winston.

"Only around girls," I said.

"We're not going to have *girls* at the party?" said Winston. "Forget it."

"This is depressing," I said.

"Not to mention that a couple of those guys are also former bed-wetters," added Winston.

"Former afflictions don't count," I said.

"That last one was merely for conversational purposes," he replied.

"I guess we're not having a party, then."

"Maybe parties are just for people like Jerry Whitman," said Winston.

"That's even more depressing."

Winston didn't seem to want to stop playing with the idea of having a party, though. "Working up a menu would be almost impossible," he said doubtfully. "Rudy and Maurice have three allergies between them."

"Stanley is lactose intolerant," I said.

"We could sit around drinking water." Winston grinned.

"But no ice!" I exclaimed. "Tin Face says cold braces make his teeth ache."

"We could sit around drinking water with *no ice*," said Winston. "Let the good times roll!"

Suddenly I got this picture in my head. It was a picture of

the losers we knew trying to have normal fun at a party. All those guys with nervous rashes, thick lenses in their glasses, and too-short dress pants seemed hilarious. Winston must have conjured up the same picture, because he and I started to laugh.

And once we started, we couldn't stop. Winston kept saying stuff like "We could have a party and make loot bags like when we were kids!"

"What would be in the loot bags?"

"Asthma inhalers!" said Winston.

"Zit cream!" I exclaimed.

"Plastic pocket protectors for pens!" shouted Winston.

"Argyle socks!"

"Study guides!"

We went on like this until we were so weak from laughing we couldn't go on any more. It was dark by now, but I wasn't tired.

"Let's do something crazy!" I said.

We were both too scared to do anything like phone a girl or go to a karaoke club without Neville. So Winston and I decided to go for a swim in the heated pool. It felt funny to be outdoors in our bathing suits on an autumn night. It was sure nippy. But once we got in the water, both of us warmed up.

Swimming always reminds me of my mother because she taught me how. She said the support of the water would make my whole body feel lighter, including my legs. So there I was moving around in the water and thinking of my mom, and feeling melancholy and good, both at the same time. The lights around Winston's pool gave everything a strange glow in the dark, which made it seem okay to say things you wouldn't normally say. We floated on our backs, saying whatever came into our heads.

"Do you think we'll be losers for the rest of our lives?" asked Winston.

It was the kind of question that demanded the truth. "I don't know," I said. "Maybe growing up will help."

"Maybe it won't."

"What do you care?" I asked. "Aren't you the one who says immaturity is the ultimate form of rebellion?"

"Good point," said Winston. "On the other hand, it might be refreshing to have people respect you for a change. Do you think that's possible?"

I looked up at the clear, calm sky. "We should think positive."

Winston floated silently for a minute. And then I heard, "Do you think my brother's really in love?"

"How should I know?"

"You have *experience*," he said. "That Julie Spenser thing."

"Winston," I said, "you know that's not true."

"You are the closest person I know to someone with experience," said Winston. "And don't tell me to shut up, because I am only trying to think positive. Maybe things are already as bad as they can get. We're regularly humiliated by Jerry Whitman. Our parents are occupied with everything besides us. How could things possibly get any worse?"

"You're probably right," I said. I didn't have the heart to tell him that because of my secret deal with Jerry things *could* get a lot worse.

"Of course I'm right," said Winston. "It's always darkest before the dawn. As my old man says, good fortune is going to come raining down on us at any moment."

That's when we heard this shot that sounded like some movie monster belching. Winston recognized the noise right away and shouted, "Incoming!" The way he said it made me realize that the Beast had fired off his crap cannon. Something plopped in the water and landed close to our heads.

"Bull's-eye!" shouted a rusty voice from the other side of the fence.

Winston and I scrambled out of the pool and onto a couple of lawn chairs. I gestured toward a dark clump that shimmered on the bottom of the pool under the bright lights.

"That doesn't look like good fortune to me," I said.

We started laughing so hard we could barely breathe. "At least it didn't hit us," gasped Winston.

"Man," I said, clasping my sides. "We must be the luckiest two guys in this entire backyard."

CHAPTER

TEN

There are times when Winston sounds like a fortune cookie. We were goofing around in the games room after school the next day when he flopped down in a chair and started to talk about the pool incident. He didn't get steamed about the Beast bombing us with crap. Instead, he went philosophical on me.

"Last night was a timely reminder of our fate." He shrugged. "No matter how well paved the path, all roads lead to Loser Town."

Translation? Just when you think things are looking up, all hope is lost. Maybe Winston was right. As Mr. Why said the other day in English class, some things are a metaphor for life. I figured the Beast's little surprise package was the perfect, concrete example of the way things were going for us. One minute you are lounging in the Olympic-sized pool of life and the next minute you are dodging incoming animal waste.

Sure, it was funny in a way. But once I'd stopped laughing, I started thinking. The thing with the crap cannon made me see that I *could* be a loser for the rest of my life. Look at the Beast. If he wasn't conclusive evidence of a fully matured loser, I'd eat the rubber tips on my crutches. I decided then and there that I was going to do something daring. Even if it proved to be the worst mistake of my life, I was going to confront our next-door neighbor.

You may think I was getting addicted to the Big C or something. But my hunch is I was feeling guilty about getting the Losers' Club involved in the Christmas lights contest. Deep down I was probably trying to make up for this by standing up to non-Whitman forms of degradation. It was the least I could do for my fellow losers. So while Winston was taking Cola on one of his extended walks before dinner, I headed over to the Beast's place and rang the doorbell.

Right beside the doorbell, there was a hand-printed sign that read:

WRITER AT WORK.

UNDER NO CIRCUMSTANCES DO I WISH TO BE DIS-
TURBED BY PEDDLERS, AGENTS, DELIVERY BOYS AT THE
WRONG ADDRESS, OR RELIGIOUS PROPAGANDISTS.

A little farther down, there was a scribbled addition: "I do not wish to be disturbed by anybody."

The Beast didn't answer the doorbell right away. But I kept pressing on the buzzer, as if I was one of Jerry's boys or something.

Eventually the Beast came to the door and opened it wide enough to give me a good view. Seeing him close up was what you might call a unique experience. His hair was sticking out in all directions, as if he had stuck his finger in a light socket. He had dark stubble on his face from not shaving. His outfit seemed to indicate he'd plunged his hand into the laundry hamper and pulled out whatever happened to be available. He wore sweatpants, big fuzzy bedroom slippers, and the pineapple shirt I had seen through the telescope. A cigarette, which was mostly ash, dangled loosely from his mouth.

Close up, the Beast was kind of disappointing. He didn't look like a beast at all. He wasn't even close to the dimensions of one of those fake wrestlers on TV. Aside from being hunched over, he looked like a regular guy with below-average hygiene and furry eyebrows. That, plus the fact that I'd watched him enough times from my window to feel I knew him, made me bold.

The Beast didn't start with a regular hello or anything, but you could tell he found me more interesting than a confused take-out guy or a Jehovah's Witness.

"Can't you read?" he asked. The Beast's cigarette moved up and down when he talked. His voice reminded me of sandpaper moving across a rough surface. It sounded as if he didn't use it much.

"Sure," I said.

"So you *ignored* the sign."

"I guess."

"Do you ignore all signs?"

"No," I said. He seemed to want me to explain some more. So I added, "I guess I pay more attention to signs that say things like 'This fence is electrified.'"

"So you think the sign needs to have a greater sense of urgency?" asked the Beast.

"Urgency is always good," I said, trying to sound like a big-time sign critic.

He nodded. "Okay. I'll allow you exactly *one* question. After that, it's up to you to hold my interest."

"How old are you?" I asked.

You could tell the Beast wasn't expecting this kind of question. For a second, I thought he was going to close the door in my face, but then I heard him say, "Thirty-two."

"You look way older," I said. And then, remembering the crap cannon, I went on rudely, "You should stand up straighter."

He stared at me — all bent over, with his big sad eyes and his even sadder cigarette. Finally, he said, "Who are you, the *posture* police?"

"You can tell a lot about a person by the way they stand."

The Beast gave a dry little smile. "You sound like my Aunt June," he said. "It is not a good thing to be your age and sound like my Aunt June." He took a puff on his cigarette. "My Aunt June was a pain in the ass."

I stayed silent, which gave the Beast enough time to elaborate on why his Aunt June was a pain in the ass. "She used to call me the human question mark," he explained. "She would say, 'Harry, slouching is the physical manifestation of a mind with more questions than answers. If you are not careful, you will be no good for anything except living in a bell tower and saving damsels in distress.'" The Beast thought for a moment. "If you ask me, living in a bell tower and saving damsels in distress is not that bad a life."

"You mean like the Hunchback of Notre Dame?" I said, so the Beast wouldn't feel like he was having a conversation all by himself.

He raised a furry eyebrow in surprise. "You read the book?"

"I saw this old movie on TV," I said. "The guy who played the hunchback was pretty good."

"Charles Laughton," the Beast said, opening the door a little wider. "A superb performance."

"I like other old movies too."

"Such as?" asked the Beast.

"Anything by the Marx Brothers."

"Groucho!" said the Beast. "Easily the greatest sloucher in history." Then — as if the thought cheered him up — he straightened to his full height. "Not that Aunt June didn't have a point," he said. "Bad deportment *is* often the unfortunate accessory of mental haziness." His cigarette nearly fell out of his mouth but decided to stay put at the last minute.

"I thought you said your aunt June was a pain in the ass."

"You can be a pain in the ass and still be right," he said. "In fact, sometimes you're a pain in the ass *because* you're right."

The Beast's cheeks were starting to get rosy with so much human interaction. "Can you recite any poems?" he asked hopefully.

"Not offhand," I confessed.

"That's okay," said the Beast. "The posture thing was good. I haven't thought about posture in a long time."

I figured I better say something else. But the Beast didn't seem to mind the silence. He filled in the time by looking me over. Then he said, "Cerebral palsy, right?"

I wanted to say something cool, but I was taken aback by the Beast's guessing abilities. So instead I said, "Bull's-eye," which came out a little more sarcastic than I planned.

He didn't seem to notice. "Don't tell me you were at the *pool* last night!" he said gleefully. You'd think I had heard him play the violin or something.

I nodded, and he cackled. It sounded like dead leaves rustling in the wind. "Some of my best work," he said. "My aim was inspired."

"I hate to spoil your fun," I said, "but I've come to ask you to stop firing crap at us."

"Wish I could help you out," said the Beast. "Trouble is — what's that dog's name? Pepsi?"

"*Cola.*"

"Pepsi Cola —"

"No, just *Cola,*" I interjected.

"I don't care if his name is Dr. Pepper," said the Beast. "The dog keeps doing his thing on *my* lawn."

"It's not really your lawn, is it?"

"It's temporarily under my watch," said the Beast. "As a house sitter I have certain contractual obligations."

"It's written down that you can fire dog shit at us?" I asked.

"I am simply *returning* dog shit that was yours in the first place," said the Beast, laughing with appreciation at his own wit. "It's a little something called poetic justice, pal."

"I guess you think it's funny spreading germs like that," I said, trying to get a little anger going. "What you are doing is very unsanitary." And then, for good measure, I tossed in, "In addition, you *stole* Winston's tennis cannon."

"I liberated a rich man's toy, which has since been converted into a tool of righteous retribution," clarified the Beast. "A man has the inalienable right to walk on his own temporary grass without being molested."

"That's not the point," I said stiffly. "Why can't you be a good neighbor, Harry?"

"Who said you could call me Harry?"

"Nobody," I replied.

"You really should wait until I give you permission," he said, sounding a little hurt. "For someone who's such a stickler for good posture, you're surprisingly weak on certain points of etiquette."

"I apologize," I said, because it seemed the right thing to say.

The Beast considered this, then stuck out his hand to shake mine. "Call me Harry," he said. "Harry Beardsley."

"How come you're being so polite?" I asked.

Harry sighed. "I miss arguing," he said. The Beast was still standing there with his hand out. After a second he remembered about the cannon and said, "Don't worry. I use tongs."

"It's not that," I said. "I don't do handshakes."

"Try it," he said. "I'll make sure you don't lose your balance."

I let one of my crutches dangle loose from my arm and stuck out my hand. At first, it felt as if I was going to fall, but the Beast took my hand and let me lean into him. I told him my name, but he didn't let go. He hung on, looking me straight in the eye. Finally, he spoke. "What made you mention the Marx Brothers a minute ago?"

I thought about making up some lie. But when a guy's got you by the hand and is looking into your eyes, it isn't easy. "I saw your poster," I said. "I've been watching you through the window."

For a second I thought Harry Beardsley was going to get mad. There was a look that flashed in his eye. And then, just as suddenly, it was gone. He let go of my hand very gently, making sure that I kept my balance. I thought I'd better say some-thing. So I asked, "What's that music you sometimes play? With the sax and all the violins?"

"*Charlie Parker with Strings.*"

"I like it," I said.

The Beast nodded. "You look tired of standing," he said. "Want to come inside for a minute?"

I wasn't sure why, but it felt as if I had passed some kind of test.

Harry let me into the living room. There were dozens of old records scattered all over the floor. Not CDs, but the kind that you find in junk shops and that are shaped like a pizza. Harry lit a cigarette with a regular match.

"You smoke?" he asked.

I told him no.

"Good," he said, taking a deep puff. "It's a foolish habit."

"So why do you smoke?" I asked.

"Because I'm a fool," said Harry, blowing a perfect smoke ring. It lingered in the air for a moment before vanishing like magic.

The Beast went off to the kitchen to get us a couple of Cokes. I noticed a pile of little pink books on a table and picked one up to see what it was. The title on the cover was *By Love Possessed*. There was a picture on the cover of a muscle-bound guy with his arm around a girl who looked as if she might pass out from being possessed by too much love. The rest of the pink books were similar, except that, in a couple of pictures, the guys had longer hair than the girls. All the pink books were written by someone named Harriet Wintergreen.

There was one book on the table that wasn't pink. It was a green-colored paperback that looked beat-up. The cover read: *Separate Lives. A Novel by Harry Beardsley.*

I flipped the book over and there was a quote on the back. It said, "Beardsley has written a first novel of great power and beauty. This is a young writer to watch for many years to come. — *The New York Times.*"

Above the quote, there was a picture of Harry, looking not much older than me. His hair was neatly combed, his face was shaved clean, and he was wearing the kind of smile that you wear when you know you've done something right. I was still looking at the photograph when Harry walked in with the Cokes.

"Hey, put that down," he said sharply.

I put it down right away, as if the pages were on fire or something. I told him I was sorry, that books made me curious. He lightened up a bit at that.

"It's been out of print for a long time," he explained. "That's the only copy I have."

"You wrote a *book*," I said, unable to hide the surprise in my voice. It came out sounding dumb, but Harry didn't seem to mind.

"I wrote all the books on that table," he said.

"Even the pink ones?"

"Even the pink ones,"

"You're Harriet Wintergreen?"

"It's a pen name," said Harry, taking a sip of his Coke. "I thought it up when I was on my last Lifesaver. If things had been different, I could have ended up as Harriet Butterscotch."

"Pink books," I repeated.

"Don't give me a hard time," said Harry. "I'm trying my

best to change colors."

Harry showed me to a chair, and we started talking about his reputation in the neighborhood. It turned out that he hadn't killed a lawnmower with his hammer. "I merely unplugged it," he said. "But then I felt so guilty I ended up mowing the lawn for the gardener myself."

"So the lawnmower wasn't even dented?"

"Oh, it's dented, all right," said Harry. "Mr. Haromito, the gardener in question…he's nearsighted and keeps bashing the thing into trees."

"That thing with the hammer wasn't true?" I asked.

"When I unplugged the lawnmower, I was *carrying* a hammer," explained Harry. "I had just finished mending a hole in the fence so Pepsi Cola wouldn't get through."

"Cola," I corrected. "There's no Pepsi."

"Whatever," said the Beast. "I would never destroy a useful piece of machinery. I have more respect for machines than for most people."

"So you didn't put a Tahitian curse on the paperboy?" I asked.

"It wasn't really Tahitian," said the Beast. "I made it up so the kid would stop throwing the paper against the door." He shrugged. "Used judiciously, the power of superstition can have untold benefits."

"I knew you weren't as crazy as Winston said."

I must have sounded disappointed, because Harry started to try to make a reasonable case for his crazy reputation. "I *am* a devout recluse who wears bedroom slippers all day long," he pointed out. "And let's not forget about the dog crap thing. Dog crap really pushes my buttons."

"It's not the same as toasting a moving lawnmower," I noted.

The Beast looked sympathetic. "Ninety percent of urban legend is an escalation of bullshit built on a tiny germ of truth," he explained. "The other ten percent comes from bored gossips trying to discourage healthy eccentricity."

"So you don't mind if people think you're some crazy hermit?"

"Are you kidding?" said Harry. "I encourage it."

"How come?"

"Because the right kind of rumor keeps intruders away better than any burglar alarm," said Harry, taking another sip of his Coke. "In case you haven't noticed, I'm not exactly what you'd call a people-person."

Harry went over to the scattered pile of records and selected one near his foot. "However," he said. "I do have a superior intellect and great taste in music, which is why I tend to prefer my own company to that of the general populace." He handed me the Charlie Parker album. "Do you have access to a turntable?"

I told him that I could use Winston's.

"I'll let you borrow this," he said. "You should listen to it a few times to get the various nuances."

"What about the crap cannon?"

"You stop looking at me through the window and I'll stop firing crap across the fence," said Harry. "Deal?"

"Deal."

"Let's shake on it," said Harry. So we shook on it, which was much easier with me sitting down.

I was ready to leave, but I had one last question. "Harry?" I said. "How come you're being so nice to me?"

Harry thought about this for a second. "Let's say you

remind me of someone." He seemed a little melancholy about my impending departure, being that he was such a devout recluse and all. "Leave the record on the doorstep when you're finished," he said. "And thanks for the tip about the sign. I'll do a rewrite."

CHAPTER

ELEVEN

Given Winston's feelings about Harry, I decided not to tell him about my visit. That seemed the best plan of action, even though part of me wanted to talk about it. But the funny thing about taking risks is that it gives you an appetite for other risky things — my baffling situation with Julie Spenser, for example. I couldn't go around letting a stranger spread rumors and kiss me on the cheek for no reason. It wasn't right.

There was only one thing to do. It took several revisions, but I eventually passed Julie Spenser a note in Mr. Why's English class. It read:

Dear Julie Spenser,

    I am deeply puzzled as to why you are spreading unfounded rumors about me to Jerry Whitman and his various associates (for example, Duane "The Watertank" Waterton). I have heard these rumors involve you and me going to the movies and the art gallery and doing assorted date-like things. Why would you say this when we have never even spoken to each other once except for the time we talked about Christmas lights? I, for one, am mystified by your actions.

I don't know what you've heard about me but I am a simple guy who just wants to be left alone. Your rumors are causing me undue hardship and I feel I deserve an explanation. If you would care to explain yourself, please meet me after school at Barney's Bagel Land. Otherwise I will be forced to tell everyone that you are a neurotic and highly strung individual who cannot separate truth from fiction.

> *Respectfully,*
> *Alexander Sherwood*

P.S. This is not *a date, just a fact-finding mission.*

I confess that it took a lot of nerve to pass the note to Julie. But not only did she read it, she sent back a reply. It read: "O.K."

At first, I was unsure about how to interpret her note. Did it mean "O.K. you may tell everyone that I am a neurotic and highly strung individual who cannot separate truth from fiction"? Or did it mean " O.K. I will meet you at Barney's Bagel Land and *explain* why I am spreading rumors"? With Julie Spenser it was hard to tell.

I finally decided it meant she would meet me after school. If not, the worst that could happen was that I would have to eat a bagel by myself. I figured I could live with that.

Of course, I was apprehensive, so apprehensive that I couldn't resist showing Julie Spenser's note to Winston and Manny. Winston said it was hard to tell anything from a couple of capital letters.

Manny begged to disagree. "Julie Spenser has chosen the abbreviated, two-letter form of O.K. as opposed to the warmer, four-letter form of okay," he argued. "Psychologically, she is showing her disrespect for your predicament."

Winston rolled his eyes. "Man," he said, "that is profoundly lame."

"I'll tell you what's profoundly lame," said Manny. "Using 'man' like that." He turned to me and said, "Suddenly, the Short One is Joe Cool."

"Joe Cool!" exclaimed Winston. "Now *that's* a really cool expression."

"You're *men*-tal, Chang," said Manny, tapping the side of his head with his finger.

"*You're* mental, Crandall," answered Winston, tapping his head even harder.

Experience had shown that Winston and Manny could go on like that for hours if I didn't interrupt. So I interjected, "Guys? My problem?"

"Your biggest problem is that Julie Spenser does not talk," said Manny. "You would be better off if she were the kind of girl who dots her i's with little hearts and has verbal diarrhea."

"Verbal diarrhea!" exclaimed Winston. And then — simply to bug Manny — he added, "Man, you're such a *Rupert!*"

"Gee, sor-ry, *Win*-ston!" said Manny sarcastically.

I shot them both a dirty look, and Winston changed his tone. "The Fat One may have a point," he said. "But you shouldn't give her the upper hand by talking too much, either."

"Want my advice?" asked Manny. "*Stare* at her." He narrowed his eyes and glared at me to demonstrate. "After a few minutes of that treatment, she'll break down and tell you the color of her underwear."

"Leave the color of Julie Spenser's underwear out of this," said Winston sternly. "The Savior has come to us with a serious problem and all you can talk about is underwear. Are you still in elementary school or what?"

"You're right, Winston," said Manny, apologetic now. "I'm sorry."

But Winston was so worked up he thought Manny was still being sarcastic. "Guess what, Sherlock?" he said. "Julie Spenser's underwear is probably *black*. Everything else she wears is!"

For some reason, this made Manny laugh. "Yeah," he said. "Julie Spenser probably puts black milk on her cereal!" This comment made Winston laugh. Soon they were both laughing. I passed the time wondering why my two best friends were a bigger mental riddle than Julie Spenser herself.

Finally, they stopped horsing around.

"Just make her explain," said Winston.

"Yeah," said Manny. "Just make her explain."

Julie Spenser was a bit late for our appointment at Barney's Bagel Land. I was so jittery that I talked to the flowered-dress lady for five minutes about whether anybody would actually consume a broccoli-and-cheese bagel. Then Julie walked in and we grabbed our own table. She slid onto the bench along the wall and hunched underneath the cartoon of a court jester juggling bagels. I placed my crutches underneath the chair and sat down.

"Sorry I'm late," Julie said, "but I noticed you managed to pass the time with that lady in the corner."

For some reason, I got defensive. "I'm a loser," I said. "Who did you expect me to be talking to? Some Hollywood starlet?"

Julie blinked. "I didn't mean it that way," she said. "Maybe we should change the subject."

"Maybe you're right," I said. "I suppose you know why we're here."

"Of course," she answered.

"Would you care to explain?" I asked. I said it in exactly the same tone I had heard some guy use in a movie once.

"Don't you want a bagel or something first?" she asked. "I'm buying."

"I don't think it's a good idea for us to be seen enjoying food together," I said.

"Oh yeah," said Julie. "This isn't a date. It's a fact-finding mission. That's almost funny."

And then Julie Spenser surprised me. She grinned. Now she looked like a *happy* raccoon.

I could feel myself staring, and so I muttered, "I wasn't trying to be funny."

"No one who's really funny *ever* tries," said Julie. It sounded like a compliment but I wasn't sure.

Suddenly I noticed Angela Marsh working behind the counter in a cap the shape of a deluxe bagel. Angela was one of Jerry's many girlfriends. Rumor had it she was very low on the Jerry Whitman girlfriend ladder at the moment. That meant she would be looking for a way to gain a rung or two. Providing Jerry with exclusive information might help boost her above the pack.

"You look pale," said Julie.

"I just saw Angela Marsh."

"What's she currently ranked?" asked Julie. "Number five?"

"More like number six."

"You think she's looking to move up?"

"Most definitely," I said. "I think she's already seen us."

"What are you looking so embarrassed about?" asked Julie. "*She's* the one in the stupid hat."

"We are getting off the topic," I said.

"Sorry," said Julie. "What's the topic again?"

"Why are you telling lies about the two of us to Jerry Whitman and the boys?"

"Well, Savior —" Julie began. "May I call you Savior?"

"If it's all the same to you, I don't like that name much."

"How about Sherwood?" she asked.

"Jerry Whitman calls me that."

"Oh," she said. "By all means, let us avoid all Jerry Whitmanisms."

"If you have to call me anything, call me Alex."

"Do you think we're ready for that, Alex?"

"You just called me Alex," I answered. "That must mean we're ready."

Julie Spenser smiled again. "What's the matter? You're all red."

"You're talking more than I thought you would."

"That's because you've done me a big favor."

"I'll bet it concerns Jerry Whitman," I guessed.

"How did you know?"

"You have that I'm-so-happy-to-have-narrowly-escaped-Jerry-Whitman look about you," I said.

"He has this idea about turning me into one of his bubble-headed girlfriends," she confided. "You know, like a make-over.

Change my hair. Change my makeup. Make me Whitman-worthy."

"You don't want to do that?"

"Not unless he can make over my brain by removing it," said Julie. "He was getting to be a real pest. You know, teasing, grabbing, and making jokes that aren't really jokes. So finally I told him I already had a boyfriend."

"There are many other pretend boyfriends you could have selected Why did you pick me?"

"Because you're the one he comes closest to leaving alone," she explained. "He would probably beat up another pretend boyfriend."

I nodded. "Being my girlfriend also makes you way less of a prize," I said. "So he can't show too much interest."

"I never thought of it that way," said Julie.

I shrugged. "As long as you know you've lost points in the non-loser department."

"Don't sell yourself short," she said. "The idea of the two of us going around together really messes with Whitman's head." Julie Spenser leaned forward as if she was telling me a juicy secret. "I kind of like that," she added.

"I can understand why you would want to keep Jerry at a distance," I offered, trying to sound understanding about it. "But you're putting me in a very difficult position."

"I don't see how."

"That's because you're not a loser."

"How do you know I'm not a loser?"

"Because you're not," I said. "I don't know much about you, but I do know a couple of things. One, you're not a loser. And, two, you're not one of Jerry's crowd."

"I hate Jerryworld," she said.

"Jerryworld?"

"That's what I call it," she said. "Jerryworld."

"For some people, Jerryworld is not such a bad place," I said. "Especially for Jerry."

Julie looked at me curiously. "Why does everything have to be in categories?" she inquired. "What's cool. What's not cool."

"Don't ask me," I said. "I don't make the rules at school."

Julie Spenser began to explain that her parents were normal and average but she liked being different — even if it meant wearing dark clothes and turning brooding into an art. "I enjoy the fact that there is no high-school category for me," said Julie. "I'm in No Man's Land."

I looked at Julie Spenser, who was really kind of pretty when you thought about it. "Is it lonely in No Man's Land?" I asked. Now this may seem like a stupid thing to have said, and maybe it was, but for some unknown reason it came out sounding reasonably mature.

"Sometimes it gets kind of lonely," she said.

Because Julie was being honest, I figured it was best to be honest back. "Just because you don't see any bruises doesn't mean that Jerry doesn't get to me," I said. "Believe me, Jerry Whitman has his ways." I leaned forward and added, "They can get very psychological."

"I wasn't thinking," she said. "Jerry gets to me, too."

"Is it bad?" I asked.

"Nothing I can't handle," said Julie, but I could tell she was trying to be low- key.

"Sometimes it's not just psychological, right?"

"No," said Julie. "Sometimes it's not."

I pretended to develop a sudden interest in the paper place mat on the table. And then the words just came out. "I suppose it wouldn't be so bad if Jerry thought you were my girlfriend for the time being."

"I guess there's a reason they call you the Savior."

"It's no big deal," I said, but I could feel myself going red in the face again.

"Jerry might start taking it out on you. You know, psychologically."

"I'm used to it," I replied. "You might say I'm the mascot of Jerryworld."

"Have you ever thought about why he cuts you so much slack?"

"He feels sorry for me," I said. "Jerry Whitman has patted me on the head so many times he has practically left a permanent handprint."

"You think that's why? Because he feels sorry for you?"

"Of course. "

"Jerry Whitman feels sorry for nobody," said Julie. "I think it's something else."

"What other reason could there be?"

"You'll figure it out." Then she changed the subject. " So I guess we'll be spending a lot of extra time together after school."

"What makes you say that?" I asked, dumbfounded.

Julie Spenser blinked her heavily mascara-ed eyes a couple of times. "Why, the bet, of course," she said. "I know you're not going to back off the Christmas lights competition. So I assume you're going to be needing help stringing up lights and stuff."

"You want to help a bunch of losers do a Christmas display?"

"Let's face it," said Julie. "There's no middle ground with Jerry. The least I can do is lend a hand after you stood up to him like that."

She was looking at me with something that could almost pass for admiration. As a natural-born loser, I felt it was my sworn obligation to wipe that look off her face before someone got hurt.

"This deal about Christmas lights," I said, "don't you think it's a little uncool?"

"That's the beauty of it!" said Julie. "It's so uncool, it's actually kind of cool." Her face was flushed with interest, and she was talking fast. To my shock, I realized this was the first time I had seen her not looking bored.

"By choosing such a dorky contest, you're playing by your own set of rules," she continued excitedly. "So what if they're loser rules? You're still rejecting every macho, sexist thing that Jerry Whitman stands for."

"I *am*?" I asked.

"Don't you see, Alex?" she urged. "Jerry thinks *he's* in control, but *you* are."

I was so stunned at this thought that I said nothing.

This didn't bother Julie, who just kept going. "We can beat him," she concluded, her eyes all shiny. "What does it matter if it's Christmas lights or marbles or hopscotch? We can *beat* him."

Before I could reply, I noticed Angela Marsh heading for our table.

"Here comes our first test in the field," whispered Julie.

Angela arrived at our table with a notepad in her hand. "Usually people come up to the counter and order," she said, giving me a special look of mercy. "But I figured this would be easier for you."

"Thank you, Angela," said Julie. And then, like she'd made a mistake, she said, "Oh, you're talking about *Alex*." She looked at me fondly, as if I was melting her heart. "I was going to come up and order for us."

"Hey, Angela," I said. "Have you been working at Barney's Bagel Land long?"

"About a week," said Angela. "Are you guys really going *out?*"

Julie Spenser didn't answer. She simply took my hand across the table while I tried to look as if she took my hand in hers all the time. Finally, Julie said, "It's kind of an anniversary for us. Isn't it, Alex?"

"Uh-huh," I said.

"How long?" asked Angela.

"Officially?" said Julie. "Nearly two weeks."

"*That* long," said Angela, who sounded surprised.

"That's not counting the summer and the beginning of school," I said. "That was unofficial."

"Alex was seeing someone else," said Julie, her eyes going misty. "But not any more."

I looked straight at Angela Marsh and said, "I wouldn't trade Julie for any five or six girls you could name off the top of your head."

"So this is a special occasion?" asked Angela, who had switched from sounding surprised to sounding envious.

"Very special," I said. "Bring us your most expensive bagel."

"We'll split it," said Julie, giving my hand a special-occasion kind of pat. She was a much better patter than Jerry Whitman.

Angela checked the menu board. "That would be the raisin surprise," she said.

"What's the surprise part?" I asked.

"The surprise part is that it's very expensive," she answered.

"I'll have coffee as well, please," Julie said.

"She likes it black," I added.

Julie and I gazed at each other as if Angela Marsh wasn't there. Angela said, "You guys really *are* going out, aren't you?"

"I think your hat's on a little too tight, Angela," teased Julie. "You're beginning to overlook the obvious."

"Congratulations, you guys." Angela said. "I think you go good together."

We thanked Angela, and she went off to get our raisin surprise. Naturally we had to sit around and eat the bagel, because Angela kept staring at us. I also noticed my friend the flowered-dress lady glancing at us and smiling. I guess it was hard not to notice the two of us. Julie laughed at everything I said, including when I asked if she would like a glass of water. The weird thing is, I think she thought some of the stuff I said really *was* funny.

But the topper came when Julie put her hand on mine and blushed. "I have a confession to make," she said. "I still like Christmas lights. Stupid, huh?"

"That's not stupid," I said, not wanting to move my hand.

She held my hand a little tighter and smiled. "I knew you wouldn't put me down."

Maybe having a pretend girlfriend brought out the best in me. It also made me wonder what having a real one would be like. I took a good look at Julie Spenser's shiny eyes again, and

I realized that I'd do just about anything to keep that non-bored expression going.

Did you ever have that roller coaster feeling? The one where you knew you were heading for certain disaster but, at the same time, you were so thrilled you didn't care? Well, that's the way I felt holding hands with Julie Spenser in the middle of Barney's Bagel Land. Because, all of a sudden, I knew I had made the right decision to take Jerry's bet and enter the Christmas lights contest. At that moment I didn't even care if I had to do the whole thing myself.

CHAPTER

TWELVE

Since I knew we would have to use Winston's house for the competition, I figured I'd start working on him first. What better place than at the dinner table? I wanted to break him in gently. So I made a nice little pork roast for supper, along with his favorite golden potatoes. While he was chewing happily, I told him how Julie Spenser had offered to help us with the project.

Winston was not impressed. "Girls are different from guys," he said. "They like to go backwards in time every now and then. You know, make mud pies and string up Christmas lights and stuff. They can do that and their reputation will not be harmed in the least."

"Why not?" I asked.

"Because they are girls," said Winston. "Girls aren't *supposed* to make any sense."

"Our reputations are already ruined."

That's when Winston launched into this long speech about how I had gone love-crazy for Julie Spenser, and how it was up to him to save me from myself. "On behalf of my fellow losers, you will not accept this foolish Yuletide bet," said Winston, concluding his lecture. "That is final."

Now, I don't like being told what to do. It's part of my addiction to freedom. But, I asked myself, what would the great Groucho Marx do? He would pretend to go along with things, then do exactly what he wanted. So I figured it would be best for all concerned to switch the subject. I began to tell Winston about the Beast and how he wasn't such a bad guy.

At first, Winston was shocked that I had been inside the Beast's lair, but then his curiosity took over. After answering a bunch of questions about the Beast, I delivered my conclusion. "Harry is merely misunderstood," I said. "In fact, I think he's interesting."

"I agree," said Winston dryly. "For instance, he has a very interesting way of dumping dog crap on us." Then he absolutely forbade me to have anything more to do with Harry.

I tried my best to stay calm, but Winston was getting way too bossy. I told him that if I wanted to live by a lot of dumb rules, I would call Francine back from Argentina.

I guess he could tell I was steamed, because he put on this cartoon face and said, "Gee, honey, I think we just had our first fight." This was so stupid it made me laugh quite a bit. We ended up playing darts with the Jerry Whitman target and eating a carton of this ice cream called Cherry Garcia.

That was the thing about living with Winston at the mansion. There were so many distractions it was easy to forget about the pressures of regular life, including that my dad was still in hiding. I never completely forgot, of course. I still made sure to go back to my apartment to check the answering machine every few days in case Dad had left a call. But the only message on the machine was from Big Garry, who said, "Hey, Shovel. You can run but you can't hide. And that goes for Shovel Junior, too."

After that, I started to slink around like a spy whenever I visited the apartment building. I always chatted with Mr. Sankey, though, in the laundry room so that he wouldn't get suspicious. As it turned out, that was the best thing I could have done, because one afternoon I had a brainwave. I decided to ask if I could borrow his vintage Christmas decorations for a school project. He said as long as I agreed to clean them up, they were mine. From then on, I spent my time down in the laundry room polishing the red noses on reindeer and the belt buckles on elves. As I worked, I couldn't help but worry. I had the decorations now, but how would I get enough help to pull the thing off?

Everything remained orderly at the mansion. Manny came over a couple of times when he wasn't looking after his mom to play pool and get his first taste of mansion life outside the club meetings. He started calling the place "Bachelor Central," as if there was a party going on twenty-four hours a day. Of course — except for the regular Thursday meetings of the Losers' Club — there wasn't. Usually there was just me, Winston, and Cola.

Cola still pined for Neville, but he took an instant shine to Manny. The dog would go completely nuts whenever Manny was in the room. He even dropped Neville's slipper so he could lick Manny's hands. Winston said that it was because Manny wore a special perfume called Eau de Pizza Grease. But I could tell that Cola's behavior around Manny made Winston jealous.

Still, life was reasonably satisfying in a short-term kind of way. After several weeks of being roommates, Winston and I had our routine down pat. Neville was happy in California. My dad was happy being anywhere that Big Garry wasn't. And there was an alarm system to provide ample warning in case of a Jerry Whitman attack. Best of all, no adults were bugging us.

One afternoon when the three of us were goofing off in the room with the giant TV, Manny looked at me and said, "You know something? Your skin is clearing up."

"His manhood is no longer being retarded," said Winston.

"No, seriously," said Manny. "The Savior is looking good."

"I've been spending some time in the Jacuzzi," I explained. "I think the steam is beginning to open up my pores."

"Maybe your zit remedy is Julie Spenser," said Manny.

"Yeah," teased Winston. "Julie Spenser."

"Come on, you guys," I said. "Julie and I are only pretending to date to mess with Jerry's mind."

"Is that why you let her pick up those books you dropped the other day?" asked Manny.

"Yeah," said Winston. "You don't let anybody else pick up your books."

"Besides, a dropped book is no excuse for you and Julie Spenser to gaze at each other the way you do," offered Manny.

"I told you," I said. "We're messing with Jerry."

"Well, don't mess with him too much," said Manny. "He's liable to send the Watertank after you."

Manny was referring to my expanding the Bank of Sherwood. I was starting to use some of the money my dad had left me to give out more loser loans, and this was cutting into Jerry's interest. In addition, it meant the Watertank did not have anything to enforce. Jerry was afraid that Duane was getting soft and lazy.

"Whitman is going to start pressuring you to take that stupid Christmas bet so he can stir things up," said Manny.

"The Savior and I have already settled that," said Winston. "I have forbidden him to take the bet."

"I haven't decided yet," I said.

"You might take the bet?" asked Manny, amazed.

"I have forbidden him," repeated Winston, puffing out his chest like some very short king.

Winston's attitude was beginning to seriously bug me. In fact, I was preparing to announce that I'd already accepted the bet when Manny related some new information he had discovered about Jerry Whitman, Sr., It seems that Whitman's old man was obsessed with anything relating to Christmas. We already knew that every December he placed special ads on the bus-stop benches. In them, he would wear a dorky Santa hat and an extra-big holiday smile. Below his face, a message read: "The best of the season, from my family to yours." But here's what we didn't know. Apparently, before his real estate business got so busy, Jerry Senior's outdoor Christmas light displays had been the talk of the neighborhood.

"Don't you see?" said Manny. "Whitman's old man is a shoe-in. Every entry has to have an adult family member. Jerry brings in his dad with all that experience and he *wastes* us."

"We'd need an adult on our team?" I asked.

"Didn't you read the fine print on the entry form?" asked Manny. "We would not only need an adult. We would need an adult *family* member. If you think I'm going to get my mom to climb a ladder…"

"It's a sucker's bet," said Winston. "And that's final."

The only thing I could do was keep quiet and let things calm down. How else was I going to convince them? As far as Winston and Manny were concerned, the only plan of action was to appease Jerry Whitman as much as possible. We had started to go to Winston's house for lunch a couple of times a week, which meant we were able to avoid the war zone of the cafeteria. At first, we thought about eating lunch there every school day, but Manny wisely realized this was not a good idea.

"If Jerry Whitman doesn't get the opportunity to hit me with a cafeteria doughnut at least twice a week, he's liable to get suspicious," he said. "He might even send the Watertank to follow us home."

"Manny's right," said Winston, who was often stuffed into his locker during the second half of lunch hour. "If we are to keep our freedom, we must allow Jerry and the boys to maintain a decent level of abuse."

That is the way losers think. If things are going well, you automatically wonder how long the freakish streak of good times is going to last. You know that something doubly bad is going to happen once that streak is done. So nobody was surprised at what Manny said the next afternoon after he had racked up an impressive score on Mr. Chang's old-fashioned pinball machine.

"I wonder how long this paradise will last?" asked Manny. "I am feeling so good right now that I'll probably step out the door and be fried by a bolt of lightning."

"Why do you have to ruin everything by talking about electrical accidents?" asked Winston.

"You guys have to get caught *sometime*," explained Manny.

"The school counselors can smell a lack of adult supervision from ten miles away."

"Who cares?" said Winston. "Let's ride the freedom train until it runs out of gas."

"Trains don't run on gas," said Manny. "They run on coal."

"Who cares?" said Winston.

"*I* care," said Manny.

Of course, nobody cared whether trains ran on gas or coal. It was getting close to dinnertime and Manny always gets a little testy when it is time for him to go home to look after his mother. "You guys are so lucky," he said. "Nobody cares where you are at any given time. If I delay opening a can of soup for my mom, she keeps moaning my name over and over." He put his hand to his forehead. "Ru-pert! Ru-pert!" he shouted, in great distress. "Where is my Campbell's Chicken Noodle?"

I thought it was a very funny imitation, but Winston was offended because Manny had said that nobody cared where he was. "My father cares where I am," he declared. "He wrote an entire report about me! Has your dad ever done that, Rupert?"

"My dad is an extremely busy stockbroker in Manhattan," said Manny, now indignant himself. "For your information, Wall Street makes any street in this dinky little town look like a back alley. In fact, it makes any place you've ever seen look small."

"Ever been to Hong Kong, Fat One?" asked Winston.

"Who cares?" I said. That seemed to defuse things for the moment.

Manny sighed. "Well, I better get going soon," he said. "If I'm late, my mom might try to open the can and cut herself."

Manny looked so depressed at the thought of quality soup time with his mom that I convinced him to take another crack at the pinball machine. By the time he was through, it was dark out. I was in the kitchen experimenting with a new chicken recipe when I heard Manny say, "Look at the time! I gotta go."

Manny was getting his coat on when the doorbell rang. Winston said it was probably some charity person canvassing for a donation. But when he opened the door, our geometry teacher was standing on the other side.

As soon as I caught a glimpse of Mrs. Loomis, I ducked back into the kitchen and watched through the crack between the kitchen door and the wall. Mrs. Loomis is well known for her impromptu visits to students. She will deliver extra homework to a sick pupil or simply pay a call to see how their cold is coming along. Most parents are grateful for this. Most students react like Winston, whose jaw was practically on the floor.

"Hello, Winston," said Mrs. Loomis.

"Hello," said Winston. He was clearly in shock at seeing our teacher on his doorstep. "Uh…may I ask why you are here?"

"I was in the neighborhood and I thought I'd deliver this in person," said Mrs. Loomis, as she thrust out a piece of paper.

"What is it?" stammered Winston.

"Use your powers of observation, Winston," ordered Mrs. Loomis. "What does it look like?"

Winston just stood there. So Manny raised his hand and said, "Last week's geometry quiz?"

Mrs. Loomis squinted into the doorway and called out, "Rupert? Is that you?"

"Yes, Mrs. Loomis," said Manny.

Mrs. Loomis stepped across the threshold to get a closer look. Manny was so freaked out that he seemed to have forgotten all about his mother's soup.

"We are not in class, Rupert," she remarked. "You may put down your hand."

But Manny stayed frozen, his hand still up in the air. Later, he would say he felt as if his fort had been invaded by hostile forces in a surprise attack.

Mrs. Loomis took Manny's hand and gently put it by his side. She looked over at Winston. "Aren't you going to ask me in?"

Mrs. Loomis was already in. Winston closed the door, and I could see that he was trying to remain calm.

"May I offer you a beverage?" he asked. "I believe we have just uncapped a fresh jug of Gatorade."

"No, thank you," said Mrs. Loomis. "Perhaps I can see an adult about your progress? Is Neville available?"

"You know about Neville?" said Winston.

"I have read your file many times," said Mrs. Loomis.

Mrs. Loomis must have been serious, because she'd been talking for a whole minute without rhyming anything. This rattled Winston. "Did my file make you smile?" he asked with a stiff grin.

Mrs. Loomis didn't bite. "No, Winston. It did not."

Winston was so shook up by now that he was babbling, "Neville's fallen in love in California."

"Is Winston failing?" asked Manny, working hard to change the subject.

"Isn't that a question Winston should be asking, Rupert?" asked Mrs. Loomis.

"*Am* I failing?" implored Winston, picking up the cue.

"Yes, you are failing," said Mrs. Loomis. "You are failing to live up to your potential."

"What if he promises to turn on the tap?" asked Manny.

In desperation, he turned on an invisible faucet at the side of his head.

"Sometimes we need help turning on the tap," said Mrs. Loomis. "Don't we, Winston?"

I could see Mrs. Loomis craning her head in my general direction. "There must be an adult around here somewhere," she said. "Something smells delicious."

The chicken had given me away, so I figured it was time to show myself and take the heat off Manny and Winston. I got out from behind the kitchen door and stepped into the hall wearing my "World's Greatest Chef" apron. Later, I would discover there was a smudge of gravy on my forehead.

Mrs. Loomis was taken aback. "Alex, are you *cooking*?" she asked.

"Winston's guardian is cooking," I said, with a little bow. "I am merely his humble assistant."

"Where *is* Winston's guardian?" she asked.

"He's at the store getting some extra vegetables for dinner," I explained.

"Will he be back soon?" she asked. "Perhaps I should wait."

"No!" exclaimed Winston. Then, calming down a little, he added, "He's very choosy about his carrots."

Mrs. Loomis explained she had recently taken on additional duties at the school. "I am replacing Mrs. Klenaman on a part-time basis."

"But Mrs. Klenaman is a guidance counselor," said Manny.

"That is correct, Rupert," said Mrs. Loomis, as if he had managed to solve a simple math problem. "She is taking a leave of absence for health reasons."

"I am very sorry to hear that," said Winston, sounding sincere. Mrs. Klenaman had been his guidance counselor for the last year or so.

"Through no fault of her own, Mrs. Klenaman has let a few things slide," said Mrs. Loomis. She looked at Winston. "I don't think she has paid enough attention to your particular situation."

"In that case, you must be especially interested in talking to Winston's guardian," I said. "Why doesn't Winston arrange for him to call you and set up an appointment?"

Mrs. Loomis frowned slightly. "I was hoping to have a little chat with him this evening," she said. "You see, I'm going out of town on a special math teachers' conference for a week."

Winston put on a concerned expression. "I don't know what's keeping my… guardian," he managed to choke out.

Mrs. Loomis looked at her watch. "Oh, dear," she said. "I'm leaving for the conference tomorrow, and I have so much to do. Would you have him call me as soon as I get back?"

"Absolutely," said Winston, who had turned as pale as a blank math test. "No problem. We have over a dozen phones."

"Does this guardian have a name?" asked Mrs. Loomis.

Nobody seemed in any hurry to speak up, so I mentioned the first name that popped into my head. "His name is Harry," I said. "Harry Beardsley."

CHAPTER

THIRTEEN

Ever notice how there are times when even your best friends can't wait to call you crazy? As soon as Mrs. Loomis had left, Winston began hopping around.

"Have you gone completely *men-tal*?" he said. "First, you provoke Jerry Whitman with that insane Christmas thing and now you drag the Beast into our lives."

Winston stopped ranting long enough to fill Manny in on who Harry was.

Manny shook his head. "The Savior has lost it. It is a dark day for losers."

"I have not lost it," I said, irritated. "Besides, don't you have to go home to your mother, Manny?"

"She'll understand this once," replied Manny. "This is too good to miss."

"What do you mean you have not lost it?" demanded Winston. "Harry Beardsley is a worse slacker than I am!"

"There's an obvious advantage to Harry," I said. As soon as I said it, I knew it was true.

"What's that?" asked Manny.

"I think he lives on the financial edge," I explained. "We could bribe him with money."

"So?" said Winston.

"So it means he'll do what we say," I replied. "I'm almost certain he'll keep quiet about it."

"We can boss this guy around?" asked Manny.

"I don't know about that," I said. "But I don't think he'll make trouble for us."

"He's too weird," said Winston. "For this to work with Mrs. Loomis, he'd have to act like an adult."

"Come on, Winston," I replied. "If we're going to get away with this, we'll need an adult at some point to sign report cards and go to PTA meetings and stuff." We also needed an adult supervisor if we were going to enter the Christmas lights competition. But I wasn't going to reveal my thoughts on that just yet. Instead, I continued, "And besides being short on cash, I think Harry's lonely."

"That's what they say about every maniac," retorted Winston. He put on a deep voice like some newscaster. "By all accounts, the axe murderer lived alone and was very much a loner."

"Harry's not a maniac," I said. "He's an eccentric."

"How much do you want to bet he has an axe under his bed?" said Winston.

Manny had been turning his head from me to Winston as if he was watching a tennis match. "Will you stop it?" he said. "You're freaking me out. Let us focus on the dilemma of Mrs. Loomis."

"Mrs. Loomis!" groaned Winston.

"I can't believe she is now a part-time guidance counselor," said Manny. "Our worst nightmare has a *badge*!"

"She is a bulldog," said Winston.

"She is a bloodhound," offered Manny.

"Mrs. Loomis is every kind of dog you don't want following you around," said Winston. "She will wreck my life, and when she is finished wrecking it, she will wreck both of yours."

"Why would she do that?" I asked.

"Because you're my *friends*," said Winston. "And because she thinks we need to be wrecked for our own good."

"She has a real appetite for that sort of thing," agreed Manny.

"Don't panic," I said. "You're forgetting something about Harry, something that's our secret weapon in the battle against Mrs. Loomis."

"What's that?" asked Manny.

I turned on an invisible faucet on the side of my head. "Harry Beardsley has potential."

Winston snorted. But Manny got interested. "What does Harry look like?" he asked.

"Like a vampire," answered Winston, "a vampire on a permanent Hawaiian vacation."

"We could clean him up," I said. "He might clean up okay."

"We can rebuild him with spare parts," said Manny, "like an old engine in auto shop."

"He's smarter than he looks," I said. "As for his appearance, there's a closet full of suits that belong to Winston's dad. I bet Harry and Mr. Chang are about the same size."

"They are?" said Manny. "Maybe it's fate."

"How about it, Winston?" I asked.

Winston looked glum. "Maybe," he said grudgingly. "There would have to be some conditions."

"What sorts of conditions?" I asked.

"*Safety* conditions," said Winston. "We'd have to check Harry out."

"How would we do that?" Manny asked.

"My dad has an account with this local security company," said Winston. "He told Neville and me we should give them a call if we had to hire someone to do home repair. You know, like a handyman or something."

"So you pretend that Harry is a potential handyman?" I asked.

"Why not?" said Winston. "My dad says this company runs a complete background check using a big computer data base. By the time they're through, we'll know stuff about the Beast that he hasn't told his mother."

"I don't know," I said. "Maybe we shouldn't go poking around in Harry's private life."

"You wanna end up dead in your bed?" asked Manny.

"Without your head?" added Winston.

"And just when your face is clearing up, too," pointed out Manny.

"Okay, so we run the background check," I agreed. "Let's say he passes. What then?"

"Then we interview him," explained Winston, warming to the idea. "Use the data to ask him a series of questions to see if he'll make the right kind of pretend guardian."

"Like an interrogation?" asked Manny. "Man, that is *so* cool."

"No," said Winston. "Like an audition. We simulate situations he may find himself in as our guardian and see how he does."

"I *like* it!" said Manny.

"But first he's got to pass the security test," cautioned Winston.

I stressed that we only had a week before Mrs. Loomis returned. Luckily, for a lazy guy, Winston could sure swing into action when he felt like it. After Manny went home, he phoned the security company and got through right away. "I need a double red-hot rush on this," he barked, as if he was a big-time executive instead of some height-deprived loser who kept getting stuffed into his own locker. "Bill my father for everything."

Winston said that the rush job would cost his dad big bucks, but within twenty-four hours, he had a fat folder that contained the results of a deluxe investigation on Mr. Harold Ernest Beardsley. He insisted on reading it first, since he didn't trust Manny and me.

The next day at lunch, he summarized it for us. "Harry has had about a hundred different jobs," said Winston. "He's been bounced from more places than an NBA basketball."

The good news? Harry was not an axe murderer. Actually, apart from the occasional visit to the racetrack and a credit history that the report described as "checkered," Harry was not your basic criminal type. Winston said the security company had even managed to dig up a few newspaper articles that said Harry used to be a famous book writer.

In some ways, I think Winston was disappointed that Harry's past wasn't more colorful. "Harry is merely your average, low-achieving has-been in a loud shirt," he said. "He doesn't even have the *drive* to be an axe murderer."

"He is wasting his life big-time," nodded Manny, as he

stuffed an economy-pack Twinkie into his mouth. Through a mouthful of cake and cream filling, he mumbled, "The guy obviously has no self-discipline." He was so intent on getting out this last part that bits of cake sprayed all over the place.

Maybe it was the crumb of wet Twinkie that landed on my left shoulder, but suddenly I was surprisingly ticked off. "You guys are hypocrites," I said. "You can't even recognize that Harry is one of us."

Winston seemed shocked that I was sticking up for Harry — not to mention that I was granting Harry entry into the Losers' Club without so much as a single skill-testing question.

"I may be a low-achiever, but I'm too young to be a has-been," he huffed. "Besides, I have a lot more life left to waste than Harry does."

"Yeah," said Manny, who seemed put out, even though the Twinkie still had most of his attention.

Despite our disagreement, you could tell Winston liked the idea of knowing all about Harry. The security report gave him the opportunity to pass off his natural nosiness as a business strategy. Back at his place after school, he pulled out Harry's file. I refused to look at it, but Winston kept feeding us bits of personal information — such as the fact that Harry had been married and divorced — quite a private piece of data, when you think about it.

After that, I told Winston that I didn't want to hear any more. "It makes me feel like we're spying on him," I said. "All I want to know is if he's cleared for the guardian interview."

"Okay," said Winston. "But some of the stuff in his file is fascinating."

"Come on, Winston," I said. "Is Harry cleared or not?"

"Check," said Winston. He was turning out to be a real pain in the ass about the security thing.

"Does that mean yes?"

"Affirmative," nodded Manny, who had obviously decided to be a pain in the ass too.

Half an hour later, I was standing at Harry's door. I hesitated for a minute, reluctant to ring the doorbell and disturb his privacy. I hadn't even played his Charlie Parker record yet, because I was waiting for just the right time. But the funny thing was I kind of wanted to see him again. And I knew he wouldn't use words like "check" or "affirmative." So I rang the bell and waited.

Harry was surprised to see me, but he invited me in and listened politely as I told him our plan. When I was done, he let out a couple of sharp smoker's coughs and said, "You want me to pretend to be someone's *guardian*? No way, man. Teachers make me more nervous than editors."

"But we can offer you a salary," I said. "Plus benefits, such as all the Mr. Chang suits you can wear."

Harry shook his head, causing his long, greasy hair to sway from side to side. "Much as I'm tempted by the offer of multiple suits, I'll have to pass," he said. "I got a system worked out here. I don't do anything that requires me to shave two days in a row."

"Are you allergic to money or something?"

"Not money," answered Harry. "Just responsibility." He rubbed his chin. "In addition to which, I have very sensitive skin."

I could feel myself getting angry, and what came out next startled both of us. "Stop bullshitting me, Harry," I said.

"Look," he growled, lighting a cigarette. "I'm going to tell you something. You remember me talking about my Aunt June?" I nodded. "She had a nickname for me. She used to call me the Teflon kid. You know what Teflon is?"

Every once in a while, my knowledge of late-night TV infomercials comes in handy. "It's the non-stick coating on the inside of frying pans, right?"

Harry nodded. "Do you know why she called me the Teflon kid?" he asked. He didn't bother to wait for an answer. "Because I would never *stick* to anything. I've been in enrolled in six different departments in six different universities. Don't even have a degree."

"So what?"

"So nothing has ever lasted. I get bored or restless or both. I'm not a good risk."

"What about the book?" I said. "The green one."

"A freak occurrence." Harry shrugged. "An intellectual eclipse."

"What does that mean?"

Harry picked up the green book and gently wiped it with his sleeve. "It means it won't happen again."

"Why *can't* you do it again?"

"I don't know," said Harry. "It's kind of like doing a magic trick without knowing how."

Harry started to shuffle through a stack of CDs. He put one on and held up his index finger to signal that I should be quiet. The song he played was all about glory days and how they can pass you by before you even know it. When it was over, he told me it was by some guy named Springsteen.

"What did you think of it?" he asked.

"I don't know," I said. "I'm a loser. Losers don't have to

worry about glory days passing them by, because they never have any glory days in the first place."

"Don't be so sure," he said. "Glory has a funny way of sneaking up on you."

We sat there for a time, enjoying the silence. "Harry?" I asked. "What does it take to be a big-time writer?"

Harry shrugged. "Big or small, you gotta have curiosity about the human condition."

"Is that why you're always staring at me?"

"I stare at you?"

"Yeah," I said. "You stare at the way I walk."

"Sorry, chief," he said. "I didn't mean to make you feel self-conscious."

I told Harry that many people stared at me and that, mostly, I was used to it. "But with you, it's as if you're more than curious. It's as if you're looking at me and seeing somebody else, somebody you already know."

"I'm thinking about making up a character like you," he said, running a hand through his greasy hair. "For my next book."

"One of your pink books?" I asked.

"Why not?" said Harry, patting his pockets for a cigarette.

"Harry," I said. "You're already smoking."

Harry let a small plume of smoke drift past his line of vision before croaking, "So I am." He took the cigarette out of his mouth. "Anyway, lots of women who read pink books dig crutches. Unlike a suit of armor, they're heroic without making you look like an open can of sardines."

"You mean you keep looking at me because I'm inspiring you?" I asked doubtfully. "You're not making fun of me, are you?"

"No way," said Harry. "In fact, you could say I owe you one."

I brought up again how Winston and Manny and I wanted to test him for the role of fake guardian. "I'm not sure I owe you that much," said Harry.

"Could you at least show up for the audition?" I asked. "I promised the guys."

"Sorry, pal," he said. "I don't like people asking me personal questions."

My face turned a little red at that point as I remembered Winston's security report. I worked on Harry for a while longer, though, mostly because we urgently needed a fake guardian. But the more I thought about it, the more I realized there could be other reasons, too.

Maybe I figured that if I could get Harry involved with people again, it might stop him from being such a loser. Or maybe I was scared, because I didn't like to think that someone with as much potential as Harry could learn to make misfortune his lifelong friend. I mean, if it could happen to him, what chance did Winston, Manny and I have for an adult life that didn't feature disappointment, loneliness, and a hundred candy wrappers on the floor?

It didn't really matter what my motivation was, since Harry was firm about turning down our offer. And that made me a desperate man. I knew that Harry's green book was probably the only thing in the whole world he cared about. So I probably shouldn't have stuck it under my shirt when he went to the other room to get a pack of cigarettes. But, to tell the truth, I had to do it. Sure, it was underhanded. But it was also the only way I could think of to get Harry to the audition.

It took about an hour for Harry to notice that the book was

gone. I was several chapters into it up in my room when the phone rang at Winston's with a call for me.

As soon as I said hello, a rusty voice demanded, "I want my book back."

"Sorry, Harry," I replied. "Not unless you come for the audition."

"That's blackmail," said Harry. "You should be ashamed of yourself."

"I am," I said, "but not so ashamed that I wouldn't tear out a page a day until you say yes."

"You're trying my patience, kid."

I told Harry that I was actually *reading* his book. There was a pause. And then he asked, "How do you like it so far?"

"The parts I understand are very absorbing," I said. "Some of it's a little over my head, though."

"But you're going to stick with it, right?"

"That depends."

"On what?"

"On whether I start to tear out pages from the end or the beginning."

"About this audition," said Harry. "Do I have to wear shoes?"

We set up the audition for the next day after school. When I answered the door at the appointed time, I could see Harry had shaved with a dull razor. His face had some bits of toilet paper sticking to it from where he had cut himself. But his long hair was freshly washed and sort of combed, and his pineapple shirt was wrinkled but clean. I looked down at his shoes. Harry was wearing scuffed-up loafers on his bare feet.

"You didn't mention anything about *socks*," he said defensively.

"Don't worry about it, Harry."

"Socks don't make the man!" he continued. "What makes a man is integrity — which you might not understand, being a page-ripping book thief."

I let that last part slide, because it was obvious Harry was more than a little skittish. On our way through Winston's living room, he even began talking to the giant stereo like it was a person or something. "Has anyone ever told you that you are a thing of beauty?" he cooed, straight into one of the speakers. "Because you are."

Manny and Winston, who were already seated at the dining room table, thought this was totally bizarre, but Harry explained the thing about an excellent stereo system was that it was completely non-judgmental. "You simply press a few buttons and that baby will play any kind of music you want, no questions asked," he told us earnestly.

It took a while to get Harry settled. Then he got nervous again because Manny — who is very anti-tobacco — refused to let him smoke in the house. Harry without his cigarettes was not exactly an obliging person.

"When do you bring out the rubber hose?" he asked Manny.

I thought it was funny, but Manny didn't laugh. He just wrote something down on a yellow pad. Then Harry took out a pack of gum and offered us each a stick. I took a piece, but Winston acted suspicious and asked if Harry was trying to bribe us or something.

"Hey, man," said Harry. "It's only *gum*. Didn't your parents teach you about sharing anything besides dog crap?"

"I am not in the mood for gum," said Manny. "Got any breath mints?"

"I'm afraid not," said Harry. This made Manny shake his head and write something else down on his pad.

Winston was so offended by the dog crap comment that he went on a major tirade about how Harry didn't even *know* the Changs. To my amazement, Harry apologized.

"These shoes are from hell," he confessed. "They pinch my toes like a twin set of maniac crabs. In addition to which, I need a cigarette *bad*." Little beads of sweat were beginning to develop on Harry's forehead.

The interview went downhill from there. First, Winston asked Harry about his employment history.

"You want to know about jobs?" Harry said. "I've been a skip tracer, a police reporter, a plumber's assistant, and a blackjack dealer."

"What's the longest time you have held a job?" asked Winston.

"Three weeks," said Harry, before throwing in, "I'm not much of a joiner."

Manny chimed in next. "Have you ever stolen anything?" he asked.

"When I was in grade three," Harry replied, "I stole a little pink eraser from the corner grocery store. I couldn't sleep for a week." He shot me a dirty look. "But I have never stolen a rare book and held it hostage."

There were other questions as well, all quite personal in nature. It was a little like one of those old TV shows where a couple of cops grill some poor guy under a naked lightbulb. Before long, I noticed a small river of sweat traveling down Harry's armpits. The sweat collected at the base of some palm trees on his shirt, creating two sweat-stained islands. Finally,

Winston asked Harry if he'd ever been responsible for looking after kids. First, Harry said yes. And then, right away, he said no.

"Which is it?" Winston persisted.

"When I figure it out, you'll be the first to know," Harry replied. He looked at the three of us in turn. "You may not believe this, but not so long ago I was a clean-cut, socially responsible citizen who carried breath mints all the time."

"What happened?" asked Manny.

"*Life* happened," said Harry. "That's what happened."

"About this guardian thing?" said Winston. "We'll get back to you."

"Have you ever worked in publishing?" asked Harry. He took a beat-up cigarette out of his pocket and placed it between his lips. Manny looked on disapprovingly until Harry said, "I'm not gonna light it, okay? I'm just gonna *hold* it!"

It was a lot for Harry to go through merely to get his book back. When I gave it to him at the door, the first thing he did was check for missing pages.

"It's all here," he said, with a look of surprise.

"I wouldn't rip up your book, Harry." I said. "I only wanted you to come out of the house."

"Did you finish it?" he asked.

"Not yet."

Harry thought for a second and then handed me the book. "Give it back when you're finished."

"How come?"

"Books are like people," he said. "It's not right to give up on them until you know the whole story.

CHAPTER

FOURTEEN

After he was gone, I argued for giving Harry one last shot. Winston and Manny outvoted me. Even I had to admit Harry had failed the audition with flying colors. But we all knew it was urgent that we get our hands on a genuine adult before the return of Mrs. Loomis.

Winston said that if we sat around and waited for the clock to run out, he'd go crazy. So, over a pool game, the three of us tried to think of what to do. We thought for so long our brains hurt, but we couldn't figure a way out of our predicament.

"We're doomed," said Winston finally.

I was getting ready to agree with him when Manny came up with an idea.

"We could hire someone to play our guardian," he said.

"That's what we tried to do with Harry," I reminded him.

"No," explained Manny. "I mean a professional. An actor."

"The Fat One has had a brainwave!" proclaimed Winston.

The three of us went to the computer and looked up local actors on the Internet. Before long, we found a website for an actor named Gerald P. Hargrove. His home page read, "There are no small parts — only small actors. Mature, family-oriented roles a specialty. Fee negotiable."

Underneath the "fee negotiable" part was a photograph of Gerald P. Hargrove, Actor. Gerald P. Hargrove looked as if he shaved every day — sometimes twice. He had neatly trimmed hair with a little gray at the temples and the type of wire-rimmed glasses you see on award-winning scientists. He was wearing a cable-knit cardigan and smoking a pipe. A tasteful plume of smoke was coming out of the bowl.

"This is our guy," said Manny. "He has 'guardian' written all over him."

"Don't you think he's a little obvious?" I asked.

"Teachers love the obvious," said Winston. "It makes them relax."

Manny and Winston were eager to contact Hargrove, even though I pointed out that "Gerald" was just another form of "Jerry" — as in Whitman. I considered this a bad omen. But Manny and Winston didn't listen to my point of view. Since my first choice, Harry, was out of the question, I let them have what they wanted.

Gerald P. Hargrove came to the house the following after-noon. Right from the beginning, Manny and Winston really hit it off with the guy. Manny even let Gerald smoke his pipe during the interview. If Hargrove minded being auditioned by three teenaged losers, he didn't show at it all.

"I am an *actor*, dear boy," he told Winston. "You may direct me as you see fit."

Gerald agreed to leave the room while we discussed his suitability for the role. Winston and Manny were extremely impressed. Winston liked Hargrove so much he said we didn't need to run a security check on him. Even Cola thought the actor was okay. Personally I thought Gerald P. Hargrove was a bigger BS artist than my dad. I didn't like the fact that he had a fake British accent and was always ending his sentences with "old man" or "dear boy." But I was outvoted again.

Gerald was clearly delighted to take on the role of Harry Beardsley, guardian. Winston showed his faith in the actor by quickly obliging when Hargrove requested a cash advance "for research purposes." And when Gerald said he needed a quiet place to rehearse, Winston gave him a spare key to the house *and* the security code. Once Hargrove was gone, I tried to tell Winston and Manny that this was a dumb idea, but their heads were so swollen from being called "old man" and "dear boy" that they refused to listen.

It was a total shock the next day when Harry Beardsley called Winston on his cell phone right in the middle of a cafeteria lunch. It was very noisy in the cafeteria. We could hear Winston, though, and he filled us in later on Harry's side of the conversation.

Winston started by shouting, "Who is this?"

"Harry Beardsley," said Harry. "I got your number out of the address book in your kitchen. Your front door is wide open."

At first, Winston thought it was Gerald P. Hargrove *pretending* to be Harry Beardsley. And so he said, "You sound just like Harry."

The voice on the phone said, "I *am* Harry, you little —. Clean out your ears."

"*Harry?*" said Winston.

Harry swore — which Winston said was very discourteous,

considering that this was Winston's personal cell phone.

"I apologize," said Harry. "I just thought you'd like to know that some strange guys in overalls are about to load everything you own into a moving van."

"What!" said Winston.

"Do you want me to call the cops?" asked Harry.

"No police," said Winston. "My dad will find out and kill me."

"Whatever you say, kid," replied Harry. "But some of these guys look pretty big. I'm not sure they'll listen to reason."

"What about Cola?"

"He's out there wagging his tail," said Harry. "He won't be any help."

Winston panicked. Jamming his cell phone into his pocket, he jumped up from the table and took off running. "My heart was pounding," he told us later. "I was about a half a block from the house when everything broke loose."

As he got closer, Winston could see Gerald P. Hargrove and several accomplices talking to Harry. The Chang color TV, the stereo, and several other high-priced items were on the front lawn. Winston said that since Harry was outnumbered, things could have gotten ugly. But just as a couple of Gerald's guys were going to gang up on Harry, he pulled a gun on them.

Winston heard Gerald ask, "Is that thing loaded, old man?"

Harry looked coolly at the actor. "You want to find out?" he said.

The gang looked at the gun, then at Winston, who was shouting for them to stop. That's when Gerald and the others piled into the empty van and took off. Winston, still very agitated, kept yelling at Harry to shoot out their tires.

"You said no cops, remember?" cautioned Harry, pointing out that nothing had been stolen.

Then Harry fired up a cigarette with his gun. Later, Winston confessed to us he was so shocked at that moment somebody could have knocked him over with one of Mr. Winecki's sponges.

Harry took a few puffs on his cigarette before saying anything. Then he told Winston, "I didn't do it for you. I did it because they scratched one of your speakers getting it out the front door." Harry blew a smoke ring and continued, "What kind of low-down animals would do such a thing?"

Winston shook his head as he recounted the story to Manny and me. He told it to us a few times, actually, acting out the various parts, until Manny had to go home to heat up his mother's soup. But I guess Winston still felt guilty about misjudging Harry. That night, as we were loading the dishwasher, he said to me, "Maybe we should have offered Harry the job."

"He is a little short on qualifications."

"I don't know about that. He *is* a dad."

"Harry's a father?" I said, more than a little astonished.

"He has a ten-year-old son named Jack who lives with his mom," said Winston. "It's in the file. Harry's ex-wife is some semi-famous movie actress. There're copies of news clippings on both of them."

I couldn't get over it. "I wonder what kind of kid Jack is?" I asked.

Winston said, "I think you should read the security report." When I didn't reply, he went and got it for me.

Harry was right. Before you judge anything, you should always have the complete story. There were many things about Harry in that report, but the most interesting thing was the color photocopy of a picture of Jack Beardsley from some magazine. He looked like any other ten-year-old, except for the fact that he had a leg brace and walked with crutches. Right away I knew he had cerebral palsy. Like me. I knew before I read it in the report.

I don't know exactly why I went next door to Harry's after that. Curiosity, maybe. Harry invited me into the living room and we sat down. At first, I thanked him for rescuing Winston's furniture.

He smiled. "It felt strange," he admitted. "It's the first thing I've done halfway right in a long time."

I don't know what made me do it, but I took the picture of Jack from my pocket and showed it to Harry.

"Is this your son?" I asked.

Harry looked at the photo. He seemed stunned to be holding it in his hand. "Where did you get this?"

"We had you investigated by a security company," I said. "Are you angry?"

"I guess not," said Harry slowly. Maybe the picture of Jack was softening him up or something. He looked at it again and said, "This picture is a little out of date. He's eleven now. His mother says he's getting tall."

"You don't visit him?"

"We write each other," said Harry. And then, as if he was making an excuse, he added, "I send him money every month."

"So what?" I said. It came out sharper than I meant it to.

Harry shrugged. "Exactly," he said. "His mother has a part

in a soap opera and makes big bucks. He doesn't need the money. It eases my conscience, that's all."

"Why don't you visit him?" I repeated.

"His mother says he has the best of everything," replied Harry. "Do I look like the best of *anything*?"

"I get it," I said, amazed that I was pushing it. "You're scared."

Harry didn't seem to mind my boldness. "I've fallen a long way down from where I used to be," he said. "I didn't notice how far until I talked to you guys the other day and saw how you looked at me. Harry seemed embarrassed. "I'm no good around young people. You all have built-in bullshit detectors." He ran his fingers though his nest of hair and confessed, "Jack makes me nervous. I haven't seen him in a long time."

"Do I make you nervous, Harry?"

"I'm cool with you," said Harry. "But you're not my *son*. You know? A father and son — that's a very complicated relationship, especially when the father's screwing up."

That's when I told Harry about my dad and how he wasn't exactly an award-winning father either. Still, I missed him sometimes. "You miss Jack, don't you, Harry?" I asked. "That's why you kept staring at me that way. I remind you of him."

"It's not just the crutches," said Harry. "It's other things, too."

It wasn't hard to see that Harry was stuck in a rut, the way a car gets stuck in the mud and keeps spinning its wheels until a tow truck arrives. I don't know what it was that I liked so much about Harry. Maybe I felt sorry for him, or maybe it was the bond that forms between fellow losers. But, right then and there, I decided to be what you might call his emotional tow truck.

I remembered a film we saw once in guidance class. It was full of people with long hair and sideburns who used words like "rapping" and "getting down." It was dumb, but it might work on Harry, if I played my cards right.

"Maybe you're rusty when it comes to hanging out with the younger generation, " I said. "Maybe all you need is a little practice."

"You think so?" asked Harry. "I never thought of it that way."

"Absolutely," I said. "You could practice relating to Winston and Manny and me. If the experiment works, you could try it out on Jack."

"It's not the same," said Harry. "Jack's barely eleven years old."

"It's no problem getting Winston and Manny to act as if they're eleven," I said. "Most of the time, the problem is to get them to act as if they're fifteen."

"I don't know," said Harry. "I don't know if I can bounce back. "

"Come on, Harry," I said. "Let's face it. You need to rejoin the human race."

"I can't run fast enough for the human race," said Harry. Then he glanced at my crutches and added, "Forget I said that, okay?"

"You want me to leave you alone, Harry?"

"It's not you personally," said Harry. "I want *everybody* to leave me alone. That scares me more than Jack, more than failure, more than anything."

"You don't have to be worry about us, Harry," I said. "We're losers. Being scared is what we *do*."

"What are you saying?"

"I'm saying that if we're going to be scared anyway, we might as well be scared together."

"It's not much of an offer," said Harry. "On the other hand, it's probably better than I deserve."

And that's more or less how Harry became our fake guardian. His first assignment was to book an appointment with Mrs. Loomis. We all knew he wasn't ready to meet her face to face, so we instructed him to stall the meeting for as long as he could. As it turned out, Harry did an excellent job. He managed to delay the encounter with our geometry teacher for ten days by pleading writing deadlines and a passionate desire to make sure Winston did all his homework. They set up a meeting for October 24, which Winston circled on the kitchen calendar in felt pen the color of blood. A lot happened in those two weeks. It was as if the four of us were cramming for some final exam with real life as the test. We worked hard, but we had fun, too.

Whipping Harry into shape in such a short time wasn't easy. He kept trying to smoke around us, for one thing. Plus, he was very attached to his ugly tropical shirt. Winston tried to convince him that the shirt was cursed with bad luck. Manny said if he had to look at those polyester pineapples one more time he was going to hurl. Finally, since time was so tight, we decided to use shock therapy.

It was Manny who tricked Harry into taking his tropical shirt off by saying that a spider had crawled up his sleeve. The minute Harry removed the shirt, Manny stuffed it down Winston's super-deluxe kitchen garbarator and turned on the switch.

"Die, evil shirt," said Winston as the garbarator churned away.

"Instant pineapple chunks!" said Manny.

At first, a frozen Harry just stood there in a black T-shirt that read "Elvis Costello in Concert." Then he moved to put his hand down the garbarator in a desperate attempt to save his most cherished piece of clothing.

"Let it go, Harry," I said. "Just let it go."

The funny thing is, once we got rid of Harry's favorite shirt, he really *did* start to change. We all noticed, even though it was over a matter of only days.

When I asked Harry about it, he said, "The cranky guy you know isn't the real me. The real me is buried under Oh Henry wrappers and cigarette smoke and hair."

"How long is it going to take before the whole real you comes out?" I asked, thinking of his appointment with Mrs. Loomis.

"More time than we've got," replied Harry. Then, when he saw the panicked expression on my face, he said, "But I figure I'll be able to fake the real me by our deadline."

Harry's voice still sounded like a bag of jiggling rusty nails, but he lit the cigarette dangling from his lip less often. Maybe it was in response to the magazine pictures of blackened, smoke-ridden lungs that Manny had cut out and stuck on Winston's fridge. And even though Harry was under a lot of pressure, he didn't yell each and every time Winston or Manny or I did something to get on his nerves. Sometimes you could hear him whisper, "Let it go. Just let it go."

Harry said he needed a good night's sleep in his own bed next door without interruption, but he came over to Winston's every day for training sessions, which sometimes lasted late into the evening. At first, these sessions mostly involved Winston pretending to be Mrs. Loomis. Peering over the top of Neville's sunglasses, he would grill Harry with all sorts of Mrs. Loomis-type questions. For example, he would ask Harry, "How important do you feel geometry is to the forming of young minds?" Being a writer, Harry was quite good at improvising.

There was also the matter of Harry's appearance. Manny got the ball rolling when he raised the issue of Harry's long, greasy hair. "No offense, Harry," he said, "but we can't have a guardian who looks like he should be playing the washboard in a jug band."

Winston got a bunch of magazines like *GQ* and *Esquire*, and we went over every page looking for the appropriate fake-guardian hairstyle. The three of us voted on the magazine haircut we liked the best. Harry grumbled about it, but he *did* go to the barber. When he returned, we were impressed with the results.

After that, Harry showered every morning and shaved daily with sharp blades. But he found using the razor hard. "It's not so much the shaving that bothers me," he admitted. "It's the looking-myself-in-the-eye part."

Manny confessed that he didn't like looking at himself in the bathroom mirror much either. Winston offered, "At least you *can* look at yourself in the bathroom mirror. All I see when I stand in front of the sink is the top of my head."

It was the kind of useless conversation that made Harry relax. Sometimes we would even take a break from training sessions to compare loser stories. Harry would tell us about the time he got so wrapped up in his writing he let the bathtub overflow in his dorm room, which wrecked the ceiling below. Then Manny would relate how he sent away for this dumb gizmo that was supposed to flatten his stomach without doing sit-ups. That led to the story about Winston sending away for a pair of elevator shoes, only to discover that they killed his feet.

After Harry had a few days to get semi-comfortable with his new grooming regimen, he agreed to try on a couple of Mr. Chang's suits. They were a reasonable fit, apart from being a little long in the legs. Manny, who was handy with a needle and thread, fixed the problem by hemming the slacks. "I'll make the stitching nice and relaxed so that, when the time comes to hang them back up, we can just pluck out the thread nice and easy," he said.

Before Manny left, Harry gave us a fashion show. He had discovered that, with the addition of some tissue paper, even Mr. Chang's shoes were a decent fit. Manny teased Harry a little, calling him Harry Handsome.

Before we knew it, there were only two days left before the meeting with Mrs. Loomis. "Now we must accelerate the brain work," said Winston. Harry was very conscientious about research. He prepared for his meeting with Mrs. Loomis by asking all manner of questions about the Chang family. He called it "creating a back story." But Harry didn't stop there. He also wanted information about Mrs. Loomis — such as if she had won any geometry teacher awards and if we knew what her favorite color was. "Never underestimate the power of concentrated charm," said Harry.

Then the big day arrived. Winston, who would be attending the meeting with Harry, confessed to a few butterflies. But as it happened, Harry had enough concentrated charm to bowl Mrs. Loomis right over. From Harry and Winston's report, it was obvious that the meeting had gone well acting-wise. But when Manny and I asked Harry what Mrs. Loomis had said about Winston, he replied, "That's between Winston, Mrs. Loomis, and me."

"Come on," Manny begged. "You can tell us. We're the only friends he's got."

Harry looked at Winston. "You want me to tell them?"

Winston shook his head. Harry said, "Sorry, guys. It's private."

Over the next few days, Manny, Winston, and I dreamed up other shady stuff that Harry might be able to do as our guardian — things like forge signatures on notes so that we could cut classes. Manny was particularly anxious to get out of gym since there was an entire week of rope-climbing coming up. But the only form Harry agreed to sign involved his adult sponsorship of the Christmas competition. I approached him about it when Winston and Manny were engaged in a hot game of table hockey. He agreed to keep it a secret from them until I could convince them to participate. I thanked him profusely, but he told me there was a condition.

"What's that?" I asked.

"I'll sign the form," he said, "but don't ask me to help in any way."

When I asked him why, Harry went into a long speech about how much he hated Christmas. "The Christmas season is a disaster for me," he said. "My old man died the day before Christmas. My ex-wife told me she wanted a divorce over the holidays. The last time I bought a present for anybody, I was mugged on the way out of the store." Harry paused to allow his Yuletide misfortune to sink in. "These days, I have a strategy for Christmas," he said. "I ignore it completely. I haven't touched a piece of tinsel in years."

"You mean you do *nothing*?" I asked.

"Well, next to nothing," said Harry. "Usually I stay at a friend's farm while he's visiting his relatives. I've discovered I have a lot in common with cows. They don't care about Christmas either."

Except for the Christmas thing, Harry didn't actually say yes or no when we mentioned the possibility of his doing something shifty. Instead, he would suggest a game of poker with various favors as the stakes. For instance, if Harry lost to me, he would have to pretend to be my dad over the phone at report card time. If I lost to Harry, I'd have to spend half an hour that day nagging Winston about his homework. The trouble was, Harry always won at poker.

After several games, I asked him why.

He shrugged and said, "I cheat." When I protested, he offered me a deal. "If you can *catch* me cheating the next time we play, you win," he said. But Harry was so good at being underhanded that none of us caught him.

In the end, Manny made up a fake allergy — complete with his mom's forged signature — so he could get out of gym class. There was a silver lining to developing this kind of devious self-reliance, which we hadn't thought about until Manny pointed it out. As he put it, "Learning to successfully con the school administration will be highly beneficial to our self-esteem."

Just in case my dad wasn't back by report card time, the end of November, I decided I'd start learning now to forge his signature and imitate his voice over the phone. I studied some of Dad's old infomercials on tape. Winston, Manny, and I also cooked up a story I could use about how my dad had fractured his leg falling off a ladder and couldn't get out of bed. This would take care of teacher conferences *plus* permission forms and report cards. As long as Big Garry didn't hear that the teachers at Marshall McLuhan High had been talking to Sam Sherwood over the phone, everything would be cool.

Apart from Jerry Whitman and my nagging worries about the Christmas contest, it looked like smooth sailing for some time ahead. But, being losers, we should have known that something would happen to burst our bubble.

It didn't take long. Less than a week after we had dodged the bullet fired by Mrs. Loomis, Manny's dad phoned from New York and got Manny's mom instead of Manny. In the past, Manny had been careful never to let his mother answer the phone. "She has this unfortunate habit of slurring her words and getting really mad," said Manny. "Especially if it's my dad on the line."

The trouble was, Manny had been spending more and more time at the mansion and less and less time looking after his mom. So one day his mom picked up the phone when his dad called from Manhattan. I guess the conversation got kind of intense, because the next thing we knew, Mr. Crandall was flying to Vancouver to put Manny's mom in one of those clinics for hard-core alcoholics.

The whole thing tore Manny up inside. On the one hand, he was very upset about his mother having to go away. On the other hand, he was definitely excited about his dad coming all the way from New York to see him. Mr. Crandall took one look at how messy Manny's condo was and decided that Manny was going to stay in a hotel suite with him. That's when things got a little too hopeful for Manny's own good.

The first thing Mr. Crandall did after putting Manny's mom in the clinic was take us all out to a big, fancy restaurant.

We convinced Harry to come along in his role as Winston's guardian because, as Manny put it, "My dad is under the impression that I have way more friends than I actually do."

I could tell right away that Harry didn't care for Mr. Crandall, who insisted that we call him Terrance. Harry kept saying nice things about Manny, but all Terrance could talk about was Manny's weight. Throughout the entire meal, Manny managed to choke down only a little bit of lettuce from underneath his shrimp cocktail.

I didn't care for Terrance either. In a lot of ways he reminded me of an overgrown Jerry Whitman. Plus, he was constantly bragging about New York. Right through dessert, Terrance kept saying what a backwater town we lived in and how Manny was missing out on so many cultural advantages. It turned out he was leading up to a big announcement.

"I am going to take Rupert to live with me in New York," said Terrance, lifting a big, fat glass of brandy. "From this day forward, he will get the kind of upbringing he deserves."

I had never seen Manny look so happy. Mr. Crandall added he had to go back home for a few days to make arrangements. I suppose Harry didn't want to spoil Manny's big moment. So, when Terrance asked, Harry told him Manny could bunk at the mansion until everything was set up.

All Manny could talk about once he got to Winston's was New York, New York. "The Big Apple awaits!" he declared. "Soon, I'll touch down on the greatest city on earth."

Winston tried to be generous about the matter, but finally he asked, "Why aren't you there right now, smart guy?"

"My dad has to smooth things over with Babette," Manny answered. "You know, so it's not so much of a shock."

"Yeah," said Winston. "We wouldn't want Babette to pass out when she sees you with more than an overnight bag."

"Hey, I'm *going*," insisted Manny. "It'll be great. My dad has season's tickets to the Knicks and the new baby is way too immature to appreciate basketball."

This went on until Terrance made the phone call. At first, Manny was excited. Then he looked really upset. Finally, he put the phone aside and ran next door to get Harry. I guess Harry could see how disturbed Manny was, because he came running across the lawn in his bedroom slippers.

Harry talked to Terrance for a minute. "I understand," he said. "Believe me, you don't have to explain." After Harry hung up the phone he said, "You okay with this, Manny?"

"Okay with what?" I asked.

"My dad and I decided that I should stick around for a while," said Manny. "You know, to make sure my mom is okay and everything." He looked as though he was going to cry.

"I said he could stay here for as long as it takes," said Harry. "That okay with you guys?"

"Absolutely," I said. Winston looked at Manny and nodded his head.

"I gotta go do homework," said Manny. But suddenly he couldn't hold it in any longer. "Man," he sobbed. "I am such a *loser*. Such a big, fat —"

We watched Manny take the stairs two at a time. No one spoke. Then Harry said, "One of you guys want to go talk to him?"

"Maybe we should leave him alone," said Winston.

Harry glanced over at me. When he saw how shook up I was, Harry's expression changed. It was as if he was making his mind up about something.

"I'll see if Manny needs some help with his homework," he said. And then he headed up the stairs to Manny's room. He was gone a long time.

Winston and I tried to loosen up by playing a little pinball, but all we could think about was Manny.

Winston said, "His old man's never taking him back."

"How do you know?" I asked.

"I just *know*," he said. "We should do something."

"Like what?"

"I don't know. *Some*thing."

I would never have thought of Winston's "something" in a million years. But that's Winston C. Chang for you — so full of potential that the tap has to come unstuck every now and then. The main idea he had was this: If Manny couldn't go to New York, we would bring New York to Manny.

Over the next few days, during the hours that Manny was visiting his mom at the clinic, Winston and I sprang into action. We bought party food and posters that featured different New York–type landmarks: the Empire State Building, the Brooklyn Bridge, Yankee Stadium. We even found a Styrofoam replica of the Statue of Liberty.

On the afternoon everything was set up, we turned out the lights in the living room. We knew Manny would be home for dinner, so we waited for him in the dark. Harry had found a tape of New York traffic sounds — honking horns, squealing tires, and cab drivers with Brooklyn accents swearing at other drivers to get out of the way. We heard Manny's key in the lock.

"Anybody home?" he called.

We flipped on the lights. Manny looked in wonder at the posters and the party food. But his eyes came to rest on the replica of the Statue of Liberty. Even Winston had to admit that it looked majestic for something that was basically a cross between a monument and a giant coffee cup.

For most party organizers, this would have been enough, but not for Winston. He had used one of his father's credit cards to Federal Express a couple of pastrami sandwiches all the way from Nate's Deli in New York. When Manny saw the Nate's Deli bag in the special cooler, he almost burst into tears of joy.

"Man," he said, blinking a couple of times. "You even remembered the coleslaw."

The pastrami creations didn't look so different from your ordinary sandwich, but Manny kept shaking his head and saying, "You guys…you guys…"

"Both sandwiches are for you, Manny," said Winston. The rest of us have plenty of ordinary food."

"No," said Manny. "We share. It's one for all and all for one." He took a knife and sliced both sandwiches in half.

"Are we the Three Musketeers or what?" Winston said.

"The *Four* Musketeers," Manny said, as he gave Harry half a New York pastrami sandwich. Harry made us hold up our sandwiches together as if they were swords and we were the good guys in some old swashbuckler. It was stupid but also kind of great. Almost great enough to make us forget there was a Jerry Whitman — or that some dads were just as happy to be without their sons.

CHAPTER

FIFTEEN

It looked as if Manny and Winston, and I would get along well as roommates. Harry spent most of his time next door, tapping away on his old typewriter, but he seemed to enjoy coming over for dinner. He even cooked us dinner once or twice. To our amazement, he was a fairly decent chef. He'd occasionally stick around for a few hours in the evening, even though he said he was in a rush to write another one of those little pink books — something called *Love's Eternal Flame*.

So much stuff was going on that I was almost able to forget about my one big problem. Almost, but not quite. It was the first week in November, and I still hadn't figured out a way to tell the guys that I had accepted Whitman's Christmas decoration challenge. I worried about this as I took long walks in the rain, kicking the wet leaves with my crutches and knowing that I would soon have to give the display some heavy-duty thought.

Since the episode with Manny's father, Harry had started to take his role as Winston's fake guardian more seriously. He bugged Winston about an upcoming geometry test, saying things like "Don't try dogging it with me, kid. I know every slacker trick in the book."

When Winston told Harry to stop bothering him about his low marks, Harry held up his hands in surrender. "Hey, I understand," he said. "If you can't do it, that's cool."

"I can do it," said Winston. "I just don't want to."

"Whatever," said Harry.

"I *can*," said Winston. He knew Harry was doing a number on him, but he was letting it get to him.

"The thing is," said Harry, "how do we *know* you're right?"

"I'm *right*!" said Winston.

Winston pretended he was greatly inconvenienced by Harry's interest, but deep down I think he liked it. I think Harry did too.

If you caught Harry when he wasn't writing, he was happy to converse about all the stuff he knew. He'd read lots of books on architecture and engineering, and he and I had some long talks about great bridges and buildings. We also talked about how much life has to offer if you keep your eyes open.

Because of all our talks, it seemed easy to tell Harry my private thoughts — stuff about how I missed my dad and how I missed my mom, and about my weird Christmas dream. I even told him about the secret stash of funds in the handles of my crutches. He tried to convince me to put it in the bank, but I said no.

"My dad is on the run from Big Garry. He may arrive in town at any moment of the day or night on a secret mission for emergency cash," I explained.

Harry was very cool about it. "It's your call," he said.

Even though Harry was cool, you could tell he was looking

out for our welfare. He encouraged Manny's artistic pursuits, too. He praised Manny's cartoons and lent him some books on abstract art. Manny started using words like "surrealism" and showing us these weird pictures by famous painters. There was this very strange painting of melting watches that Manny claimed was an important artistic statement on the fickle nature of time. Winston said the melting watches reminded Manny's subconscious of grilled cheese sandwiches, which was the actual reason he liked the picture so much. But Manny simply grinned. He was so inspired that he made his own bizarre collage by clipping pictures out of magazines. He stuck it up on Winston's fridge next to the picture of the black lung. Harry said Manny's collage was very striking.

Not that Harry had become a pushover or anything. One evening Winston explained that he wanted to get Mr. Winecki, the janitor, a special birthday present.

"It's a rare kind of beer from Slovakia called Golden Star," said Winston. He asked if Harry would go to the specialty liquor store and buy a bottle for him. "It is practically the last beer label Walter needs to complete his collection."

Harry said he would run the errand only if Winston's geometry mark improved.

Winston shot Harry a grumpy look and said, "I think I liked you better when you were firing dog crap at me."

Still, I noticed that Winston spent more time with his geometry text that evening.

We were just settling in to our new routine when a number of unexpected things happened. The first was that Harry went to an open house at Marshall McLuhan High in his role as Winston's guardian. We were showing him the library when

Ms. Maculwayne stopped Harry dead in his tracks. She broke into a warm smile.

"Excuse me," she said. "Aren't you Harry Beardsley, the novelist?"

Harry was taken aback by the question. "Yes, I've written a novel." he said, but he said it as if he had been accused of forgetting to pay a parking ticket or something.

Ms. Maculwayne got all excited. "I've read *Separate Lives* several times!" she exclaimed. "It's one of my favorite books."

Harry blushed, mumbling that he was surprised she had recognized him.

"Oh," gushed Ms. Maculwayne. "You've changed remarkably little from the picture on the back of your book."

Comparing notes later, Manny and Winston and I discovered that we all had the same thought at that moment: You should have seen him before the makeover.

Harry thanked the librarian. Then she said, "I've looked everywhere for your second novel. But I can't seem to find it."

"There isn't a second novel," said Harry. "I've had what you might call an extended dry spell."

Ms. Maculwayne looked so disappointed at the thought of Harry's extended dry spell that I almost mentioned *Love's Eternal Flame*, but Harry had caught Ms. Maculwayne's sad expression too.

"I've been kicking around an idea for a sequel," he said. "Do you think that's a good idea?"

Ms. Maculwayne said she thought it was an excellent idea. Then they made a date for coffee. I think Harry was in shock about the whole thing, but Ms. Maculwayne said she'd always wanted to discuss books with a real writer.

We couldn't resist teasing Harry about his coffee date on the way home. He stayed pretty reasonable about it, though. "It's no big deal," he told us. "It'll be a nice change to hang around someone who doesn't use zit cream."

I had made up my mind to break the news about the contest to Winston and Manny the next day, but something else intervened. Mrs. Loomis called Harry and asked him to come down to the school immediately. As Harry told Manny and me over dinner, Mrs. Loomis sounded so pumped up he figured Winston had passed out inside his locker or something.

When Harry got to the school, he found Mrs. Loomis and Winston waiting for him in the main office.

Before Harry could say anything, Mrs. Loomis turned to Winston. "Tell Mr. Beardsley what you got on your geometry test, Winston," she commanded.

Harry said that Winston looked very embarrassed. He told us you could barely hear him mumble his answer.

"Louder, Winston," said Mrs. Loomis. "Your guardian can't hear you."

"A perfect score," said Winston, a little louder.

"A perfect score!" exclaimed Mrs. Loomis. Harry told us later that she looked like the happiest geometry teacher he'd ever seen. She peered at Harry and said, "Aren't you proud?"

Proud? Harry was so proud that he went right out and bought a bottle of Golden Star beer without waiting for Winston to give him the money. He even put a ribbon around it so that it would be all ready for Mr. Winecki's birthday. Winston told us it was the luckiest Thursday of his entire academic career.

It only figures that everything would come crashing down around Winston the next day, which Manny would later call

Black Friday. You may have the impression that every Friday at Marshall McLuhan High is black. But, for Winston at least, November 8th made every other Friday look like a dignified gray.

That morning Winston went to the janitor's room for his regular bacon and eggs with Mr. Winecki. He even brought his perfect geometry test to show off. But when Winston got there, Mr. Winecki was sprawled on the floor. At first, Winston thought Walter might be drunk. But when he tried to shake him awake, Mr. Winecki didn't respond. Winston called 911 on his cell.

When the ambulance arrived, the paramedic told Winston that — although Mr. Winecki was still alive — he'd probably suffered a heart attack.

After the ambulance took Walter away, Winston phoned the house and told us the news. At school, the principal made an announcement over the PA system about Mr. Winecki. There was even a little bit about Winston Chang and how he had acted so calmly in a crisis. But Winston wasn't calm at all. He looked upset in homeroom, and he vanished shortly afterwards.

Manny and I figured that Winston might be in the janitor's room in search of a little privacy. I remembered that Winston had once told me Mr. Winecki kept a spare key hidden in the ledge of the doorway in case he ever locked himself out by mistake. Manny and I checked at lunch. We found the key, all right, but nobody was in there.

It was Manny's idea to take Mr. Winecki's root beer bottles and pour the secret contents down the sink. He said it would be undignified if the administration discovered what was inside.

As he was pouring, Manny suggested, "Maybe Winston went home."

"I doubt it," I said.

I had the idea that maybe Jerry and the boys had been low enough to stuff Winston into his locker on the worst day of his life. So I went back upstairs and looked through Winston's locker vent. Winston was scrunched up into a ball, but I could see the top of his head.

"Winston," I called.

No answer.

"Come on, Winston," I said. "It's me. I can see you."

"Leave me alone," said Winston. His voice came out shaky, and it sounded as if he had been crying.

"Did Jerry do this?" I asked. "Was it the Watertank?"

"No," said Winston. And then, a little weaker, "Leave me alone."

"Manny dumped out the booze in Walter's fridge," I said.

"That's cool," said Winston. "Thank the Fat One for me."

"I will."

"Now go away."

It was then I noticed there was no lock on Winston's locker. I took a deep breath and said, "Maybe he'll be okay, Winston."

"You didn't *see* him."

"Why do you expect the worst?"

Winston didn't answer. Finally, he said, "Why do you always have to try to *fix* everything?"

"I don't know," I answered.

"Well, *stop* it," said Winston. "It's starting to piss me off."

"Come out and we'll talk."

"Leave me alone. Just leave me the hell alone."

I realized the best thing I could do for Winston was walk away. So I moved on to my next class before someone caught me talking to Winston's locker and forced him to come out.

Eventually, Winston crawled out of his locker and walked home. He might as well have stayed in there for all the talking he did. His eyes were red and puffy. When Manny and I tried to engage him in conversation, he said, "Nothing's ever going to work out for us. You know that?"

He kept repeating it until I mumbled, "That's not true, Winston."

But Winston was on a roll. "Do you even know where your old man is?"

"Not at the moment," I said.

"Not at the moment!" said Winston. "How long has it been? At least Manny and I know where our parents *are*. Not that it makes any difference."

"Come on, Winston," I said. "Knock it off."

"I'll knock it off when you stop pretending everything's going to work out fine," he said. "You know what life is about? Friends have heart attacks, parents don't give a shit, and Jerry Whitman is going to keep kicking our asses until he gets too tired to kick." Winston took a deep breath and continued, "Which is *never*."

After that, Winston didn't say anything, and I didn't say anything back. The only person who could get Winston to say anything positive that night was Harry. He got Winston to talk about Walter and all the things they shot the breeze about over bacon and eggs. Then, when Winston started laughing, Harry gave him a little pep talk. "Don't count Walter out just yet," he said. "A guy like that isn't going to cash in his chips until he completes his beer-label collection."

CHAPTER

SIXTEEN

The next day was a Saturday. I thought I might get a break from my troubles by going to the drugstore with Julie Spenser, but unfortunately we bumped into Duane as soon as we got there. The Watertank cornered me while Julie went off to do some shopping, and he immediately started to rub it in about the Christmas contest.

"Jerry's really getting into the spirit of the thing," said Duane. "His old man is going to help him do a big Christmas lights tribute to real estate. Jerry is taking great pleasure at the thought of kicking your holiday ass."

"Thank you for that uplifting piece of information," I said.

"Did you and Julie come in here together?" asked the Watertank suspiciously.

I nodded. "Black lipstick is always on sale after Halloween," I explained. "She's stocking up."

The Watertank did not laugh, but he did mention that his little sister, Diane, was in the store looking for some post-Halloween bargains too. Now, you may think it is unusual for someone like the Watertank to hang out with his little sister. But Diane uses a wheelchair, and Duane likes to steer it around for her.

As soon as Diane saw me, she wheeled over to say hello. I've known Diane since elementary school. She's is a nice kid. In fact, she's so nice that you can barely believe she's related to Duane.

"Hey, Diane," I said. "I haven't seen you in ages. You look way more grown-up."

"Don't tell my big brother." She smiled. "He still enjoys pushing me around."

"You're not the only one," I said. But I could tell from Diane's expression that she had no idea of the Watertank's secret life as Jerry Whitman's number-one enforcer, so I switched the subject. "What grade are you in now?"

"Seven. Next year, I'll be going to your school."

I looked over at Duane and said, "You're lucky you're a girl. Some of the guys there get picked on for being different."

Diane looked concerned. "They don't pick on you, do they?"

"Not really," I said, still looking at the Watertank. "Not like some."

"Because if they did, Duane could help you out." She turned to her brother. "You'd help Alex out, wouldn't you, Duane?"

"Sure," said Duane. He was staring at the floor as if he'd discovered an especially interesting square of linoleum.

"Why don't you come over to the house sometime?" asked Diane. "Duane's too shy to ask, but I'm sure he'd like to see you."

"We talk at school sometimes," I said. "To tell you the truth, we hang out with different crowds."

"Well, think about it, anyway. Duane's kind of stupid," Diane teased affectionately, "but he has his good points."

Just then Julie came up to us with a plastic basket full of black eyeliner and lipstick. Diane struck up a conversation with Julie, and it didn't take her long to ask if I was Julie's boyfriend.

"Isn't it obvious?" Julie said.

Diane smiled.

This was too much for the Watertank, who would have to report the encounter to Jerry. "Come on, Diane," he said. "Let's try the place down the street."

"Nice girl," said Julie as the Watertank pushed his sister toward the door.

Harry and Winston spent Saturday afternoon visiting Mr. Winecki in the hospital. Mr. Winecki was hanging in there, although the doctors said he'd had a major heart attack. Winston told us that Mr. Winecki spent most of the time with his eyes closed, but once, after Winston told him this stupid joke, he opened his eyes. Winston said his speech was slow and slurred, but he could make out the words, "Pretty funny, Win." That's what Mr. Winecki liked to call Winston. Win. He said it was his own nickname in high school.

Mr. Winecki was in the intensive care ward, Mrs. Crandall was in the alcohol clinic, and my dad was nowhere to be found. It was enough to give a person a case of the November blues. At the same time, it made the Four Musketeers feel closer. Over the next few days, each of us began to open up about things that we would normally keep to ourselves. Without really meaning to, Manny and Winston and I told Harry about how Jerry and the boys extorted money from the losers at school. Harry was in favor of telling Ms. Maculwayne about it, but we made him promise not to.

"The teachers will only make it worse," I said. "We'll come up with our own way to deal with Jerry Whitman."

Harry said he understood, but he put a time limit on our arriving at a solution. "You better think fast," he said. "Because this can't go on much longer."

I suppose Harry thought we'd been through a tough weekend, what with Mr. Winecki and all. He came over on Monday afternoon to prepare stew for us while Manny was visiting his mother. Winston was going to join us following an after-school appointment with Mrs. Loomis. I was in the kitchen talking to Harry and chopping vegetables. I knew it bothered him that we wouldn't let him step in and solve the Jerry Whitman dilemma, but neither of us had counted on Jerry and the Watertank following Winston home from school that day and pushing him around. It was less than two months before Christmas, and Jerry was hoping to squeeze some extra cash out of his most prosperous client.

Whitman and the Watertank started giving Winston the usual treatment right in front of his own house, bullying him in an efficient and businesslike way. It wasn't anything that Winston hadn't endured a thousand times before, but Winston was feeling bad about Mr. Winecki, and that made him stubborn about handing over more money. The other big difference was that Harry and I saw what was happening from the kitchen window. Both of us dropped our half-peeled potatoes and headed for the scene.

Unfortunately Harry had put on this frilly apron of Mrs. Chang's for making dinner, and he was still wearing it when he charged into the street.

"Who's this? Your mother?" Jerry asked Winston.

Harry ignored the question. "You guys want to even up the odds? Me and Winston here against the two of you."

"I don't think I'll be much help, Harry." Winston said.

Harry shrugged. "Just me, then."

"What do you mean?" said Jerry. You could tell he was nervous.

"I mean I'll take one of you at a time or both of you at the same time," said Harry. "Your choice."

"Big talk from a guy in an apron," said Jerry.

"Oh, the apron," said Harry. "That comes off." He threw the apron on the ground.

"I'm bigger than you," Duane said.

"You're also stupid," said Harry. "It evens out."

"Harry, it's okay, really," Winston pleaded.

All of a sudden, Jerry held up his hands and said, "I'm cool."

"I'm cool too," the Watertank said.

Harry looked at them both. "Well, I'm *not* cool. Whatever scam you've got going at school is your business, but this is my turf. Understand? After school, these are *my* kids."

Jerry and Duane nodded, then they walked off, trying to look as if nothing had happened — except they were moving a little faster than usual.

Even though the altercation was over, Harry looked agitated.

"Are you okay, Harry?" Winston asked.

Harry nodded. "I'm sorry about that, Winston. I wasn't expecting to get so worked up. It came out of nowhere."

"That's okay, Harry," said Winston, picking up Harry's apron off the ground. "I've been there."

Winston, Harry, and I went back in the house to finish

preparing dinner. When Manny came home, Winston and I related the incident to him over stew.

"Just my luck," said Manny. "All this excitement, and where am I? Sitting at the bus stop with my ass next to a picture of Jerry Whitman, Sr."

Harry looked at Manny and said, "Don't be crude at the table."

The more time we spent with Harry, the more it made me wonder about how my dad was doing. I was still waiting for my next message from Uncle Vito. The next afternoon I noticed a familiar face outside the school grounds. It was the guy in the hat who used to stand outside my apartment. I don't know what came over me. Maybe I was tired of being followed around. Or maybe I was sick of Jerry Whitman and I wanted to take it out on a stranger. Anyway, I went right up to the guy.

"Why don't you leave me alone?" I said.

The guy gave me a card. It said that his name was Carl Evans and he was head of Carl Evans Investigations. "You know who I work for?" he asked.

"Big Garry," I said.

Carl Evans nodded. "You want me to leave you alone? Tell me where your dad is."

"I don't know where my dad is."

Carl Evans studied me for a couple of seconds, then said, "You really don't, do you?"

"No, I really don't."

"Well, keep the card," he said. "Garry and your old man have a few things to work out. If he contacts you, let me know."

"Oh, I'll be sure to do that, Carl," I said sarcastically. "As soon as I get the call."

"Let me ask you something, kid," said Evans. "What kind of lowlife ditches his only son and doesn't call? You think about it. And don't lose my number." He walked off without another word.

I guess what Carl Evans had said got to me. I didn't feel like going home. Instead, I walked for a long time with no idea where I was going. I picked up a fair-sized rock and shoved it in my pocket for something to do. After a while, I got kind of stiff, but I kept walking anyway. Deep down, I suppose I knew all along where I was going.

I stopped in front of my dad's old high school, then walked up the front steps. From there, I opened the big door, walked down the main hall, and ended up in front of the display case with my dad's old picture and all his running medals. Suddenly I got that feeling again, like the best part of my dad was trapped behind the glass and I had to let it out. I took the rock out of my pocket. I thought about breaking the glass into a thousand pieces. For a few seconds, it was like this irresistible urge. I'm not sure what stopped me, but it could have been Dad's picture. The more I stared at it, the more it looked like me.

I put the rock back in my pocket, went out the big door, and headed for home. Later that evening I sat in Winston's living room with the lights off. I played Harry's Charlie Parker record on the stereo and sat very still. I didn't even have to ask Manny and Winston to leave me alone. They just knew.

CHAPTER

SEVENTEEN

I must have been especially tired from my encounter with Carl Evans and all that walking, because that night I had the Christmas dream again. Only this time it was more intense — deeper and more vivid. What happened in the dream was different, too. This time, the whole Losers' Club was working on the Christmas display. We were laughing and making jokes about the decorations. Nothing mattered except that we were working together against Jerry's boys and having a great time building something stupid, goofy, and *ours*.

Of course, it was only a dream, but when I woke up, my mood was lighter. I didn't expect it to last for the entire day. However, then I got another lift.

I was passing through a secluded area of the school when I noticed that Duane was putting the squeeze on Davey Swanigan. The Watertank didn't see me because he was so absorbed in the business of extortion. Davey was shaking. You could tell he was really scared. As for the Watertank, he sounded annoyed.

"What's the matter with you, Davey? Don't you *learn*? I keep beating on you and you *still* don't have the money."

Davey kept quiet, as if he was preparing to get himself bruised. I was about to step in to provide a distraction when the Watertank stuck his hand in his pocket and pulled out a bill. He gave the bill to Davey.

"Now give the money *back* to me, Davey," he said.

"But it's your own money, Tank," said Davey, amazed.

"Just do it!" commanded Duane.

Davey gave him back the money. "You are paid in full," said the Watertank. "See you next week." Davey kept standing there until Duane added, "And if you tell anybody about this, I'll break your face *with interest.*"

After that, Davey took off. Everything would have been cool if Duane hadn't turned and seen me standing there.

"How much did you catch?" he asked.

"Enough," I said. "How many times have you paid losers out of your own pocket?"

"None of your business," warned Duane, who seemed very sensitive about the issue. "And if you spread this around, I'll never do it again."

"Don't worry," I said. "Your secret is safe with me."

A third thing that day put me in an even better frame of mind. It was the after-school bagel I had with Julie Spenser at Barney's Bagel Land. Not the bagel *itself*, but what we talked about while eating it.

"Remember when you said there was a reason Jerry Whitman left me alone?" I asked.

"You thought it was because he felt sorry for you," said Julie. "And I told you that wasn't it."

"Right," I replied. "You said I would figure it out. Well, I haven't figured it out yet."

"Want me to tell you?"

"Of course," I said. "I'm a loser. If you leave it up to me, I'll never figure it out."

"You may be a loser, but you're the *king* of the losers."

"Julie," I sighed. "I don't get it."

"Think about it," she said. "There's not a loser in the school who doesn't have the highest respect for you. As far as they're concerned, you're the *man*."

"So I'm the king of losers," I said. "So what?"

"So Jerry can't do anything major to you because your people would rebel."

"My *people*?" I blurted.

"There are far more losers in the school than there are Jerry's boys," said Julie. "Harness the raw power of losers and you can do practically anything."

"Loser power," I said. I liked the sound of it.

"Exactly," said Julie. "Think of all the energy that non-losers spend on dating and other socially rewarding activities. With losers, it's being wasted on cleaning their rooms and building model spaceships."

I had been panicking about the Christmas competition up to this point, but at that moment, inspired by Julie Spenser, I decided to pitch the idea to the entire membership of the Losers' Club at the next day's meeting. Julie even offered to attend to lend moral support. That night I lay awake formulating a plan. We would use Winston's mansion, naturally. But Winston's mansion was enormous and would require tons of Christmas lights and decorations. It would take a supreme effort from each one of us. Sketches, plans, labor — and, most of all, lights.

The next day flew by. Before I knew it, the Losers' Club was assembled in Winston's games room, and I was presenting my argument as logically as I could. Initially I didn't think the idea was going to catch fire. Tin Face Facelli was the first skeptic to voice his doubts.

"It's way too big," he said. "We are not a bunch of slaves building the pyramids." After a pause, he added, "Plus, the Watertank won't like it."

Then Randall Wattkiss piped up. "Has anyone considered that our homework will suffer?"

As if this wasn't bad enough, Herbert Jardine put in his two cents. "As we know, losers are very uncoordinated," said Herbert, whose major hobby was fretting over everything. "I feel it is only prudent to mention the very real possibility of someone falling off Winston's roof without the benefit of personal liability insurance."

Next Manny chimed in about how Christmas in our city was so second-rate it wasn't even worth celebrating. "You should see Christmas in Manhattan," he said. "It's a hundred times better." And then — as if he was picturing his dad and Babette and their fat little baby under a big Christmas tree — he said, "I'm skipping Christmas this year."

Winston seconded the motion. "For once, the Fat One has a good idea," he said.

I thought we were sunk. If there's one thing I know about losers, it's that negativity can spread easier than peanut butter on toast. But then something interesting happened.

In a quiet voice, Howard Beal said, "I can rig up safety

harnesses so that nobody falls off the roof."

"Why would you want to do that, Howard?" asked Manny.

"It's simple," said Howard. "I despise Jerry Whitman with all my heart."

Howard's comment was the turning point. It reminded everyone of how much they hated Jerry. One by one, the losers stood up to say how much they wanted to beat Jerry and the boys at something — even if it was something as dorky as a Christmas display.

Ronnie Rosenblum, who was probably the quietest loser in the entire tenth grade, clambered onto a chair and made a speech.

"As you know, I am Jewish," he said. "I don't even celebrate Christmas. But if there's the slightest chance of humiliating Jerry Whitman, I'll put up lights until my fingers bleed!"

There was a big round of applause. Finally, Julie Spenser spoke up. She was a loser only by association but that didn't stop her from making a decent speech.

"I've heard what the Savior has done for you," she said. "He's started the Bank of Sherwood! He's shielded you from all manner of flying debris in the cafeteria! Are you going to let him down in his time of need?"

Maybe the guys were stirred up by having a girl on the premises. But for whatever reason everybody started to yell things like "No, we can't let the Savior down!" This was followed by the kind of chanting you hear at football games. Everybody was shouting "Sher-wood! Sher-wood!" It was actually very cool. I just hoped the feeling of inspiration would last.

The next afternoon the club got to work on plans for decorating the mansion. Harry was on deadline for his next pink book. This, combined with his bleak attitude toward the Christmas season, meant that we had an adult sponsor in name only. We tried not to let this get us down. After taking a vote on a theme, we made Manny draw up a quick sketch for the display right then and there. The sketch was titled "Santa's Crazy Workshop." The idea was to have the elves working on various toys. Manny wasn't perfectly happy with his drawing, but I thought it looked really decent.

The others must have thought so too. I have never seen a bunch of guys work as hard as the Losers' Club did over the next little while. Losers cut back on their after-school and week-end pursuits of homework, stamp collecting and clarinet lessons to devote time to the project.

I went to see Mr. Sankey about getting his Christmas decorations for the display. He was busy renovating some of his suites and was a little preoccupied as I explained that I was staying with Winston while my dad was away on business. I must confess I didn't exactly tell Mr. Sankey the whole truth. In fact, I strongly hinted that Neville was looking after us. Luckily Mr. Sankey proved true to his "live and let live" nature and was very cool about the whole thing. He even used his lunch break to load the decorations into his van and transport them to Winston's mansion.

Assorted losers brought in decorations to add to the ones I had borrowed. To help us buy the lights, guys donated what little money they had after being bled by Jerry Whitman's Christmas collection fund. And in addition to the safety harnesses, Howard Beal rigged up a fancy system of pulleys and ropes so that we could get the lights and decorations up faster.

At first, the general hatred for Jerry Whitman acted as

high-octane fuel for the project. "We are going to wipe the floor with Whitman," you'd hear someone say. Or, "We are going to kick Whitman's butt." I began to notice some changes in my fellow losers. For example, Rudy Zennetti got into wearing his old man's tool belt, which affected his normally conservative disposition. Rudy was usually very sensitive about coarse language, but all of a sudden he was walking around scratching himself and saying, "We are not only going to kick Whitman's butt. We are going to kick his *ass!*"

Julie Spenser came up with a name for our project: "Operation Jingle Bell."

If only that spirit of goodwill had lasted. However, all too soon, things started to unravel. To begin with, it was just a bunch of little things. Someone would trip over his shoelace, then laugh about it. Somebody else would lose his balance after going off on a sneezing jag. Rudy cut his finger on a broken reindeer's antler and couldn't find a Band-Aid. Clearly, none of us were cut out to be handymen. As Winston said, "Remember the Greek myth about Pandora's box, where some goddess flips back a lid and unleashes different kinds of despair? Well, that is what a tool box is like for losers."

Then, on Saturday morning, Manny spilled a thermos of hot cocoa all over his sketch for the display. After that, things went seriously downhill. Everybody's personal fears and phobias came into play — fear of dust, fear of electrical currents, fear that Jerry and the boys would pay us a surprise visit. That weekend alone, there were dropped ladders, tangled wires, and *two* broken windows. So many things went wrong that Manny dubbed our project "Operation Jingle *Hell.*" Soon everyone was calling it that.

"This project is cursed," said Manny, who kept threatening to go on strike. "And there is so little time for snacking that I am going through Twinkie withdrawal."

The members of the Losers' Club were used to small-scale science projects, like ant farms or papier mâché volcanoes. But Winston's mansion had a very complicated roof with many sharp peaks, round corners, and flat surfaces, and decorating it proved to be harder than anticipated. Not that we didn't take precautions. Gordie Heffernan's dad owned a second-hand sporting goods store, and he was so happy his kid wanted to actually *use* the equipment that he let us borrow it for nothing. The protective gear alone could have supplied a couple of Roller Derby teams. One day I counted eight bike helmets, six elbow protectors, four mouth guards, and at least one set of goalie pads. And those guys weren't even on the *roof*. Have you ever watched somebody try to climb a ladder in goalie pads? It defines the word "pathetic."

Even with all the padding, things were grim, injury-wise. Herbert Jardine tried to drive a nail with a hammer and broke his thumb. Tin Face Facelli got tangled up in a string of Christmas lights and tripped, twisting his right ankle. Winston, who got severely depressed when he noticed that one of the decorative elves was taller than he was, said it would probably be a good idea to have an ambulance on twenty-four-hour call. Manny added that having an ambulance on the premises might be the only way we could make sure we had a flashing light that *worked*. The whole undertaking reminded me of a line from this song I heard once: "If it wasn't for bad luck, I wouldn't have no luck at all."

One afternoon, Randall Wattkiss was working away on the

roof in one of Howard Beal's safety harnesses. The harness was actually more like a bungee cord, with one end hooked to a brace on the roof and a little seat that looked like a giant diaper attached to the other end. Randall was wearing the diaper when he slipped off the roof and down the front of the mansion. The cord didn't break. Instead, it sort of bounced up and down. Randall managed to hang on to it while emitting a savage scream. On the plus side, he looked a bit like Tarzan — if Tarzan had worn a diaper. On the minus side, he kept swaying back and forth like a human pendulum.

None of us knew what to do. Rudy Zennetti — who had won several science prizes at school — tried to reassure us by saying, "Eventually, gravity will restore his equilibrium." But we felt useless watching Randall swing back and forth like that. After a while, the rope *did* calm down, and Julie Spenser managed to get a ladder under him.

Even when Randall was on solid ground again, he remained freaked out. Although he unhooked himself from the rope, he didn't bother to climb out of the diaper. We attempted to get him to sit down on the grass, but he preferred to stagger around on Winston's front lawn like a big-eyed baby learning to walk. A couple of times, he tried to say something, but no sound came out. It was a minute or so before he slowed down enough to lose his lunch all over a plastic replica of a singing choirboy.

After that, everybody refused to use Howard's baby-diaper harness. This led directly to another decorating calamity — a calamity that also revealed Winston's lifelong fear of heights, a fear that Winston had somehow managed to keep secret from everyone.

Afterwards, Winston would say he'd felt being short was bad

enough without having every loser in the school know he got dizzy every time he climbed past the second rung of a stepladder. It took major guts for him to climb that long, long ladder to the roof, but he said he was getting tired of the guys calling him a slacker because he didn't spend any time up there.

Winston pointed out after the fact that he was also tired of being inadvertently put to shame by Julie Spenser. Julie — who wasn't even an official member of the Losers' Club — was doing enough work for several nerds. In fact, she was toiling so hard on the roof that the sweat made her mascara run down her face in little black rivers. Winston said the sight was so bizarrely inspiring that it momentarily blocked out his phobia.

At first, everything seemed okay. Once he was on a flat part of the roof, Winston began to bark out orders as if he owned the place — which he kind of did. But then he looked down and froze. He froze so completely that anybody who didn't know him would have assumed he was part of the display.

Julie tried to help Winston, but the sight of a girl offering him her hand only made him panic all the more. He moved just far enough to grab onto Mr. Sankey's giant holiday hula girl, which was waiting to be braced to the roof. Winston hugged the smiling mannequin desperately from behind, his short arms stretching across the naked area between her plastic coconut-shell bra and her grass skirt.

Later, Manny would theorize that Winston grabbed the hula girl for psychological security. In other words, while it didn't make much sense, it made Winston feel better about being so high up in the air. It was as if he *would* fall if he let go. As Manny says, the brain is a very mysterious mechanism.

Even though we couldn't see anything but Winston's

skinny arms wrapped around the giant mannequin, we could tell he was having a major panic attack.

Every time somebody tried to get near him, he would yell, "Get away" or "Don't touch me." Every once in a while, he would try to make it closer to the ladder by pushing the hula girl forward. We stood with our mouths open as the hula girl did her Hawaiian dance closer and closer to the edge of the roof. It was not hard to picture Winston splattered all over the ground next to a dummy in a grass skirt.

I had narrowed down our options to getting Harry or calling the fire department when Manny suddenly started up the ladder to the roof. Once he got there, he casually sauntered across a section of flat roof toward Winston.

"Hey, Short One," he called. "I see you have yourself a new girlfriend." He moved closer and added, "She is very exotic, but she seems a little heavy for your taste."

Hula-Girl/Winston told Manny not to make him laugh right now.

So Manny asked, "Do you like being up here?"

"No, I don't think so."

"So don't you think we better get down?" asked Manny.

"*No! I don't think so!*" Hula-Girl/Winston shrieked.

Manny continued to talk, pointing out that he carried more weight than your average individual. "Do you think this spot on the roof can support two losers *and* a giant Hawaiian Christmas dancer?" asked Manny.

Hula-Girl/Winston said he was pretty sure it could.

"What if I started jumping?"

"Why would you want to jump at a time like this?" Hula-Girl/Winston asked.

"You're always bugging me to get exercise," explained Manny. "Suddenly I can't contain the urge to do some special jumping jacks."

"Don't jump," Hula-Girl/Winston pleaded. And then he tossed in, "*Please.*"

"Will you let go of your new girlfriend and come down from the roof?"

"No way."

So Manny jumped up and came down with a thud.

Being Manny, he was a rather sluggish jumper, but a couple of guys who were also on the roof said you could feel the vibrations from several feet away. You could even see the hula girl shake a bit, like a doll on the dashboard of some big old car.

"You know, Short One," Manny said, "if I jump again, I could make a hole in the roof and we could go all go falling through it like a bunch of losers in some crazy cartoon. Do you think this is better way to die than trying for the ladder?"

Winston finally said he would let go of the hula girl and try for the ladder. Manny was standing beside him at that point. He pried Winston's fingers from around the mannequin's waist and offered the Short One his hand. At first, Winston did not want to take it. But then Manny said, "Look at my hand, Short One. Is it not the biggest, fattest hand you have ever seen?"

Winston had to admit it was.

Then Manny said, "It is also a hand that will not let you fall."

Anyway, that's how Manny coaxed Winston off the roof. He took Winston's hand and led him to the ladder as if the Short One was some kid off to his first day at school. Manny is a pretty big guy by any measure, but I have never seen him move so gently. All the while, Winston kept repeating, "Think *tall*….Think *tall*." Winston thought tall until he was all the way down the ladder.

When they both got safely down, everybody let out a cheer. Manny was definitely the hero of the hour. But all anybody could get him to say was "I hate Christmas."

CHAPTER

EIGHTEEN

Much as I hated to admit it, "Operation Jingle Bell" wasn't working out too great. As Winston expressed it, "It's almost the beginning of December, and all we have to show for it are some festively colored bruises."

In addition to the injuries and assorted mishaps, nothing seemed to be coming together. The guys were bickering. We needed more labor and more money. Plus, we needed someone who knew about wiring. I was over at Harry's house the next evening, complaining about all this, when he said, "It's Christmas, man. Bad karma all around."

I suppose I was stressed out from working on the display. Otherwise I wouldn't have yelled at Harry like I did.

"Why don't you *help* us?" I shouted. "That's what Christmas is supposed to be all about. The rest is just for kids."

Harry blinked a couple of times. "Hey, chill out," he said.

But I didn't chill out. As a matter of fact, I let Harry have it. I told him a lot of stuff that I had been holding inside — how all he cared about was finishing his little pink book, how I was afraid my dad was never going to come back. Then I yelled at him some more.

"I can't help it if bad things happen to you at Christmas," I said. "Maybe if you did some good, your luck would change."

I was all set to leave when Harry said something that blew me away. "You already know I spent some time in engineering," he said. "It was one of my more sustained attempts at higher education. But I never told you what kind."

"What kind of engineering?" I asked.

Harry smiled. "Electrical," he said.

That's how Harry became our supervisor on "Operation Jingle Bell." He did a good job, too. With Harry's help, everything started to gel. Soon all the lights worked, and the elves and reindeer and Mr. Sankey's big Santa on a sleigh all had specific places. The gigantic Fat 'n' Happy Turkey sign looked fantastic on Winston's front lawn. Harry even anchored the giant hula girl to the roof, just in case Winston felt the need to grab onto her again.

Our display didn't look like a motion-picture extravaganza or anything, but Mr. Sankey's decorations scored very high in the originality department. And even Winston admitted that the hula girl added a special touch. Everybody was impressed with the result except Manny, who surveyed our display with a pained expression. When I asked him what was wrong, he would only say, "Someone better tape down the hula girl's skirt in case there's a sudden gust of wind."

Unfortunately a new piece of information made us think Manny's reservations might be prophetic. Unbeknownst to us losers, Julie Spenser had taken it upon herself to go on a spy mission. She started hanging around Jerry Whitman's house, chatting with Jerry long enough to find out about his old man's "Tribute to Real Estate" Christmas display. When she reported back to us, the news was not good. Julie did a little sketch of what the Whitman display was going to look like. It featured a few houses outlined in lights — including Santa's place at the North Pole. In addition, there were many moving parts. All in all, it was depressingly spectacular.

"We are doomed," said Winston.

"We are doomed a thousand times," agreed Manny.

Julie attempted to cheer us up. The Whitman display was still a work in progress, she reminded us. "Who knows if they'll manage to pull it off? Getting the two Jerrys to work together is a problem in itself."

"What do you mean?" I asked.

"Mr. Whitman really pushes Jerry. There's a lot of tension between them."

"What kind of tension?" asked Winston.

"The non-productive kind," said Julie. "Jerry's dad doesn't cut him much slack."

"You must be mistaken," I said. "The Whitman family looks like the kind of family you get when you buy an expensive picture frame."

"They are perfect," nodded Manny. "It is a well-known fact."

But if there's one thing I know, it's that nobody's perfect. Interestingly, we soon had another indication that all was not well in Jerryworld.

That afternoon Duane came up to my locker at lunch to deliver a warning.

"I wanted to let you know that Jerry isn't too happy these days," he said.

"My heart bleeds, Duane," I said.

"You don't understand," said Duane. "He's wound up because his old man's riding his ass about the stupid Christmas contest."

"What are you trying to say, Duane?" I asked. "That Jerry's going to win the contest and get everything he wants?"

"That's just it," said the Watertank. "Even if you gave Jerry everything, it wouldn't be enough. The power's getting to him. He's out of control."

"Yeah, well, someone should tell him that there are only so many loser bucks to go around."

"You think it's about the money?" said Duane.

"No? What's it about, then?" In spite of myself, I was curious to hear what Duane had to say.

The Watertank addressed me gravely. "Jerry is the type of guy who sees the sun come out and right away thinks how great it would be to fry a crowd of ants with a magnifying glass," said Duane. "Only instead of ants, he uses losers."

I thought about this for a second. "Jerry may be looking through the magnifying glass," I said, "but you're the one holding it for him."

Duane got red in the face. "Forget it," he said. "This was a stupid idea." And he walked away as if I wasn't worth talking to.

That evening, for a change of pace, Winston, Manny, and I decided to go to the movies to take in a special showing of a Marx Brothers double feature. It was late when we got home. Between that and all the evenings we'd spent working on the display, we were bagged. I remembered later that I'd heard some thumping in the night, but I was too sleepy to worry about it. So it was a total shock the next morning when the three of us got up to see that our Christmas display had been wrecked.

Winston's front lawn was covered in broken colored glass. All the display figures had been thrown off the roof, then twisted and stomped on. The neon lettering on the Fat 'n' Happy Turkey sign was bent out of shape. It was a big mess.

We stood outside with our mouths agape.

"Holy shit," said Winston. That about summed it up for all of us.

"Who would *do* a thing like this?" said Manny after a minute. He was obviously flustered, because it was a very stupid question.

"Jerry and the boys," I said.

Winston asked, "Why would Jerry wreck it? He was going to win anyway."

"That doesn't matter," I said. "He wrecked it because it was *ours.*"

We stood around like idiots for a while. We swore and cursed at Jerry and the boys until we couldn't think of anything more to say. Then Manny and Winston took a couple of tarps from the garage and covered the mess. Manny said it was like covering a dead body or something.

At school that day Jerry and the boys didn't say anything, but they kept giving us these secret smiles.

"Don't get mad," Manny urged Winston and me. "That's what they want."

But I *was* mad. I couldn't help it.

The word about what had happened spread fast. All day long, losers kept coming up and offering loser-type condolences.

Finally, Manny said, "If one more loser comes up to me and says we wouldn't have beaten Jerry Whitman anyway, I'm going to put my fist through the front of the Twinkie machine."

It was so depressing that Manny, Winston and I cut the last class of the day. We didn't care if we got caught. We figured things couldn't get any worse. But, as usual, we were wrong.

Harry had his own key to Winston's house, and he often left us notes while we were in school. But his note that day was different. It read:

Alex:

Had to leave town. Sorry about the display, but I know you guys will be okay. I'll be back as soon as I can. Needed to borrow some money. Look in the secret place.

Harry

The three of us sat down in the kitchen, staring at the note on the fridge and letting the worst day of our entire lives sink in. Harry had deserted us. Even for losers, this was harsh treatment. How much harder could life kick us in the butt?

Finally, Manny said, "What's the secret place?"

"How could he just *go* like that?" I said. I was so upset I couldn't say any more. When Manny asked about the secret place again, I heard Winston whisper, "Give him his space, Manny."

I went up to my room and unscrewed the handles of my crutches. I counted the bills and found out there was a thousand dollars missing. In its place was an IOU note from Harry. He must have taken the money while I was napping or in the Jacuzzi or playing pinball. It really didn't matter. The money was gone, and so was Harry.

I went back downstairs and filled Manny and Winston in. At first, they were ticked off to hear about my secret stash.

"Wow," said Manny. "You were rich and you didn't even tell us."

Winston glared at Manny. "Can't you see the Savior has things on his mind?"

"Yeah," said Manny. "First, his old man takes off and now Harry."

"Shut up, Fat One," said Winston.

"You shut up, Mansion Boy," said Manny.

I was going to tell both of them to shut up, but it was sort of comforting to hear them arguing again.

"Why would Harry take off so suddenly?" Manny asked.

"Maybe he was sick of us," said Winston.

"Who can blame him?" said Manny. "We're losers."

"Harry is a loser too," said Winston.

Our pointless conversation was interrupted by a knock at the door. That's when we realized that it was a Thursday, and we were going to have one of the largest turnouts ever for our regular meeting of the Losers' Club. When we went outside, we could see that someone had removed the tarps. I thought maybe the guys would start to clean up, but they were too busy gawking at the damage as if it was some major traffic accident.

The only non-loser to show up was Julie Spenser.

"Oh, Alex," she said, "I'm so *mad*, I could —" Julie stopped right there, fuming. But she didn't have to say anything else. I knew exactly how she felt.

Just then, I noticed Jerry, the Watertank, and a few of the boys calmly walking toward Winston's house. As they got closer, a bunch of losers automatically moved to make space for them.

Once Jerry was within earshot, I called, "You can't let us have anything, can you?"

"You think I had something to do with this, Sherwood?" asked Jerry innocently. "Why don't you guys admit it? You're cursed with bad luck."

"Congratulations, Jerry," said Julie. "You've hit a new low."

"Somebody did you guys a favor," said Whitman. "There's no way you could have beat us with that collection of junk. My old man's spending a fortune on our display."

"What's the use?" said Winston, looking at the mess. "Nothing ever works out for us."

"Now there's a loser with the proper attitude," said Jerry. "Right, Tank?"

Duane said nothing.

So Jerry shot me one of his slimy grins and said, "Right."

There was something about Jerry and his boys standing there enjoying the wreckage that got to me. I threw aside one of my crutches so that it made an ugly sound on the sidewalk and started clearing debris from the lawn. I tried to move the big plywood cutout of a sleigh with one hand, but it wouldn't budge. I tried again, and I slipped on the grass and fell. I got up and stood as straight as I could. Everybody was looking at me.

"What's the matter with you?" I shouted. "We can start over." I could feel my voice going high and out of control, but I didn't care. "Come on. We can build it over."

It was quiet for a minute. Out of the corner of my eye, I could see Jerry Whitman smirking.

"They'll only wreck it again, Alex," Manny said.

"We can't leave it like this!" I shouted. "Don't you see? If we do, we're everything they say we are. We're nothing but a bunch of losers."

Nobody budged. So I went back to the plywood sleigh and

attempted to move it. I kept slipping on the grass. Julie Spenser took the other end and tried to help. She did her best, but the sleigh was too heavy.

Then something totally weird happened. It could be that Duane was fed up with cleaning park benches. Or maybe he was trying to repay me for that hot dog thing in elementary school. In any case, the Watertank shook his head and said, "No more." He helped Julie and me put the sleigh upright and then moved on to some of the other heavy stuff. All the while, you could hear him saying, "No more. No more."

After that, several losers started to pick up the smaller items. Before long, everybody but Jerry and his flunkies was cleaning up and sorting. Jerry was furious.

"Hold it," he yelled. And it was a tribute to the power of Jerry Whitman that everyone did just that. "I shouldn't do this, Sherwood," he said. "But, in my own way, I like you. So this is what I'm going to do."

Right there on the sidewalk, Jerry Whitman offered me a deal. It was the same as our earlier deal, with one big difference. If he won the contest, I would close down the Bank of Sherwood *and* go to work for him as his personal collection agent. As long as I agreed to that, we could rebuild our display and his boys would leave it alone. "You can even have Tank," said Jerry. "He's all used up anyway."

A couple of losers gasped. Manny was the first to speak. "Don't do it, Alex, " he pleaded. "Whitman is sure to win and he will make you his slave."

"He's going to have you cleaning benches and pestering us for our last dime," said Winston. "He'll take away your freedom."

Even the Watertank said, "Listen to them, Alex."

Whitman stood there with his arms crossed like some sort of king. "They're right, Sherwood. Why not give up and let my representatives keep bleeding your friends for cash?"

"You're such a slimeball, Jerry," snapped Julie. "You could win a thousand contests and you'd still be garbage."

Jerry eyed Julie disdainfully. "I had such high hopes for you," he said. "But you're not going to cut it after all. You belong with the rest of the losers, Julie."

"Suits me," she replied. "The company's better."

Jerry looked angry but he turned his attention back to me. "So what do you say, Sherwood? Is it a deal?"

I probably would have taken the advice of my fellow losers if I hadn't heard Manny say something illuminating at that very moment.

"It's not so bad," he offered. "We're used to losing anyway."

I stared at Jerry with his ferret-like smile, so positive that I was going to back down. I knew exactly what he was doing, but I didn't care.

"It's a deal," I said. "You have my word."

"Excellent," said Jerry. "May the best man win."

Jerry and the boys walked off, leaving Duane behind. Nobody said anything for a while. Then Winston noticed his old friend the giant hula girl. She was all beat up and lying on the ground with her fake grass skirt in a very undignified position. Winston went over to her and adjusted her skirt back to normal. Then he got amazingly fired-up for a terminal slacker. His hands were balled into fists and there was a vengeful spark in his eye. He turned to the Watertank.

"What are we waiting for? Christmas?" he shouted

"You heard the man," Duane yelled. "Let's get to work."

CHAPTER

NINETEEN

We started to build our whole display over again, but not without a few expenses. I took some money out of the handles of my crutches, since even Winston had depleted his extra funds. The Watertank also chipped in a few bucks. He said he had been planning to quit enforcing for Jerry and the boys next year anyway, when his kid sister came to our school. He cautioned us not to be too optimistic, though.

"Jerry will only replace me with someone else," he told me. "And they may not be as understanding."

"He has to beat us first," I said. But although I tried to hide it, I was feeling discouraged. There were only two weeks left before the contest deadline. It was getting colder, and my fellow losers were having difficulty keeping their spirits up. And without Harry to guide us, we had no idea how to put the display of lights back together. Lying in bed at night, I would think about Harry and how he had deserted us in our hour of need. I guess I'd been wrong about him all along, and that hurt.

Things seemed hopeless, all right — until we got some

encouragement from an unexpected source. Winston had continued to visit Mr. Winecki, who was out of the hospital by now and recuperating in a convalescent place. Walter couldn't move his mop arm, and he still had some difficulty talking, but when he heard from Winston about what Jerry and the boys had done to our display, he made his feelings clear.

Apparently Mr. Winecki was a real Christmas kind of guy. When Winston made some comment about how maybe we should quit working on the display, Mr. Winecki sat up right in bed and made his good hand into a fist. "That's a hell of an idea," he said to Winston. "Let's *all* give up." And then he glared at Winston C. Chang and asked, "You think I should give up, Win?"

Winston said certainly not. There were still a lot of floors that needed Walter's special touch. Mr. Winecki laughed then, Winston informed us. "I'll make you a deal," Mr. Winecki said. "You guys don't give up and *I* won't give up either." According to Winston, that's when Winston shook Mr. Winecki's good hand and said, "Deal."

Winston may have been a devout slacker, but he was also a good friend to Mr. Walter Winecki. This last part won out and made Winston determined to live up to his part of the bargain. As he put it that night over macaroni and cheese, "If Walter can give a damn while lying in bed and eating Jell-O with his one good arm, then who are we to sit around on our loser butts feeling sorry for ourselves?"

Winston is slow to get fired up about something, but once the spark takes hold, he's hard to resist. Manny and I had to admit he had a good point. "We are losers," said Manny. "But we are young and healthy losers who can eat Jell-O with both hands." Okay, so Manny did not make the greatest speech in the world, but Winston and I knew what he was saying. We had to see the Christmas contest through to the end, no matter what.

The next afternoon I went to see Mr. Sankey, who had almost finished his renovations to the apartment building. He had some free time now, and when he heard about our predicament, he volunteered to repair the decorations *and* supervise putting up the lights. When I thanked him, he belched and said, "It sounds like more fun than sticking my head in a broken-down dryer."

As it turned out, the damage to the decorations wasn't as bad as we thought. Things were bent and twisted, but not beyond repair. Basil Whiting brought over his woodworking tools and fixed a few elves under the watchful eye of Mr. Sankey. Randall Wattkiss, who had been getting so much mileage out of his stunt with the safety harness that he confessed to feeling like a genuine loser celebrity, went back up to the roof and even had his picture taken with one of the reindeer. Rudy Zennetti strapped on his tool belt like some gunslinger in an old western.

It was inspiring to see all the losers come together again over the next few days. Tin Face Facelli got a dab of red paint on his nose as he was repainting Santa, but his smile was so wide I could see a generous slice of metal. When I asked him why he was so happy, he said, "I like being outside without having to worry about Jerry and the boys."

I knew what he meant. Call it Loser Pride. After years of cowering in corners, we could be open about who we were. We had a *project*. We had a *goal*. We were still losers of, course, but nobody was going to put us down if we held a handsaw the wrong way or let our safety glasses fog up. We could be ourselves.

I was so inspired, in fact, that I got up my nerve and went

to see Alvin of Barney's Bagel Land. When I explained that our Christmas display had been destroyed, Alvin offered to donate some money —on one condition. He had recently commissioned the creation of a giant inflatable bagel that read: "Barney's Bagel Land: Spread a Little Holiday Goodness!" where the giant dab of cream cheese was supposed to go.

"It's a replica of my latest creation," he told me, "a spinach and red-pepper bagel in festive tones of red and green." He got more and more excited as he talked. "I was going to put it on the roof here," he said, "but I've got a much better idea. Why not make it the centerpiece of your display?"

I wasn't sure about the giant bagel, but I couldn't very well say that to Alvin in light of his generous offer. That didn't mean I had to *like* it, though. Once he'd gone back to his office, I got into this long, involved conversation about the whole thing with the old lady in the flowered dress. Actually, it was more like a confession.

It must have been the kind way she looked at me, but I started to blurt out how I'd got my friends into the middle of something that was probably going to be a disaster, how we'd worked so hard, and how life was so confusing and unfair. Before I knew it, I had told her all about Jerry and the boys and what was going to happen when we lost the contest to the Whitman "Christmas Tribute to Real Estate."

The old lady listened patiently, then said a bunch of stuff about how the important thing was "pulling together" and "thinking outside the box." I just smiled at her. She was a nice old lady — but she was way too eccentric to understand about Jerry and the boys.

While I prepared dinner that night, I tried to figure out a

way to tell Manny and Winston about the giant inflatable bagel. Finally, as we sat down to our chicken, I decided just to come right out with it. Like me, they weren't exactly thrilled with the concept.

"We need something inspirational," said Winston. "Not some overgrown chunk of bread."

From an aesthetic point of view, Manny was disgusted. He also raised a practical concern.

"Who's gonna blow up an inflatable bagel?" he asked.

I told Manny that Alvin had a special pump, but that didn't cheer him up much.

I was chewing on my chicken and thinking about how horrible it was going to be like working for Jerry Whitman when Cola started barking and wouldn't stop.

"He's out in the backyard," said Winston. "Let's get a couple of flashlights and see what's going on."

In the yard we discovered Cola barking and snarling at the archway of his doghouse. Like the mansion, the doghouse was palatial. Knowing that there was room in there for everything from a family of cornered raccoons to a pack of wandering coyotes, we were a little nervous. Winston gingerly aimed his flashlight at the opening. Suddenly, I could see a set of very familiar eyes staring back at me. Winston moved the flashlight around some more.

"*Dad?*" I called. "Is that you?"

"Guilty, son," said my dad. "I'm coming out now, okay? Can you call off the dog?"

The dog was still barking, but when Manny said, "Take it easy, Cola," he started to wag his tail.

My dad came out of the doghouse, which was so big he

didn't even have to duck his head. He looked apprehensively at Cola, then apologetically at me.

"Sorry, son. I would have gone back to the apartment, but I was afraid one of Big Garry's guys would have it staked out."

"Come on, Manny," Winston said. "Let's give them some privacy." He turned to me. "You okay out here, Alex?"

It was a mild night for December, and I liked the cold air.

"Here is fine," I answered.

Winston gave me his flashlight and went back to the house with Manny and Cola. My dad and I were left in the yard with nothing but that flashlight and a few streetlights for illumination. The weird thing was, I think both of us preferred it that way.

"What happened?" I asked. "What are you doing here?"

"Harry Beardsley tracked me down in Vegas," said Dad. "He explained everything, and I thought it was best if I came home." He handed me a note from Harry. I opened it, training Winston's flashlight on the words. The note read:

Dear Alex,

Remember how I told you I was once a skip tracer? Well, I had some contacts in Vegas and decided to find your old man. Don't be too hard on him. He's broke and Connie has dumped him. I think he's also kind of scared. But he misses you so much that he is willing to return and face the whole mess with Big Garry. I'd say that takes a fair amount of guts. Sorry for borrowing the money, but I needed plane fare and stuff. I'll pay you back as soon as I can. I've decided to go to L.A. and spend some time with Jack. Wish me luck.

Merry Christmas,
Harry

I looked at my dad. "How long have you been sitting in the doghouse?"

"For a while," he replied. "Harry gave me the keys to the house next door, but I didn't feel like going inside."

"Why didn't you knock on Winston's door?"

"I don't know. I guess I wasn't sure what sort of reception I'd get."

"You don't look so good, Dad."

"I don't *feel* so good, son. I'd like to sit down. Do you mind if we go back in the doghouse?"

Winston had told me that Neville liked to hang out with Cola in the doghouse sometimes and read magazines. It wasn't much like a doghouse at all. There was a space heater, a couple of chairs, and a big futon for Cola to sleep on. There was even an overhead light, but we didn't switch it on.

As we settled in the two chairs, Dad said, "This is Buckingham Palace compared to my more recent accommodations." After that, I clicked off the flashlight and we talked in the dark for a long time. We said a lot of things that cleared the air between us. During the months he was gone, I'd been through quite a few changes. Still, he *was* my dad. Plus — no matter how you looked at it — we had missed each other.

Dad told me about the exact moment he had decided to come home. "Let me set the scene, son," he said. "Harry and I are sitting in this tacky motel outside of Vegas. He's looking around the room and he notices this big fat roach crawling across the floor. So there we are, watching this bug crawl toward the bathroom, and Harry starts to explain about how you three guys gave him a chance."

"A chance?" I asked. "What sort of chance?"

"A chance to be different," Dad answered. "He said something about you turning on his tap."

I laughed at that.

Then Dad said Harry had asked him if he'd ever wanted to be different. "I've thought about that over the last while," said my dad. "And that *is* what I want. A chance to be different from what I've been." Even in the dark, I could tell Dad meant it.

Things were still a bit awkward between us. Dad had been honest with me, though, so I decided to bring him up to date on the Christmas display. I could feel him listening intently, for there is nothing my dad likes better than to hear how a goal is progressing. He was interested in every little detail.

When I was done, my dad leaned over and said, "I always thought you were more like your mother, but there's a lot of me in you, too."

"I know that, Dad."

"I'm not sure that's such a great thing," said Dad, "but I must admit to feeling good about it."

"At least I don't have to call you Uncle Vito any more," I said. We both laughed at that one.

My dad sighed happily. "A project. You have a *project*." And then, "Can you hear it, son? Can you hear it?"

"Hear what, Dad?" I asked.

"The most beautiful call in the world," he said. "The call of *science*."

CHAPTER
TWENTY

I guess my dad had really missed creating things. He threw himself into helping on the Christmas display with a passion I hadn't seen since Insta-Dye. Dad still had access to the garage where he conducted his experiments. Once he had cleaned out some of his junk, he used the space to team up with Mr. Sankey and to fix the rest of the decorations Jerry and the boys had wrecked.

With assistance from Julie Spenser, the full membership of the Losers' Club, plus my dad and Mr. Sankey, the new display was going up surprisingly fast. Sometimes I would stand back and watch everybody scurrying around like organized ants. Mr. Sankey kept things light by drinking a giant bottle of ginger ale and burping his way through the entire alphabet. As he explained it, "All work and no play is bad for the human condition."

Neither Dad nor I wanted to go back to the apartment, so I stayed with Winston and Manny in the mansion. Dad moved in next door to look after the place for Harry. Repairs to the display were going better than I could have imagined. Still, I couldn't get over the feeling that something was missing. I didn't figure out what that something was until one night I opened my window and discovered Manny sitting on the roof in the dark surrounded by nothing but elves and reindeer.

I figured he must have crawled out from his bedroom window. It was a clear, cold night with lots of stars. I crawled out onto the roof to sit beside him. As you know by now, I am not the sort of guy who generally goes crawling around on rooftops. But then I've ended up doing many things in the last few months that I never thought I'd do in a million years.

"Hello, Savior," said Manny, like as if we met at this elevation every day of the week.

Being up there reminded me of the hula girl incident, and I mentioned what a brave thing Manny had done getting Winston down off the roof.

"It wasn't brave at all," said Manny.

"What?" I replied.

"You know when I was jumping up there?" asked Manny. "Part of me wanted to be funny, but part of me didn't care *what* happened." He paused for a few seconds before adding, "I mean, part of me wanted to make a hole in the roof and crash through until I was swallowed up or something."

"A lot of guys would care if you got swallowed up," I said. "Me and a lot of guys."

Manny was looking up at the stars now. "Don't you ever get tired of caring?"

"Sure," I said. "Just not right now."

Manny nodded, but he wouldn't look at me.

"What's wrong, Manny?"

"What *isn't* wrong?"

"Pick something we can change," I said. "I know there's something that bugs you about the Christmas display. Is it the bagel?"

"I don't want to put our display down or anything," said Manny. "I mean, I was the one who made the original sketch."

"Everyone voted on it," I reminded him. "You don't like it?"

"Well, the design is above average," said Manny. "It's kind of strange and surrealistic with the hula girl and the bagel and everything — which is cool."

"But?"

"But it doesn't say anything about *us*," he continued. "It doesn't say anything about us as losers."

"You mean like a statement?" I asked.

"I mean like an *artistic* statement," said Manny. "Something that tells people we're here and we're not going away."

I thought of Tin Face, with the dab of paint on his nose and his full-metal smile. "You have an idea, don't you?"

"I may have to borrow your dad."

I told Manny he could borrow my dad any time. We sat for a few minutes longer looking at the stars. Then I told Manny I was going to need help getting back through my bedroom window. He put out his hand and said, "In that case, I'm your man."

Manny *did* borrow my dad. The next day was a Monday, so Manny skipped school to work on his idea. Dad said he was fine with that, given the educational nature of what they'd be doing. Manny and my dad went into Dad's garage workshop first thing in the morning, and they were still there when Winston and I went over there around four. There was noise and shouting and the sound of power tools, but we didn't go in. Manny said he wanted his masterpiece to be a surprise. When Dad and Manny brought the display to Winston's that evening and unveiled it for us , we were more than surprised. We were totally amazed.

What they had done was fix the big Fat 'n' Happy turkey sign. Correction: they didn't just fix it — they *altered* it. The chubby dad, who now bore a passing resemblance to Manny, was still about to stuff a big turkey sandwich in his mouth. But now there were crutches leaning against one kid's chair. The other kid was noticeably shorter and looked sort of like Winston. In the window behind them, Manny had painted a bunch of faces that we recognized as fellow losers. There was a smiling guy with braces on his teeth like Tin Face Facelli, and a guy with big round glasses like Stanley Horton. There was even a guy who liked to tuck a pencil behind his ear, like Maurice Lieberman.

But that wasn't all. Remember how the attached neon sign used to read: "From All the Boys at Fat 'n' Happy…Wishing You a Happy, Closer Holiday!"?

Now it read: "Be Fat 'n' Happy…Wishing You a Happy, Closer Holiday!"

Only Manny being Manny, *that* wasn't all either. The first C in the last line had been rigged to flash on and off when you plugged the sign in. So what you got — in bright-red neon lettering — was this: "Wishing You a Happy, Closer Holiday!"

And then: "Wishing You a Happy, loser Holiday!"

After we had finished admiring that, Manny said there was a special detail you had to get up very close to see.

"Take a good look at the back end of the turkey," he instructed seriously.

At first, Winston and I couldn't see anything unusual. But finally we made out the ghostly face of Jerry Whitman staring at us from the butt end of the bird. Manny had clipped a picture of Jerry's face from the annual and delicately layered it with brown paint so that you could still barely see the image. The two of us laughed so hard we had to work to catch our breath.

"I'm glad you like my finishing touch," said Manny, grinning. "I've titled the whole thing 'Merry Christmas, Jerry Whitman.'"

Winston grinned back and declared, "If you can't be cool, then play the fool!"

"Immaturity is the ultimate form of rebellion," I added.

Manny waved his fist in the air and shouted, "Fat power!"

Dad was modest, but I was proud when Manny went on about what a big help my dad had been in creating "Merry Christmas, Jerry Whitman." And if that wasn't enough, Dad had discovered some leftover stock of a glow-in-the-dark version of Perma-Paint. It enabled our decorations to dazzle against the night sky. Manny said we had the first radioactive hula girl ever to be in a Christmas display.

Winston got into the act by taking a mop from the janitor's office and fixing it to look as if one of the elves was mopping the floor. It was his tribute to Mr. Winecki. With all the finishing touches that other people wanted to add, we completed the display just in the nick of time. Manny joked that he would have collapsed from exhaustion but he was far too busy to make time for it.

Before we knew it, it was the day before the preliminary round of judging for the contest. The way it worked was that one member of the jury would scout out each display and report back to the other judges. The following evening the finals would take place, with all the judges on the scene.

That night we turned on the whole works for our fellow losers. Against the dark sky, we could see the giant hula girl, Santa and his elves, and what appeared to be the biggest bagel in the universe. Down on the lawn, Manny's "Merry Christmas, Jerry Whitman" glowed brightly.

"I wish Harry could see this," I said. "He'd really appreciate it."

We agreed that Harry would. Then Manny confessed. "I'm a bit scared for you, Savior."

"Why?" I asked.

"We're not going to win anything," he said. "This is too *us*."

"Exactly," agreed Winston. "Way too us."

"I wouldn't have it any other way," I said. And I meant it.

Nonetheless, that night I tossed and turned in bed. And then, when I thought I was finished, I tossed and turned some more. I'd be willing to bet that none of the other losers were sleeping either. Let's face it. We needed some kind of Christmas miracle to beat Jerry Whitman.

Finally, I decided to go downstairs for a glass of milk. I guess Winston had the same idea, because he was already at the kitchen table with his own glass. We sat there, sipping our milk, in no hurry to go back to bed. Then Winston said, "Whatever happens, I want you to know I'm glad we did it."

"Thanks, Winston," I said.

"Me too, Savior," said Manny, who appeared outside the kitchen door in his pajamas.

"Thanks, Manny," I said.

The three of us sat around the kitchen table drinking milk

for a while. Then Manny said, "I sure could use a New York pastrami sandwich right now."

I waited for some kind of crack from Winston. But all he said was "Me too."

Manny looked shocked, but Winston C. Chang just shot him a grin and said, "Well, it was *good*."

Manny had a big laugh over that one. "Short One," he said, "sometimes you really take the Twinkie."

We managed to make it through the next day at school but all we could think about was what the preliminary judge for the contest would think of our display. He turned out to be a sour-looking guy who kept writing things down on a notepad. He didn't smile once. Manny got worried as he watched the judge out the living-room window.

"The man doesn't get it," he fretted. "I am doomed to be an artist ahead of my time."

Winston tried to think of things to make Manny feel better. "The guy looks as if his shoes are too tight," he whispered. "He obviously has no taste."

The next day at school we tried to forget about the reaction of the preliminary judge. While we were at it, we also tried to forget the rumor that Jerry Whitman's display was the greatest thing since the invention of electric light. None of us but Julie Spenser could bear going past the Whitman house to take a look. Reporting back, she grimly described their display as "eye-popping."

But something happened that evening that helped to balance out all the Jerry Whitman-like things that go on in the world. When the judges came around to look at our display, I noticed that the head judge was none other than my old friend the lady in the flowered dress. She came right up to me and Manny and Winston.

"I've been meaning to introduce myself," she said. "My name is Elvira Mumford."

"Of the Elvira Mumford Foundation?" I asked, my jaw dropping about a mile.

"Precisely," she said. "I sponsor this event. And I'm happy to say that yours is the most original display I've seen in the history of the contest."

"Don't you think it's a little…?" Winston asked.

"Out there?" interjected Manny.

"Certainly," said Elvira Mumford. "But I happen to *like* out there."

When the judges had left, Manny looked at the hula girl and at Alvin's giant bagel. He looked at the reindeer and at the elves and at the blinking sign on Winston's front lawn.

"Well, there's only one thing I can say," observed Manny.

"What's that?" I asked.

Manny smiled the biggest smile I'd seen since the last time he scored a bull's-eye on the Jerry Whitman dartboard. "Merry Christmas," he said.

The judges announced the results later that evening in front of Winston's house. Jerry Whitman was shocked when the Losers' Club won first prize in the Festival of Light competition. Jerry and his dad were awarded the second-place trophy for their "Tribute to Real Estate." Jerry Whitman, Sr., was very quiet for once.

A lot of people in the crowd wanted to congratulate us, including Mrs. Loomis and Ms. Maculwayne. Mrs. Loomis threw her arms around Winston and told him that our display was a fine example of realized potential in action. Then a few newspaper reporters started making a big fuss over Manny, Winston, and me. They even made us pose in front of the Fat 'n' Happy turkey for some special photographs.

My moment of glory was interrupted by the call of nature. I went inside the house to use the bathroom, and I was about to go back out when I heard an argument coming from below. It was dark, and the bathroom window was only open a crack. When I looked down, I could make out Jerry Whitman and his dad in the soft glow of the surrounding Christmas lights. There was no mistaking Mr. Whitman's angry voice. I guess Jerry Senior figured that since they'd moved around to the side of the house, nobody could overhear them fighting, but I could hear them just fine.

"Do you know how humiliating this is?" demanded Jerry Senior "Do you know how much *business* this is going to cost me?"

"I'm sorry, Dad."

"Sorry!" said Jerry's old man. "You know what you are? You're a *loser*!"

"I am not," said Whitman. But his voice was very small.

That made Big Jerry even madder. Through the crack in the window, I could see him wave his shiny trophy in front of Jerry Junior's face. For a second, I thought he was going to brain his son with it. "What does it say on this thing?" asked Jerry's old man.

"Second place," replied Jerry.

"And second place is what?" asked Big Jerry as if he already knew the answer.

"Bullshit," muttered Jerry.

"That's right, *bullshit*," agreed Big Jerry.

For a minute, Jerry Junior tried to defend himself. "How come you're blaming me for taking second place?" he asked. "You had more to do with our display than I did."

Jerry's old man said nothing at first. Then he hissed, "That's exactly what a loser would say. I'm blaming you because I'm bigger and smarter and because I *can*." Then he added, "You got a problem with that?"

Jerry Whitman, Jr., kept his mouth shut, which was how his old man wanted it. "Now let's see if you can go out there and at least *act* like a winner," he ordered. The two of them headed back around to the front of the house.

By the time I got outside, Jerry Whitman, Jr., was trying his best to act like a winner in front of everybody. He was concentrating so hard on being cocky that he got a little too successful. Jerry began bugging Cola, who was standing around enjoying the festivities with Neville's slipper in his mouth. Whitman pulled the slipper as if he was going to take it away. Winston tried to warn Jerry about the danger of such a rash action, but Whitman merely sneered.

"Are you kidding?" he said. "I know this dog. This dog is a pussycat."

While Whitman was saying this, he managed to get Neville's slipper out of Cola's mouth. The rest seemed to happen in slow motion. There must have been something in the dog's expression that told Jerry Whitman to run in the opposite direction as fast as he could. He took off like a scared rabbit. Unfortunately Jerry forgot to drop Neville's slipper along the way. So Cola went running after him as if he saw Jerry as some kind of giant chew toy. Winston and Manny then ran off in pursuit of Cola.

Suddenly Gordie Heffernan yelled, "I'm not going to miss this!" He took off to see if Cola was going to catch up with Jerry. This started a chain reaction of other losers eager to witness Cola taking a bite out of Jerry Whitman, Jr. Stanley Horton was the first. He gave himself a blast from his asthma inhaler and shouted, "What are we waiting for? Let's go." Pretty soon, a whole pack of huffing and puffing losers were running down the street to see what they could see.

My dad glared at Jerry Senior. "Aren't you going to see if your son needs some help?" he asked. Whitman's dad looked around at the crowd as if calculating how many potential real estate customers were there. Finally he flashed a big embarrassed smile and went jogging off with the second-place trophy in his hand.

Julie Spenser and I stood watching our friends swarm away from us over the hill.

"You were right," I said to Julie. "There *are* a lot more losers than winners."

"You think they'll catch up to him?" asked Julie.

I nodded. "But they won't hurt him," I said. "They'll be out of breath. And besides, they just won something."

Julie Spenser took my hand and kissed me then, right under the giant hula girl. "So did you," she said.

"I did?" I asked, trying not to blush.

Julie nodded. We stood out there under the starlit sky and held hands. For a minute, I felt kind of strange. But then I realized that I was experiencing something most losers can't identify with. I felt lucky.

This is more than I can say for Jerry Whitman. According to Manny and Winston — who told Julie and me the whole story later — Jerry couldn't manage to out-run Cola. In fact, Cola was so upset that he managed to tear a nice big chunk from the bottom of Jerry Whitman's neatly pressed khakis before Jerry managed to make his way up a tree. Winston told me that a very scared Jerry was still holding Neville's slipper when Cola tried to climb up after him.

By that time, things were getting kind of crowded. A whole bunch of losers were clumped around the base of the tree, waiting to see what would happen next. That's when Manny took charge. He finally got control of Cola and called up to Jerry, sounding just like one of those TV detectives trying to talk some very upset guy out of giving up his weapon.

"Okay, Jerry," said Manny, in a very soothing voice. "Just drop the slipper. Nice and easy."

Whitman dropped Neville's slipper, and Cola picked it up, his tail thumping happily against the trunk of the tree. But Jerry wouldn't come down until his old man arrived on the scene and ordered him to.

After that, the best Jerry Junior could do was look at Winston all embarrassed and declare, "Someone is going to pay for these pants!"

Jerry Senior, who, Winston said, looked pretty disgusted, told his kid to shut up, and hurried him from the crowd.

As they left, Tin Face Facelli said in a kind of sing-song-y voice, "Some-one is go-ing to pay for these pa-aa-nts."

It was kind of hard to hear if either Whitman said anything back because all the losers were laughing so hard. They kept laughing too. Right there in public. I guess it just felt too good to stop.

The next day was a Saturday, which Manny proclaimed

"Victory Day." The three of us did stupid things that made us feel good. For example, Winston stood at the top of the stairs and tore up little bits of toilet paper, which he dropped over the railing as Manny ran around below with our trophy and exalted, "We are the champions!" Manny said it was like getting a ticker tape parade down Fifth Avenue for winning the World Series or something.

To top it off, there was a big picture of Manny, Winston and me in the morning paper. Winston went out and bought copies for his relatives in Hong Kong. Manny even sent a copy to his dad.

That night, people from all over the city cruised by Winston's house to see our display. Mr. Winecki came by early in his wheelchair for a special showing.

"Win?" he asked. "Is that my mop up there?" When Winston told him it was, Walter looked proud. "Mops are a more important part of Christmas than most people realize," he said.

Even Big Garry stopped by to pay his respects. At first I thought there might be trouble because Sam was up on the roof when he arrived, making a few adjustments to the lights.

I was proud of my dad, though. He didn't try to hide from Big Garry. He climbed down the ladder and went right up to the guy. Big Garry looked intimidating in his black wool hat. For a second I thought maybe he would punch my dad in the eye. But then he looked at the Christmas lights twinkling against the sky and this calm expression came over his face.

When Big Garry took off his hat, you could see that most of his hair had grown back. He told us that all of the Insta-Dye clients had started to grow back their hair. Manny, in an aside to Winston and me, called it the second Christmas miracle of the season. Big Garry lingered on the lawn with his hair standing on end, trying to figure out what to do.

Finally, he held out his hand. "What the hell," he said. "Merry Christmas, Shovel." And he and my dad shook hands.

Neville did not feel so cheery when he got back from California the next afternoon. Winston told us that his brother had had a big fight with his girlfriend. Neville made it home just in time, beating Mr. and Mrs. Chang by only twenty-four hours.

It's funny but, looking back now, I can see that after we won the Christmas competition, a few things started to go a little bit right once in a while. Manny put it best when he said, "We are still basically miserable. But every now and then something good happens so we can tell just how miserable we are the rest of the time."

Winston's parents were so impressed with their youngest son's improved geometry mark that they told him they were thinking of buying him a car for his sixteenth birthday. Winston worked up his courage and said he would rather see them more often. That's when Mr. and Mrs. Chang got out their matching Daytimers and pledged to spend four extra days in Vancouver during the coming year.

Winston was pretty philosophical about his parents' promise. "I'll be lucky to get two extra days out of the deal," he said. "And for one day of *that*, my mother will be busy in the escape room, totally engrossed in her puzzle of the Taj Mahal." Still, Winston C. Chang considers it a stroke of good fortune to have his brother back — even though Winston has made me swear not to tell Neville that he now knows a whole bunch of useful laundry secrets.

The losers at school have stopped being so scared of Jerry

and the boys. It isn't only because the Watertank had resigned from the enforcement business, or because the losers all saw Jerry Whitman run like a rabbit. It's also because Jerry Whitman, Sr., convinced that Jerry was becoming a serious loser, transferred his son to a private school over the holidays and started watching him like a hawk. Winston said he heard that it's the kind of school were you have to salute before you can go to the washroom.

Manny is being cautiously optimistic, but he still thinks like a loser. A couple of times, he's gone on this rant about how Jerry Whitman is going to come back to Marshall McLuhan High after undergoing secret, private-school Ninja training on how to make our lives worse than ever. I guess it's hard for us to accept that life doesn't have to be a living hell where your wallet is always empty and you are constantly being assaulted by week-old pastry.

At first, Manny couldn't believe we no longer had to move around in a safety cluster. "I kind of miss having you as a human shield," he told me. But Manny still has his problems. Manny's mom is back from the rehab clinic and they have started to see a counselor. Even though the sessions are a big hassle and can get pretty intense, Manny told me he tries to be optimistic. Manny being Manny, he says at least it gives he and his mom something to talk about besides chicken noodle soup.

Julie Spenser and I are kind of an item around school. She still calls me king of the losers sometimes, but in a very cool way. She kisses me in the hall on occasion, too. But at least now I'm prepared for it.

Dad is out of the invention business for good. At the beginning of the New Year, he got a job hosting a local TV show called *Ask Mr. Science*. It doesn't pay much, and we're still living in our old apartment. On the other hand, nobody is threatening him with lawsuits and he has yet to blow up anything on the air.

Late in December, Winston, Manny and I had chipped in to buy Harry a special Christmas present — a new shirt with pineapples all over it — and sent the package to him in Los Angeles. Harry wrote us to say the shirt was very nice but we had already given him a present by making him rejoin the human race. He mentioned in his card that he was trying hard to write a serious book again and also spending a lot of time with his son. Sometime soon, he hopes to be back in town to visit us and Ms. Maculwayne. In the meantime, he's paying back in installments the money he borrowed from me.

Harry also said I could keep his favorite record, *Charlie Parker with Strings*. I listen to it on an old portable record player my dad bought. The music makes me think of different things. Sometimes I think about my mom. Sometimes I think about Julie. And sometimes I think about the night before we took down our Christmas display.

It was midnight, the day after New Year's. The rest of the Changs had gone to bed, but Winston had arranged to meet with Manny and me for one last look. Everything would be coming down the next morning, and we knew it was important to fix a picture of it in our minds.

The three of us stood there admiring our display. We were saying good-bye to more than just a bunch of Christmas decorations. We all felt it, but we kept quiet about it and concentrated on the lights. Manny's giant piece of artwork was blinking in the night: "Closer…loser…Closer…loser."

Finally Manny said, "How come losers never know the right thing to say?"

"Sometimes you don't need to say anything," said Winston.

And he was right. Sometimes you don't need to say anything at all.

ABOUT THE AUTHOR

John Lekich is a freelance writer who has been working as a journalist, movie reviewer and essayist for 18 years. His work has appeared in such publications as *Reader's Digest, The Los Angeles Times* and *The Hollywood Reporter.* John is the recipient of numerous magazine awards on subjects ranging from the arts and human rights issues to business and medicine.

As a movie critic, he has interviewed people on dozens of film sets. He has had the good fortune of comparing noses with Steve Martin on the set of *Roxanne* and he once shared a beverage with George Plimpton. He was kissed by the legendary film actress Audrey Hepburn and believes he holds the record for the longest consecutive interview with novelist Michael Crichton.

John has co-written two feature-length screenplays. He now adds to his list of accomplishments that of book author. In addition to *The Losers' Club,* he is the author of *Reel Adventures: The Ultimate Teen Guide to Great Movies.* He lives in Vancouver, British Columbia.